Children of the Gods

BOOK 1

Oppression

To Sarah,
Keep writing ! I hope you
like my book :)

JESSICA THERRIEN

ZOVA Books

Los Angeles

ZOVA BOOKS

First ZOVA Books edition 2012.

For information or permission contact:

ZOVA Books
P.O. Box 21833, Long Beach, California 90801
www.zovabooks.com

ISBN 13: 9780984035045
ISBN 10: 0984035044

Cover Design © Daniel Pearson

TO MY MOTHER AND SISTER

FOR BEING MY CHEERLEADERS
ALONG THE WAY.
AND TO MY HUSBAND FOR BEING
MY INSPIRATION.

1.

IT WAS DECEMBER 12, 1973. I remember because it was my fiftieth birthday, and Christmas was coming, so the snow was to be expected. In this area of northern California, we rarely saw anything but a white Christmas. Chilcoot was nestled high up in the Sierra Nevada Mountains. A small rectangular green sign was the only evidence that the small town actually existed: Chilcoot, California, Elevation 5000 ft, Population 58. A distracted driver could easily pass through the two-mile stretch of road that touched its borders without realizing he'd seen it.

We were on our way into the city, the closest to our house being over an hour away, and Daddy was grinning ear to ear as he drove his new forest green Cadillac Coupe de Ville into the oncoming flurries. He loved that car.

"Now, make sure the tree is sturdy, Elyse, and nice and tall," Daddy said.

"I know, Dad. I think I've picked enough trees in my

life to know a good one. Besides, you never let *me* choose it anyway," I mumbled under my breath. I saw my mother's cheeks lift into a smile. She must have heard me, and she knew it was the truth. We'd had this birthday tradition for the last twenty years. I was supposed to be the one to pick out the Christmas tree, but my choices hardly ever passed Daddy's final inspection.

"Don't you like this one?" he'd ask. "Yours is a little thin on the bottom. This one's much better, right?"

"Right," I would mutter mechanically.

"See, Sarah, she's a good sport, knows a good one when she sees it."

My mother never argued. He was too much of a perfectionist to let anyone else handle those sorts of things. It was kind of funny really, one of his little eccentricities that I overlooked in my youth.

It was two o'clock in the afternoon, but the day was dim. The sun had been swallowed up by the all-consuming white. I was gazing out the back window as it happened, trying to judge the visibility through the whiteout. I couldn't see far, just beyond the edge of the fence that ran alongside the road.

"Richard, slow down!" my mother shouted. The words triggered the incident like she had seen it coming. The car drifted into the next lane, and I felt the loss of control as the paved road became slick ice. My body stiffened in response to the awkward gliding sensation, and I braced myself for the impact. Every second of the slow motion tumble seemed an eternity as I prepared for the last moments of life. I clung to those seconds, taking in the final images that my eyes would see, and listening for the closing lines that would mark the end.

"Ellie!"

My mother's panicked voice rang out in the hollow silence of the cab with a sort of knowing uncertainty just before we hit.

***

It had been thirty-nine years since the accident, and still these photos stirred up the last memory I had of them. I stared down at the faded pictures, the delicate paper worn on the edges. I would never forget. The last words of my parents, the flickering image of a deep red that stained the snow like an open wound on the skin of the earth, and the crumpled Cadillac flipped over in the bank.

The photos were old, too old for me to be in them, but I was. My mother's silky brown hair billowed over her shoulders, and I was glad I still remembered the rich chocolate color of it because the gray and white image didn't do it justice. The lack of color masked her would-be golden brown eyes and rosy cheeks. She was gorgeous. My father, to her left, was looking far too concentrated on the camera, furrowed brow and closed mouth. His skin, dark from working in the sun, nicely contrasted his short blond hair which he wore parted and combed to the side. I was at his feet, and we were posing in front of the tree like a typical storybook family. It was the Christmas of 1939. I looked three years old, but in truth, I was much older.

I was born in 1923 with a rare genetic abnormality. Like my

mother and father, I aged five times slower than the average person. I'd been alive for eighty-nine years making me almost eighteen in the eyes of the rest of the world, and for the most part I felt young. I was living in San Francisco now. I found the city much easier to hide in than the small towns I had been moving to every five years or so since their death. In the city, I was just another face, another body in the crowd, completely invisible amongst the masses.

"We've gone to great lengths to live as we do, Ellie. It's for your safety," my father had always insisted. "Our bodies are durable and strong, but that's a blessing and a curse. The secrecy of our identities is precious, and there is no telling what could happen if we were to be found out. People like us could not live a normal life if we were exposed."

It was all I ever learned about myself and why I was so different, why I had to live in secret. Looking back, there was so much more I wanted to know, so many unanswered questions. What about my grandparents? What about my future? Was I destined to be alone? How did my parents find each other? Were there others? My father never went into detail. Instead, he avoided my questions, always suggesting a distraction that would divert my attention for a while.

"In time you'll learn to live under the radar as we've done. For now, why don't we get you a puppy?"

They bought me a Border Collie. She was black with white spots and white feet. I named her Sweetie, and I loved her like I had never loved anything. She went with me everywhere, and in my friendless world, Sweetie became the best friend I'd ever had. The attachment we'd formed seemed unbreakable, but as nature would have it, Sweetie died when I was nine. On that day, I fully understood why my parents had not wanted me to have friends—friends who I would love, who would age, and leave, and die.

The phone rang loud and unexpected, waking me out of my nostalgia. I returned the old photos to the small gold chest I kept them in and stumbled over unpacked boxes trying to get to the receiver. I had just moved in about two weeks ago, and the naked living room, void of furniture, was a scattered mess. I picked up on the third ring, still lost a little in my own head.

"Hello?" I answered, expecting the only person who had my number.

"Ellie?"

"Hey," I said, happy to hear from her. "I know I haven't called. Sorry."

I caught my reflection in the hallway mirror, still so young. My dark brown hair was tied back in a loose ponytail, my cheeks wrinkle-free and rosy. I felt guilty listening to Anna's older voice. Over the years, she'd become a woman of forty-eight, and I'd barely changed.

"Are you moved in?" she asked, excited.

I sighed, looking around at the cluttered floor. "Getting there."

"How are you?"

"Okay," I lied.

She knew me too well. "You want to come over?"

"I don't know. Not yet. I know it's been a while but . . ."

"I'm sorry," she said. What are people supposed to say when

your second mother dies?

"I still wake up and listen for her thinking maybe I dreamed it."

"She lived a long, happy life, Elyse. Eighty-nine years is longer than most of us get."

"You know that's how old I am, right?"

"I know."

I felt my throat tighten and the tears come. There was no stopping it. Hadn't I cried enough?

"So, how are you?" I asked, throwing myself back into the conversation. I didn't want to think about Betsy's age. "How's Chloe?"

"I'm good," she answered. "Yeah, I'm good." I heard the pain in her voice, the fear, the worry. "Chloe misses you. She's worried about you. We both are." Her words hung in the air.

Talking about it was too much. "I, um, have to call you back, Anna."

I had to get out. Sulking wasn't going to do me any good. I would go to the grocery store. I needed food. I needed buckets of ice cream to get me back to a normal weight. Betsy would have been so angry.

"You've got no meat on your bones," she would have said. "It's not healthy, Elyse." I could imagine her aged brow creased in the center, her lips pressed together in disapproval. I missed that look. There was so much love behind it, such motherly concern.

I tried all day not to think about Betsy. I watched movies, cleaned and unpacked, read, did crosswords. Now here I was again remembering. It seemed like all there was to do was remember. After a while, I let myself give in to the urge and stopped resisting the memories. They flooded me with all their weight—an avalanche of nostalgic sorrow burying me in the depths of my own mind.

The daylight broke through the open blinds of my bedroom window, waking me before my alarm. I glanced at the clock by my bed with a sigh, 7:22 a.m. The memories of life with Betsy had continued throughout the night, weaving in and out of my dreams. I suppose that was to be expected. She had arranged all of this for me, a new social security number, a license, a place to live. She had prepared me to start a new life, prepared me for her death in a way. I owed her those memories.

Today, I needed to look for some sort of job to keep me busy. It wasn't that I needed the money. My parents and Betsy had set plenty of that aside for me. But I wanted to be done grieving. It seemed like no matter what I did, I couldn't escape the guilt I felt for having so much more life to live. I knew eventually I would have to learn to turn my emotions off— witnessing death just seemed to be part of my existence—but for now it was out of my hands.

Although I'd been here a couple of weeks already, I still wasn't used to my new place. It didn't feel at all like home. My unit was one of three that sat above a café in the Lower Haight on the corner of Waller and Steiner. It was a classic-looking building with a vintage façade. There was a door for each apartment lining the sidewalk, all opening to narrow stairs which led up to the second story. The entry opened into the left side of the kitchen with its blue and white plastic floor and maple cabinetry, and transitioned into the living room with a simple change in flooring, from linoleum to tight knit gray-blue carpet. To the right of the living room was a single hallway with a bathroom on the left and a solitary bedroom on the right.

My clothes were still packed away in the suitcases I'd brought them in. I wasn't a complicated girl, so it didn't affect my lifestyle much. I chose whatever outfit was on top, usually jeans and an old baseball shirt. I wasn't trying to impress anyone. In fact, I was aiming for the opposite, so it didn't matter much what I walked out the door wearing.

I wasn't used to public transportation, but the Bay Area had an underground metro system close by, a convenience I was still growing accustomed to. I didn't intend on stopping at the café downstairs on my way out, but I was looking forward to passing by the place this morning. It was a silly reason, one I probably wouldn't admit to anyone if they asked. From time to time *he* would be there, one of the workers at the coffee shop. I didn't know his name, but he seemed to linger outside, clearing tables or taking his break.

We'd never spoken a word to each other, at least verbally. Most of the time our eyes did the talking. A quick smile said enough. It was an innocent exchange, safe, yet exciting.

As I headed down the stairs, the thought was trivial and foolish, but I hoped he'd be there. The last time I had seen him, he'd been leaning against the wall, digging his shoe into the concrete waiting for someone. His arms were crossed, head down, his hair falling forward, following his downward gaze. He didn't see me at first, but as I passed by, he looked up and directly at me. His expression was pleased, as if he'd been waiting for *me*. When our eyes met, it was like he'd known me for years, as if we'd already shared a hundred secrets. Or maybe that was what it looked like when two people were in love. *I shouldn't think like that*, I thought, reprimanding myself for even considering the idea.

When I stepped out the door and didn't see him, I sighed with disappointment. I took my time rummaging through my bag and locking my door. Despite my stalling, he didn't show. It wasn't like me to care so much about these things. I didn't allow myself to get involved with people. I should think of his absence as a good thing, less of a temptation. Still, I found myself staring at the sign that read CEARNO'S for far too long. I don't know what possessed me, but I decided to go in. I hadn't eaten yet this morning. That's how I justified it.

It was my first time inside the café. In full daylight, it didn't brighten up the way it should. The only windows were at the front of the store, and even those were covered by long brown curtains—but it was comfortable, like the den of an old friend's house. Cushioned seats lined the walls and a jukebox sat next to a pool table in the far right corner.

"What can I get for you?" asked a young guy from behind the counter. It was him.

When our eyes met, I lost my ability to speak. He was gorgeous, and I felt intimidated. What did he ask me? I was too busy trying to figure out what it was about his handsome face and soft mouth that had me so flustered.

"Cat got your tongue?" he teased, tucking his grown out waves of golden hair behind his ears. He stared into me as I tried to understand the connection, the mysterious closeness between us that I couldn't put my finger on.

"No." I had to look away from him to respond. "Just thinking." I needed to pull myself together. "Just . . . um . . . I'll have a medium iced mocha and a blueberry muffin." Maybe it was the way he was looking at me. His lips were hiding a smile, and I wondered if I had toothpaste on my cheek or something.

A grin flickered across his face as he glanced in my direction, his busy hands making the drink. "So you live upstairs, huh?"

"Yeah," I answered simply. I looked away from him again, trying to deter my interest in continuing the conversation or any kind of unnecessary flirting.

"I'm William," he offered. "We were all wondering when the mystery girl from upstairs was going to show."

"Oh, really?" I eyed the mocha.

"You know, the last person who lived in your place was a regular customer. No pressure though."

"I guess I'll have to start drinking more coffee."

"I was hoping you'd say that."

It would be a pretty good excuse for me to ensure I'd see him every morning, something to look forward to, but in my mind, things had already gone too far. This was a secret crush that broke all of my rules.

"The real fun starts at five though," he said. He seemed amused by something. I wiped my cheeks casually, just in case.

"Does it?"

"You should come down sometime."

"Yeah, maybe I will," I lied.

The door chimed as another patron walked in. I would hardly have noticed her, but as she walked toward the counter, voices hushed, and William tensed. The young woman had wild curly black hair that folded around her chin, but her rough apparel didn't seem to match her delicate demeanor. Shiny black army boots completed her distinct grunge punk style.

"Don't hate me for this," William whispered as he intentionally poured the entire mocha down the front of my white tee and jeans.

I inhaled with surprise as the ice cold liquid saturated my clothes and chilled my skin.

"Oh, would you look at that," he said, faking concern and rushing around the counter. "So sorry." His eyes stayed on the girl in the army boots, as he grabbed a hold of my hand.

"What are you doing?" I asked, yanking it free, but his touch left a lingering warmth.

He grabbed it again without reason. "Come on, I have towels in the back, I'm sure we can get that out."

He pulled me with him as he shoved his way through a swinging door, leaving no one to tend to customers. As we burst into the back, I noticed another employee busy taking an inventory of supplies.

"Sam, I need you to work the counter," William demanded with an anxious look as he grabbed white cleaning towels from a shelf. Our hands, still pressed together, grew warmer.

"Seriously? I'm almost done," Sam protested, but when his eyes found me, they widened and he smiled. "Yeah. Sure. No problem."

I pressed the towels against my coffee-soaked clothes. "Look, I'm fine. Really," I tried convincing him as Sam left us alone.

"No, you're not. We have to go," he said, removing his apron and grabbing my hand once again.

"Go where? I have plans . . . I'm not . . ."

"Well, now you have new plans. They're following you, Elyse. Just trust me okay?"

I pulled my hand free, but I could still feel the heat on my palm. "Who's following me? And how do you know my name?" I had made a point not to tell him.

He stopped his rushing and looked me in the eyes, realizing I wasn't going to just follow him in his crazed state for no reason.

"I know more than your name, and I'll tell you everything, but you have to come with me, all right?"

The way he looked at me before was more than just an accidental glimpse in my direction. There was obviously more going on here, and what was it about him? Being so close had me surprisingly on edge. He glanced at the swinging door and back at me.

"Elyse, we need to go. You have to trust me okay?"

"Okay," I agreed, heart pounding.

The next thing I knew, he was dragging me along behind him, rushing me through alleys and across busy streets. I didn't know who we were running from, but I forced my muscles to push on. Heat pulsed beneath my clothes, and I breathed heavily as we dodged cars and cabs halted in the morning traffic. Horns blared and people shouted, but William ignored them all. He was busy searching, looking in all directions with quick eyes like we were being hunted.

"Where are we going?" I asked out of breath as we slowed for a passing car.

"I'll explain later, just come on." With another tug, he led me into a MUNI station, pulling me by the warm grip he had on my hand. Just as a train was leaving, we slid through the closing doors, and William watched out the window, smiling at something, or maybe someone in the distance.

I didn't know why I followed him. It could have been my attraction to him or the excitement I felt when our eyes connected, but something drew me to him, in a very dangerous way. As I sat in one of the gray plastic seats, I tapped my feet against the floor anxiously. What was I doing? This wasn't smart. He turned to look at me. We smiled slightly at each other, but his focus quickly turned to the people around us.

Something had compelled me to believe him, but when we squealed to a stop at one of the next stations, I hesitated. What was I doing trusting some stranger who was leading me who knows where? I waited for everyone to come in or out, hoping he wouldn't suspect my next move. Just as the doors began to close, I jumped onto the platform, leaving him pressed against the glass as the train rolled away.

I stood alone in the station wondering if I had been smart or made a mistake, but as I hiked back up the steep cement stairs, I came to the conclusion that people in this city were crazy. There was no telling what might have happened. Besides, I would have noticed if I was being followed, wouldn't

I? Suddenly aware, my eyes scanned the streets, looking for a clue, a mysterious or recognizable face, but there was nothing. I was paranoid.

As I climbed the rolling paved hills heading home, the close proximity of things made me a little claustrophobic. I tried to forget about what had just happened, but I couldn't help feeling on edge. The whole morning was so bizarre, and now I was drenched in coffee and needed to go all the way back home to change. My stomach rumbled, and I realized, on top of everything, I never actually got to eat my blueberry muffin. This wasn't my day.

"Hi," a voice came from behind.

I noticed the girl right away. She was quite beautiful, even in her army boots. She didn't look threatening, but after William's warning, I quickened my pace.

"Wait up," she called.

Did she know me? I couldn't remember ever meeting her before. A glint of a smile dashed across her face as I glanced back and saw that she had already caught up.

"We haven't met," she said, answering my unspoken question. "I'm Kara."

I looked her in the eyes for the first time, almost suspicious of her greeting.

"Hi," I returned. It was best to keep it short and sweet with people. Less complicated.

"Where's your boyfriend?" Her question was abruptly too personal.

"What?" I shot out, unable to contain my immediate reaction. I didn't even know this girl. "He's not my boyfriend."

She laughed. "I know."

"Are you following me?" I asked bluntly.

"Yes."

I wasn't expecting her to be so honest, but it prompted me to be just as forward. I felt my eyebrows sink low into a scowl. "Why?"

"You really don't know anything do you?"

Her knowing smirk made me nervous. Maybe I had made a mistake.

"About what?"

"Come on. I know you're hungry. Let's get something to eat."

I had no idea what kind of a person she was. Sure, she looked harmless. A woman in her mid-twenties with a stern but pretty face wasn't exactly what I'd expect in a stalker, but she did admit to following me. I didn't like how things were playing out.

"I think I'm just going to go," I answered.

"Elyse." Like William, she knew my name without me telling her. "Relax, nothing is going to happen. God, you're high strung."

"You don't even know me," I retaliated.

She rolled her eyes. "I know a lot more than you think."

"Like what?" I asked, calling her bluff in the middle of the street.

"You're lonely. You like writing poetry. You eat microwave dinners for most meals. Most importantly, you know nothing about yourself."

She did know a lot about me, more than I was comfortable

with. It made me wonder how closely she'd been watching, how long she'd been following me. I had to know why. Maybe this would be my second bad decision of the day, maybe not.

"Are you coming or what?" she asked.

Okay, so I was hungry, really hungry, and I used that as an excuse to follow her into the diner around the corner.

The eatery was fairly large and crowded. People spilled out onto a patio with umbrellas and talked loudly as they ate. The floor was black and white tile, like a chessboard, and there was a single counter that had trays at the beginning and a register at the end.

"They have breakfast burritos. I know you like those."

"Why did you say it like that?"

"Like what?"

"Like you know I like it."

"I do."

I sighed. "Whatever."

Kara chose the far back corner table. I waited until we were seated to interrogate her.

"So are you going to tell me what it is you claim I don't know about myself?"

She thought about it before she answered. "No."

What the hell was this girl getting at? I couldn't figure her out.

"Why not?" I asked.

"The less you know about yourself, the easier my job will be."

My eyes narrowed. "Your job?"

"Yeah," she answered a bit uncomfortable. "Look, the only

reason I wanted to talk to you was so I could give you my spiel. Before you figure out who I am, who you are. Maybe you'll be able to see things from my perspective one day down the road, and not hate me."

I had no clue what she was talking about, and I didn't like the sound of it, but I needed to know.

"Let's hear it."

"I guess the best way is to give an analogy. For example, you eat meat." The statement was slightly accusatory.

"Yeah," I answered, waiting for there to be more.

"Do you believe in murdering animals?"

"Excuse me?"

"It's just a question. I mean do you?"

I stared at the sausage spilling out of my burrito. "Well, I . . . just because . . ." The whole question had me stuttering with frustration.

"That's my point. It doesn't make sense. Part of you speaks morally and logically, understanding that killing is wrong. Something in you is disgusted by the thought. The herding of chickens and cows in tiny, cramped quarters, living a predetermined, torturous life, it's wrong. You know that. Yet on a day like today, you find yourself standing in line, craving that breakfast burrito with spicy sausage, and you can't resist. It's in you—the instinct to survive. Your body tells you it needs meat, food, sausage, and so you eat it. You could choose the egg and cheese, but you'd think of it as a sacrifice."

The blunt confrontation with my choice had me tense and defensive. It wasn't any of her business what I ate, but somehow I'd still lost most of my appetite.

"Okay so you caught me. Are you going to turn me in for moral hypocrisy?"

She laughed subtly, but answered with undeniable sincerity. "Look, don't feel bad. I ordered the same thing you did. I only wanted to make a point in my defense. People criticize. It's in their nature. They'll pass judgment on almost anything that involves them. Citizens blame the government for their own shortcomings while they rely on the fruits of its existence. They damn the use of oil and its effect on the environment but they drive their cars to work and heat their homes. Do they have a choice? Could they survive without it?"

"So what is your point?" I asked with slight hostility.

"I'm sure you'll understand it soon enough." Her voice was almost too cheerful, which made it even more antagonizing.

"So that's it?"

"That's it." After she took the last bite of her burrito, she stood to clear her tray. "See you around, Elyse," she said. Without another word, she turned and walked out of sight, leaving me completely unsatisfied.

I thought about going home, but after such a strange morning, I just felt like getting lost in the city. I caught a bus and let it take me downtown. Since moving here, I'd quickly grown to love the eclectic feel and buzzing streets. I appreciated the fact that I could walk around in my coffee-stained clothes and nobody would care. People were free here, and could be, look, act, or live any way they pleased. It reminded me of the circus, accepting of outcasts and those who were different, including me. San Francisco was where I belonged, and it was the perfect place to be alone, but not by myself.

Today the sun shone brightly through the strong-willed trees that grew up through the concrete, casting shadowy patches on the sidewalk. I was grateful that nature refused to surrender here. Even amidst the man-made machine, it persevered.

I stayed out until dark, trying to figure out the strange girl who claimed to know me better than I knew myself, but I couldn't understand her. Then there was William, who had been right all along. If I wanted answers, I knew he would have them. Or at least I hoped he would.

2.

WHEN I GOT HOME, I remembered what William had said about Cearno's after 5:00 and hoped he would still be there. Before I even had a chance to get to the café door, a hand grabbed my arm and pulled me into the shadowed alleyway between my building and another.

"It's me," he said, taking my hand. I could feel the warmth beginning to build beneath our palms.

I sighed. "Jeez. You scared me."

"Good. Now we're even."

His looks were distracting, his eyes a dusty green and mouth seductive by nature. "I'm sorry."

He shook his head and laughed with relief. "Well, as long as you're sorry, and not dead."

"Dead? Look we need to talk, this is . . ."

"We should go somewhere else. I don't know if it's safe here."

"Okay," I answered, but he seemed hesitant, remembering

my last attempt at ditching him. "I believe you."

He nodded. "My car is around the corner."

He drove a silvery blue Honda Civic, and once we were inside, he relaxed.

"I'm sorry we're meeting like this." He laughed to himself. "Things haven't gone *exactly* as planned, but I think the night can still be salvaged." He looked at me, gauging my reaction. "You probably think I'm crazy."

"A little," I admitted with a smile. I wasn't supposed to be encouraging this sort of thing, but I couldn't help myself. "How *did* you plan it?"

My question seemed to perk him up. "Oh, you know, kick up the charm, dinner, flowers, a movie. The way normal people do it."

I wasn't sure what I'd gotten myself into or what was going on, but for some reason I trusted him. It was a nice thought to imagine myself on a date. I'd never been on one.

We ended up at a small public library. As we walked toward the white granite building, he reached out for my hand again, and I instinctively pulled it away before he had a chance to weave his fingers through mine. It was a quick defensive movement, almost as if I was afraid of his touch, and maybe I was. I was afraid that it might mean something it couldn't, that I might like it.

"It's not what you think," he said.

"It's nothing, I just . . ."

"Just don't want me to hold your hand," he finished for me. "I get it." We continued walking in silence, but his eyes were looking for something, or someone. "You know if we were on a date, you'd expect me to hold your hand."

"Only this isn't a date," I answered.

He stopped, trying to think of how to explain. "If we're touching, it protects us."

I was starting to get irritated. "From who?" I asked, but he ignored my question.

"Can you feel it?" He lifted my limp fingers and pressed his palm to mine. The warmth was subtle at first, but emanated the longer we held them together.

"What is it?" I asked.

He took a deep breath with new hope in his eyes, as he slowly and cautiously folded his fingers into the grooves of my knuckles. "Friends can hold hands, right?"

"No," I said with a modest smile, but I didn't pull away. "I don't even know you."

"You will."

I was right. His touch was dangerous—I liked it too much.

When we reached the basement level of the library, he set me free, dragging his loose fingers across the rows of books. The place was silent and smelled like old paper, but in a good way. If there was anyone else on this level, they'd kept hidden and quiet.

"I love it down here," he whispered. "There's so much knowledge in this little room."

I'd never thought of it that way, but he was right. There must have been thousands of books filling row upon row of the freestanding shelves. Truth, science, love, art, a seemingly endless collection of knowledge free for the taking.

"And still, there's nobody here," I observed. It seemed

strange that so much knowledge could be so easily disregarded.

"There never is," he said, making himself comfortable on the floor of one of the aisles. "I come here a lot."

I sat down beside him as he began picking through the books, pulling out interesting titles.

"So what is this about? Do you know who's following me?"

"Yes," he answered simply, tilting his head as he scanned the book spines, looking for a specific title.

"Well?"

"After what happened on the train, I thought about it, and I decided to keep it a secret a while longer."

"Why?"

"You won't believe me, and I don't want you to run off again like I'm some crazy person."

"I do believe you. On my way home, Kara found me. I talked to her, and she admitted it. You were right. She was following me."

He froze and looked at me with alarm. "You talked to her?"

"Yeah. She wouldn't tell me anything though. That's why I need you to tell me," I urged.

"I can't believe you talked to her. She's dangerous, Elyse."

"She seemed pretty normal to me."

"She's not."

As much as I was enjoying cozying up to William in the cramped and narrow hallway of books, I had a reason for being here.

"Look, do you know anything or are you just trying to seduce me in the abandoned aisles of the library basement?"

He laughed. "I'm not trying to seduce you, not unless you

want me to," he said with a look that was far too honest.

The thought reminded me that it was just the two of us down here, alone together. All I'd have to do was say 'yes, I want you to,' and maybe he'd kiss me right here, on top of all these books.

"I've never been seduced. I've never even been kissed," I admitted. "I'm not sure it would work." What was it about this guy? I was saying things I knew I shouldn't. Friends, I told myself in an effort to shut out the fantasy I had let run wild in my head. The most we could ever be was friends.

"Oh, trust me," he promised through a confident grin. "It would work."

"You're probably right." What was I doing? Talking to him was like playing with fire, and it had me testing my limits. "Better not then."

I pretended to change my focus, and started looking through books as if I was actually reading parts of them. I wasn't.

"I find it hard to believe that you've never been kissed."

I blushed. "Believe it."

"It's sort of adorable."

"That's not exactly what I was going for. I mean, I try to make a point to divert any attention from myself."

"I don't think it's working."

"Well, I'm pretty sure I put out the vibe."

"What vibe?"

"The 'not interested so leave me alone' vibe."

He merely lifted an eyebrow to this apparently crazy suggestion.

"So you're not going to tell me who's following me?" I asked, trying to change the subject.

"Here," he said pulling an ancient copy of *Homeric Hymns* from the bottom shelf. It was dark red with gold print and looked like it had been read from cover to cover more times than it could handle. He slid across the cheap industrial carpet toward me. We were sitting so close we were touching. "I wanted to show you this."

"Okay," I said, not seeing the connection.

He looked at me, suddenly so much more serious than he had been. "There are so many books here. It's like you could find the answer to any question if you just looked hard enough, you know?"

"Yeah," I answered skeptically, trying to read the insinuation in his words.

"Can I read you some of this? I'm hoping it will help you."

I was completely lost. "Help me what?"

"Not all of it is true of course. Only pieces. They got so much of it wrong."

"Who?" He might as well have been talking nonsense, but his eyes were so sincere, I had to take him seriously.

"Just listen, okay?"

The book was dog-eared. I didn't know whether he had done it, but he flipped right to the page he wanted. As he read, I tried to focus on the words, but his low purring voice was thick as honey, distracting me more than I'd expected.

"Thereupon Aphrodite the daughter of Zeus answered him: Anchises, most glorious of all men born on earth, know that I am no goddess: why do you liken me to the deathless ones? Nay, I am

but a mortal, and a woman was the mother that bare me."

He looked up from the book, and glanced at me quickly before scanning down a bit further.

"And Anchises was seized with love, so that he opened his mouth and said:

"If you are a mortal and a woman was the mother who bare you, and Otreus of famous name is your father as you say, and if you are come here by the will of Hermes the immortal Guide, and are to be called my wife always, then neither god nor mortal man shall here restrain me till I have lain with you in love right now; no, not even if far-shooting Apollo himself should launch grievous shafts from his silver bow. Willingly would I go down into the house of Hades, O lady, beautiful as the goddesses, once I had gone up to your bed."

We sat in silence for a few moments after he finished. I knew he was eagerly awaiting my response, but I didn't know what to say.

"It's really good," I managed.

A breathy hopeless laugh escaped his lips. "I'm glad you liked it."

"I don't get it."

A smile cracked through his hardened expression. I could tell he was disappointed, but what did he expect?

"All right," he said. "Forget the book. I'll make you a deal."

"What kind of a deal?"

"You let me take you out tomorrow, on a date," he added hastily, "and in exchange, I'll tell you everything."

"If there's even anything to tell. This sounds like a scam or something."

"It's not a scam."

"I don't really date," I confessed, still tempted by his offer. "Can't you just tell me now?"

"No, I don't think so," he answered, pleased with his arrangement. "My way is a lot more fun."

We stayed until the library closed, and he drove me home, leaving all of my questions unanswered.

"Okay, so I'll pick you up here at 6:30 tomorrow," he said as he let me off in front of my apartment. "Don't 'forget,' because I'll just see you around, and then you'll have to come up with an excuse. It'll be weird."

"Well, I guess I have no choice then." I played along.

"Nope." His smile was like a blow to the chest—its brilliance overwhelming. How could I resist?

3.

THE NEXT MORNING I caught myself eyeing the only piece of paper stuck under a magnet on my fridge—Anna's phone number. I had to tell somebody.

The first day of fifth grade was the day I met Anna, and it stood out in my mind like a beam of light cutting through the clouds. The schoolhouse was a two story red brick building that was much more intimidating than my years of school at home. It wasn't the school that had me nervous though. I knew it would be fairly easy. It was finding and having friends that worried me.

Betsy took my hand without hesitating and led me through the front doors.

"Don't be nervous, Ellie," she comforted. The tension in my body radiated through the firm grip I had on her hand.

As we entered the school hall, the air smelled of wood and dust. I could tell the place was old. The numerous feet that had traveled the school's single corridor had beaten the wood floors thin and uneven. Classroom doors lined the two parallel walls like rows of ready dominoes set to fall in on me at the first sign of a wrong move. What had I gotten myself into?

Ms. Kay's 5th Grade Class was indicated on a colorful sign taped over the window, and Betsy let me go in on my own. The classroom was bustling as I entered. Hardly anyone turned a head to look. There were nearly twenty kids running frantically around asking each other questions and scribbling their answers on paper.

"You must be Elyse," Ms. Kay greeted me, and I responded with a timid "yes."

I continued to watch the students running around in what seemed to be complete disorder. This was not how I imagined structured education.

"They're playing multiplication bingo," she began to explain.

"BINGO!" yelled a freckly redheaded boy, confirming the reason behind the chaos.

"All right, Benny, excellent. Everyone take your seats," she addressed the class. "Elyse, you may sit wherever you like."

Great. I was in the spotlight already. My heartbeat was so loud and hard I was sure everyone could hear the deafening thud, but the pressure was quickly relieved. A button-nosed girl with hair like black silk gestured for me to take the seat next to her.

"I'm Anna," she whispered to me. "What's your name?"

"Elyse," I answered.

"Okay everyone, before we check Benny's bingo card, let me introduce our new student."

"Her name is Elyse," the silky-haired girl interrupted.

"Yes, her name is Elyse. Everyone please make her feel at home, okay? Anna, why don't you let Elyse look off of your bingo card while we go over the answers?"

"Okay," she agreed scooting her desk so it was flush with mine. I saw her hand slip into her pocket. She passed me something in a closed fist and waited with a smile as I examined it.

"Don't let Ms. Kay see," she whispered. "It's a secret."

I slipped the wrapped candy into my pocket—the first of many secrets we would come to share.

From the moment her desk grazed the edge of mine, we were inseparable. Our friendship came naturally. Being with Anna was effortless, comfortable.

I was nobody but myself around her, and she was the same. There were no secrets, no secrets but one, and for the next three years, that secret was mine and mine alone.

Middle school was a vicious beast of cliques, bullies, and peer pressure, a monster that would have eaten me alive if not for Anna. Her gruff and forward personality countered my timid demeanor making us two perfect halves of a single entity.

The level of education was still a breeze, so school became a place to congregate, a place where we could join forces and slip into our own little world far away from the workings of junior high savagery. The summers, however, were boundless. How and where the days were spent didn't matter, as long as they were spent together, but this happiness was two-faced. The more I grew to love Anna and need her, the more pain I would feel at the loss. With every second, the joy of friendship burrowed deeper, so that when the time came for it to end, I knew it would rip out my soul.

"Did you ever hear of blood sisters?" Anna asked from the bed. She was lying on her stomach flipping through our newly printed yearbook.

"No," I told her. "What is it?"

"Just something April said at school."

"Well what did she say?" I pressed from the floor of my room. I skipped to April's class photo in my own yearbook. She was such a bully. She even looked the part.

"She said her and Susan should be able to get their picture taken together because they were sisters. Of course I told her 'no you're not,' but she said they were blood sisters, because they put their cuts together and mixed the blood."

I thought briefly about what Betsy would say, how the nurse in her would disapprove. "Elyse, that's how people spread disease. Be safe."

Anna must have taken my silence to mean that I too was contemplating the decision to make ourselves blood sisters.

"We're more like sisters than they are. Susan doesn't even like April that much. I think we should do it. Best friends for life, right?"

I froze. It *wasn't* safe. Not because Anna wasn't healthy, but because I wasn't . . . normal. Would something happen to her? What if I made her sick? My condition was something I hadn't considered in a long time. It had been so easy to push reality into the back of my head over the years, to pass off my growth-stunted body as being petite, small, or fragile, but here it was, staring me in the face. Anna wanted to test the biology of it all. She didn't know what she was getting herself into.

"Here, I'll pick this scab on my knee from yesterday. Do you have a scab or anything?"

"No. It's okay though, we'll do it later or something."

"Oh come on, don't be a baby. I know you have a blister on your hand from the monkey bars."

She grabbed my right hand and pulled open the cracked skin without warning.

"Ouch! Are you crazy?" I yelled as I yanked my hand back to examine the damage.

"Hurry, before it dries," she insisted.

Before I knew it she had my palm to her knee, rubbing the two sores together.

"There, see?" she asked looking for my approval, but I couldn't respond. My eyes were locked on her face. I wasn't sure what I was expecting, but I was waiting for it to happen. Her expression could have meant anything—a blank stare somewhere between concern and amazement.

"What?" was all I could say.

"It's gone." She searched my eyes for answers.

"What's gone?"

She took my hand and turned it over with a gasp, pulling the evidence close to her knee for comparison. Aside from the smeared blood, the skin on her knee was flawless. She licked her hand and wiped the surface clean just to be sure. Nothing. I ran my thumb over the skin of my palm, but not even a scar remained.

Betsy's footsteps gave warning of her approach, so we hid our bloodstained skin and tried to look busy.

"Hey girls, how are you doing?" she asked from the doorway.

"Good," we said in unison. She was too distracted to notice our robotic responses or the immense tension in the room.

"Good. Listen, Anna, I called your mom. She is on her way over to pick you up. I need a night alone with Ellie, okay? Don't worry, you're not in trouble," she said reassuringly, and she turned to leave.

"Do you think she knows?" I asked worried.

"No," Anna answered confidently.

I knew there was no hiding the fact that I had caused the healing. Anna knew me too well. She knew what I was thinking before I spoke.

"Look, I didn't know that would happen . . ." I said, trying to find the words that would save my friendship, words that would make me look like less of a freak, but she stopped me.

"I won't tell, Elyse," she said with earnest eyes. "Ever."

All these years later I was still sharing my secrets with Anna, and before I knew it, I was dialing her number.

"You think maybe I'm being conned?" I asked after telling her about my day.

"Maybe," she answered, "but all he's really roped you into is a date. He didn't ask for money, right?"

"No. Neither did the girl, but he knew my name. They both did."

"Elyse, you just moved in above the place he works. Of course he knows your name. The landlord is probably his boss."

"What about the girl? How would she know?"

"She's probably his crazy stalker ex-girlfriend."

I thought about it. "I don't know. He said *they* were following me. You know, my parents kept me in hiding for a reason."

"I doubt they were hiding you from a young guy that works in a coffee shop," she laughed. "I think you should go. You're just coming up with excuses. I never understood why you were so opposed to dating."

"You know why."

She paused. "Well, you know I don't agree with you."

"What if the guy wanted to get married?"

"So you marry him." Her voice spiked as though the answer was obvious.

"Eventually he would find out about my age," I argued. "We wouldn't be able to grow old together. What about kids? I don't even know if I can have kids."

"Why do you always have to play it out to the very end? Dating isn't getting married, Elyse. What's the harm in having fun?"

We'd had this conversation before, but Anna never let things go. Did she not understand the most obvious reason? What if I fell in love? What would happen when I outlived him? It would be more than heartbreaking to watch him grow old and die while he left me behind trapped in a time warp. It would destroy me. If there was even a chance, why risk it? I didn't want to talk about death with Anna, though. I didn't want to face the fact that I only had fifty years with her at most, and then I'd be alone. My heart felt heavy thinking about it.

"I'm not going," I concluded.

4.

AS SOON AS I got off the phone with Anna, I changed my mind. She was right. Dating didn't mean a lifetime commitment. Why not have fun? All morning I dwelled on the details of the night before, paying no attention to the logical warnings of my conscience.

When four o'clock rolled around, I let myself get ready. I took an extra long shower, shaving and shampooing twice, and as I blow-dried my flat hair, I realized I had never really had a reason to care about my appearance. I stared through the mirror into my chestnut eyes, trying to decide if I was pretty. Maybe I was. I could be if I tried.

I shouldn't care, but I was excited, a little too excited. I shut off the drier before I'd finished and tried to think objectively, to ignore all the reasons that fueled my curiosity. Was it really worth it? What if this was a trick? And even if it wasn't, what then? I couldn't allow myself to fall in love with someone. I had always known that. True love was *not* in my destiny.

As I began to second guess my decision and think my way out of it, I heard a knock at the door. It was way too early for William to be here, and I wasn't expecting anyone else. I sat on my bed and stayed quiet, hoping the person would think I wasn't home. They knocked again, but I didn't want to answer. This whole thing had made me so on-edge. I felt too vulnerable.

"Elyse?" The sound of William's voice got me on my feet. I grabbed my robe and went to answer the door.

"Hi. Sorry. I didn't know it was you," I said, grateful that I had gotten those first words out before I had a good look at him. He was even more gorgeous than my memory had given him credit for, and I felt speechless in that moment. His skin, the color of caramel, his jaw, strong and defined, every piece of him invited my attention.

"Hey. I know I'm a little early, but I've just been waiting at home all day to take you out."

"Okay," I answered, still unsure. "Yeah, just let me throw something on." I turned to head up the stairs, and realized I couldn't just leave him out there. I turned back. "Come on up."

I hadn't really considered what I was going to wear. I thought I had up to two hours to figure that out. After deciding that the worn out jeans and faded t-shirts in my closet wouldn't do, I began digging through old clothes I hadn't unpacked yet.

"Sorry there's no furniture," I yelled from my room.

I settled on a summery floral dress that Betsy had gotten me for my eightieth birthday. My hair still hung damp and limp, and the only shoes that matched were the black flip-flop sandals I'd been wearing every day.

When I got up the courage to reenter the living room, I found William making himself comfortable on my makeshift blanket couch.

"You look great," he said with raised eyebrows.

"Thanks," I mumbled back. I felt a little self-conscious in a dress, but I had to admit I liked the attention. I liked it too much. "So how is this going to work?" I grabbed my shoulder bag, reminding myself that I was doing this for a reason. "Are you going to tell me what you know?"

"Straight to the point, huh?" He laughed to himself. "I'll tell you tomorrow, once the date is over."

"Why not tonight?"

He shook his head. "It'll ruin it."

"All right." I accepted too easily. At least it would mean another reason to see him again. "Where are we going?"

"I was thinking we could see *Annie Hall*. There's a theater downtown that plays older films."

"I love that movie," I beamed, forgetting all the doubts and worries I had seconds before. "I saw it the day it came out." I stopped, catching my careless words as they fell out of my clumsy mouth.

"In 1977?" he asked, bright eyed and casually.

"I mean, on DVD," I corrected. I laughed my nervous laugh. Ten minutes into this and I was already acting like a complete idiot and letting things slip.

"Well, I thought you might like it."

"You did?" I sounded too pleased. He'd been thinking

about me, thinking about what I might like. Obviously any attempt to be indifferent toward him was hopeless.

"Yeah, you seem like the hopeless romantic type. Am I right?"

He sure had the hopeless part right, and as for romance, yes I suppose that was hopeless too.

"Yeah, I guess I am." No need to go into detail about my romantic hopelessness, right?

"I like your little nest of blankets," he chimed. "Maybe you should go into interior design."

I smiled. He was good at breaking the ice.

"Shut up," I shot back playfully. I was surprised at how easy it was to be myself around him. Despite the obvious paralyzing affect he seemed to have on me, I felt I could say what I pleased and act how I wanted and that was just fine with him. He was easygoing and calm in his demeanor, confident and unafraid of his surroundings. I wasn't sure how I was going to handle a whole night alone with him, but things seemed to be going smoothly.

"What kind of music do you like?" he asked once we were in his car. "I've got all kinds."

"Um, I don't know." I wasn't really familiar with what everyone was listening to these days. Betsy and I listened to a lot of the music from the forties—Billie Holiday, Frank Sinatra, Bing Crosby. I thought about asking if he had any of them, just to test his claim that he had all kinds, but I kept quiet.

"How about . . ." he paused as he flipped through one of his several books of CDs, "Foo Fighters?"

"Sure," I agreed, nodding my head at the unfamiliar name.

"Have you ever heard of them?" he asked.

"No."

He glanced up at me and smiled wide before brushing his long hair back with his hand.

"Wow," he said as he slipped the CD in. "You really have been sheltered."

The theater was old and rundown. *Rocky Horror Picture Show* flyers were tacked to the vintage ticket booth. William paid our admission without question, even though I offered to pay for my own. We decided not to stop and get snacks at the neglected concession stand to save room for dinner. The theater only had one projector screen in a room that seated nearly forty, so I expected to see at least some people, but the place was empty. The walls were wooden with carved patterns of angels and peeling white paint. It had a musky smell and a dingy look that only added to its authenticity. It looked like it might have been an actual acting theater in its prime.

"I used to come here a lot," William said. "It's been sort of neglected, but it was a really beautiful place once."

"How do you find these kinds of secret places?" I asked.

"People with secrets need places to keep them."

I stared into him, like maybe if I looked hard enough I'd be able to figure things out on my own. "I wish you would just tell me what's going on."

"I told you I'd tell you everything, but you still owe me half a date."

The lights went down almost as soon as we took our seats even though we were still the only two in the theater. Since it was just us, we could have talked, but we didn't. I wasn't sure where William's mind was, but mine was all over the place. In between playbacks of our night in the library, my thoughts picked up on the feel of his arm against my own or how his knee seemed to drift toward the bare skin of mine. Although my eyes stared in the direction of the movie screen, they were not watching.

"This is my favorite scene," he whispered into my ear. We were alone, so there was no need for the intimacy, but I liked it.

The whole experience seemed to flicker by in a matter of seconds, and I wished I could bargain with time for just a few more precious minutes. When the credits began to roll, I was reluctant to leave such close proximity—closeness that made my skin tingle. I waited until the very last words left the screen before I dared break away from it.

"Hungry?" he asked.

Jose's Mexican Food was written in red letters on the front of the building. A sombrero hung off the hook of the 'J' and a set of maracas was painted on the end. The place had character, making me think it probably wasn't a chain restaurant. It had simple brown stucco, a red roof and Spanish tiles. Inside, the walls were painted pastel green and pink, and the Mexican flag hung proudly in the entryway.

"Do you want a margarita or something?" he asked me after we seated ourselves in the corner booth.

"Not twenty-one yet."

"Right," he answered with a chuckle. "Me either."

"Hey kids," said a heavyset Mexican woman greeting us.

"What can I get you to drink?"

"Just some waters. Is that okay?" he asked me.

"Yeah, water is fine." I'd probably drink straight cod liver oil just to sit next to him.

"All right. Here's some menu's. I'll be back," the waitress said, excusing herself.

"So what do you do for fun when you're not being forced to go on dates?"

I laughed. "Yeah, because that happens every day." I practiced looking away from him, something I found extraordinarily hard to do. "I don't know. I like to write poetry, do crosswords, boring stuff."

"Sounds like you need to get out."

I shrugged. "Well, what about you? What's your idea of fun?"

"A night out with the one and only Miss Elyse Ellen Adler, of course."

I looked away again. He knew my full name. I hadn't expected that. My gaze stayed down, but I noticed how his eyes tended to fall intently on me when he thought my attention was elsewhere. Luckily our waitress came back fairly quickly with our drinks and flipped open her note pad.

"Okay, here's some chips and salsa with two waters. You ready to order?"

William nodded for me to go first.

"The grilled chicken burrito for me," I answered.

"And some carne asada tacos," he added.

"All right. Let me take these," she said picking up our menus.

As soon as she left, William started back up with the questions. I liked his questions. As pathetic as it was, it made me feel like he really was interested in me, and I let myself indulge in the feeling, something I might never feel again.

"Have you noticed anyone else following you? Any new friends since you've moved here?"

"Aside from Kara? No, and as new friends go, you're pretty much the first," I answered truthfully.

"Good."

As long as we were asking questions, I had one for him.

"How did you know my name?" I asked.

"I've always known it."

I grabbed a chip and began nibbling nervously.

"How? Do you work for the government or something?" The question sounded ridiculous. He was too young, too casual to be anyone official.

"Oh yeah. I'm a super spy," he said with a straight face. Then his expression cracked. "No, I don't work for the government, but you're right to be cautious. You shouldn't be so trusting of people."

"Of you?"

"Luckily, I'm the one person you can trust."

I found myself immensely curious about him.

"I'm just glad I found you first." He took a drink of water, staring at me over the brim.

"Here we go. A grilled chicken burrito and carne asada tacos," our waitress announced, breaking the intense moment. "Anything else I can get for you?"

"No, I think that's it," William answered.

I kept my eyes on him as he spoke to our waitress.

"Can I ask you something else?" he asked, turning back to me. "Getting back to our date."

"Sure," I shrugged, biting into my burrito.

"If you could sum up your whole life into a single flavor, what would it be? What do you think your life would taste like?"

I laughed. "I don't know. That's a strange question." I thought about it though. It would have to be something bitter, but still sweet in a way, something that looked better than it tasted.

"Maybe . . . semi-sweet chocolate?"

"Only semi-sweet?" he observed.

"I have my reasons," I defended. "What about you? Something sugary and delicious?"

"Hmm, I have to rethink it. It's definitely changed since I met you."

He smiled at me, and I recoiled a little into the cushion seat of the booth, throwing my eyes immediately in a different direction—away from his.

"Peanut butter," he decided.

"Why peanut butter?"

"I have my reasons," he mocked.

"It's not very sweet."

"No, but it goes well with chocolate."

"Oh," I said as my face flushed with heat and I took another bite to try and hide my obvious smile. "I like peanut butter." I wasn't used to these sorts of flattering comments.

"You know," he said. "I might have to change it to carne

asada tacos . . . these are pretty good."

It was already dark outside when we left the restaurant, even though it seemed like we had just come from my house. The hours had flown by unaccounted for.

"I just want to make one more stop," he said, putting on new soothing music. Every once in a while I'd glance over at him, tapping his hand on the steering wheel and bobbing his head to the beat. It was hard not to enjoy myself. I didn't really care where we went, but I wasn't expecting it to be the grocery store.

"I'll be right back, okay?"

"Sure," I said. At least this would give me some time to think.

I needed to decide what to do. The earlier I ended things the less it would hurt, so I would have to say something tonight. The knot formed in my stomach again. It wasn't fair. I felt tears of frustration begin to form, and the constant battle between head and heart raged through me. I had no choice. I would tell him at the end of our perfect night—I would be the one to ruin it all. At least it would be done, and I wouldn't be tempted to continue things after the morning.

"It's not semi-sweet or anything, but I hope you actually like chocolate," he said opening the car door with a box of ice cream cones in his hand.

"Who doesn't like chocolate?" I answered cheerfully. His charm was revitalizing. All the conflict seemed to melt away with a single glance and a smile.

"So what now?" I asked. "Where should we go?"

"Feel like stopping by Cearno's?"

"Are there a lot of people there?"

He seemed excited. "Yeah, I'm sure there are."

"I don't know," I said, hoping to get out of mingling with people I'd have to avoid befriending.

"Okay. Then, I have another secret place I want to show you."

We found ourselves at a park, left neglected in the night. The jungle gym and picnic tables were the only company it kept. The moonlight filtered down through the clouds lighting the ground with a peaceful glow.

"Do you want to get out?" I asked.

"Yeah, let's crack open the ice cream before it melts."

The large rooted trees that hovered over the weathered picnic tables and swings had littered the ground with dried leaves that crunched under my feet. William handed me a chocolate dipped cone, and I sat on the worn tabletop letting my legs dangle off the side.

"So, aside from working at Cearno's, do you go to college or anything?" I asked.

"I guess you could say I go to school," he answered.

"San Francisco State or what?"

"No, you haven't heard of it. It's more of a private institution."

"What are you majoring in?"

"Greek Mythology," he answered, trying not to smile. Maybe he was embarrassed about it. At least now, last night's reference to the *Homeric Hymns* made more sense.

"I've had a lot of fun tonight. For not being a people person you are pretty easygoing."

"For a bribe, yeah," I teased. "It's actually been a good time."

"Hey, at least I'm winning you over."

"We'll see." Winning me over wasn't an option. "Once you've delivered on your side of the bargain."

"The suspense is killing you, isn't it?" I could tell he was having fun with this. "Come on, I'll drive you home."

I worried about our goodbye all the way to my apartment. I had to draw the line, cut him off, or shut him out. This was the first and last wonderful night we would have together. After tomorrow morning, I would make a point to avoid him. He walked me to my door. This was it.

"Listen William, I just want to say that . . ." When I turned to look at him, his eyes were piercing, as if his gaze could penetrate all boundaries. All of a sudden a sense of euphoria clouded my judgment, and I felt completely vulnerable. My eyes shifted quickly to his mouth as the edges curled into his dimpled cheeks, and my heart began to race making my body warm. The warmth was overwhelming, not like heat, not like anything I could describe.

Something was happening. *He is doing this to me*, I thought, but all the confusion seemed to drift away as the euphoric feeling spread. I hadn't looked away from his lips, still wearing a faded smile. I couldn't. I imagined brushing them with my own. I wanted to be closer to him. The warmth had spread to my head, leaving an empty feeling in my chest. I needed him. The emptiness was a hole that only he could fill. He was the relief. It pulled from every direction, this yearning for him. All he needed to do was speak the words, "kiss me," and I would obey.

I found his eyes again, that penetrating gaze. I was desperate, searching for any sign of reciprocation. His expression fell, but it was there. He felt it too. I knew it.

Suddenly his lids closed, and the fog began to lift. Only fuzzy remnants of the feeling lingered as proof of my short-lived intoxication.

"Sorry," he said in a low voice. I waited for him to continue, but he turned to leave instead, and rushed off down the street.

"William?" I asked after him, but he didn't look back.

I wanted to chase him down or scream after him, *what was that*, but my head, now clear of his strange hypnotic hold, told me to be smart and go inside.

As I lay in bed that night, I relived each moment over and over again, hoping to pick up on something I might have missed, but always, it was the same inconclusive ending with his unexplainable goodnight. I tried considering the idea that maybe *I* had caused the strange euphoric rush that made me need him more than the most addictive of drugs, that had me willing to do anything he asked in return for his approval, but the vivid image of his intense eyes made me certain it was him.

I wanted more than anything to be straightforward and simply ask him what happened. Maybe there was a perfectly good explanation for the incident. I imagined how the conversation would go: "So, last night when you cast some sort of debilitating love spell on me . . . what was that?"

Realizing the absurdity of my question, I pictured his puzzled expression as he thought, *this girl is crazy*.

It was too risky. I was curious, but not willing to make a complete fool of myself. Maybe he'd explain in the morning. If not, I would have to be subtle, not come off too insane.

5.

IT WAS STILL DARK outside when I woke up to the sound of somebody in my apartment. The noises were faint, someone's unsuccessful attempt to keep quiet. My mind immediately became aware and defensive, like an animal that knows it's being hunted. Careful not to make a sound, I quietly crept out of bed and tiptoed my way to my desk, hoping to find something to use as a weapon. Without much luck, I grabbed the only thing that seemed somewhat feasible, a heavy square edged jewelry box the size of my palm. Deciding I could throw it at the intruder or maybe use it to pack a heavier punch if there was no chance of escape, I grabbed the piece and clutched it tightly in my trembling hand. My heart began to stutter, stumbling unevenly with each beat as the thuds became so loud I was sure they would give me away.

I moved on to the door, turning the knob soundlessly with gritted teeth hoping that the hinges would refrain from their sporadic creaking. They did, but even so, the panic began to take hold of me as I inched along the hallway wall that led from my bedroom. The noises had stopped.

There were only two viable scenarios. The first, it was a burglar, and with this place being so small, he would eventually find me, and then who knows what? The second and most probable thing that crossed my mind made me seize up with fear as I considered it. I was being followed, and whoever was behind it had sent someone to collect whatever it was they wanted, maybe even my life.

There was no telling what would come of me. I breathed quickly and silently, trying to decide whether I should wait or run. Sweat began to stick to my cotton pajamas as I listened for any hint of a sound. Nothing.

I moved closer, almost ready to make my move when a hand covered my mouth from behind, and my whole body tensed up from the inside. With a finger to his lips, William let go and moved to peer around the corner. I held my breath as he turned toward the kitchen and out of sight, leaving me alone in the hallway.

One second the place was silent, the next Kara was diving into William, knife drawn and ready. They rolled and scuffled on the floor of my living room, while I watched, too stunned with shock to scream.

She had him pinned beneath her, the blade pressed up against his neck.

"Wait," I shouted, but she didn't acknowledge me. Seconds passed, minutes. Then with a careful hand, Kara handed the knife to William and kissed him on the mouth.

"What the hell?" I said aloud.

"Jesus, Kara," he said, shoving her off. She huddled shyly against the wall.

"What's going on?" I demanded. "She was trying to kill you and then . . ."

"I wasn't trying to kill him," Kara answered defensively. "He was going to attack me. It was self defense."

"Well if you weren't creeping around her apartment, I wouldn't have to attack you."

"Look who's talking. What are *you* doing here?"

"Don't turn things around. You know why I'm here. Answer the question." William paced back and forth between the two of us, like a wolf guarding its den.

"I was looking for proof," she answered. "I want to know if she is who you *think* she is."

William glared at her. "Get out of my head, Kara."

"I know you're curious. Let's see her prove it."

Kara stood and William took a defensive step toward her. "I don't need her to prove anything, and neither do you."

She ignored him and kept her eyes locked on me. "OK, so *I'm* curious. I want to see it with my own eyes."

"Careful," he warned her. "Don't test me."

I waited in silence for one of them to make a move.

"Do they know?" he demanded.

She shrugged. "They know what I tell them."

"So, what have you told them?"

I had no idea what they were talking about, but the way Kara looked at me had me ready to defend myself.

"Nothing. Yet."

"Told who what?" I spoke up with force. "I'm tired of being

talked about like I'm not here."

That's when the tiny blade went flying through the air, sticking me in the leg. I let out a cry of pain, and grabbed my right thigh. William had seen it coming, and pinned Kara to the wall in a matter of seconds.

"Not okay," he seethed through clenched teeth.

She didn't struggle, but her words were fierce. "Let me go."

"Do yourself a favor and keep it to yourself."

"Don't threaten me," she choked.

"Get. Out," he spat, releasing her.

She fell to the floor and scampered toward the stairs, staring daggers at him. "Do *yourself* a favor and don't get on my bad side."

"Dammit," he cursed as she slammed the front door behind her. Then, realizing I was still frozen from shock, he returned to me. "Are you all right?"

"No!" I shouted, letting him escort me to the pile of blankets on my floor.

"Just thought I'd ask."

He knelt down beside me and straightened out my leg, gripping the edge of the blade with his strong fingers. "One, two . . ."

"Ouch!" I yelled at him as he pulled the metal from my flesh. "You didn't even say three."

"Three is for wussies."

He gently rolled up the loose cotton of my pajama pant to examine the cut.

"Who are you people?"

"Well, *she's* apparently a raging lunatic," he said with a

smile, "and I'm just the guy trying to keep you safe."

After looking carefully at the cut, William took Kara's knife and slid the sharp edge against the pad of his thumb, cutting deep enough to draw blood.

"What are you doing?" I asked, appalled.

"Always with the questions," he answered, shaking his head. "Just hold your horses, Ellie."

He moved to press his thumb against the cut on my leg, and I almost stopped him, but didn't. He knew. Somehow he knew it would heal me.

"How do you know?" I whispered the secret question.

When he lifted his thumb, both of our cuts were gone. He wiped the fresh blood with his shirt, and stared at the flawless skin.

"I know what every Descendant knows," he answered. "That there is a girl, the last healer, who has been hidden. The one we've been waiting for. The one who will change everything."

"But I'm—"

"I know that makes no sense to you," he interrupted. "There are others, Elyse. You're not alone. That's the first thing you should know."

My mind picked out the one word that had meaning. "Others?" He was right. I didn't believe him. "I want proof."

"All I have right now is a picture my dad gave me," he said, coming to sit next to me on the blankets. "I've been carrying it around just in case. He told me your parents had the same one, but I'm not sure you've seen it." William handed me the photo. "If you need more proof, I was planning on showing you, but we have to wait until the morning."

I couldn't register the words he was saying, or maybe I just refused to believe them. William's face was nervous, and he stared hard back at me. I tried to read the reason behind all of this, tried to understand how it could be true. I was so stupid, so naïve to trust him, to trust anyone, but I did.

I looked down at the picture I had been holding but not really looking at, and to my surprise, I *had* seen it. It was black and white and old, just like the one I had in my gold box, but this one was in much better condition. A group of people stood outside against a wall as if to take a class photo. All the faces were smiling, including my mother and father.

"There next to your parents, that's my dad," he affirmed.

I couldn't believe it. Things like this didn't happen to me, couldn't possibly happen, but the evidence of it was right in my hands. I had no words, no thoughts, no reaction, or maybe just too many of everything to clearly define an emotion. It took more than a minute for my first real thought to surface.

"And you, you're . . . one of them?" I asked with quiet hopefulness. My skin flushed hot and red as my pulse quickened. I prayed he didn't notice.

He flashed his brilliant white smile at me. "A Descendant? Yeah, of course."

Suddenly all of the misshapen pieces of my life that never seemed to fit clicked into place. There were others. I wasn't alone. For the first time, I felt like anything was possible, like my future could be full of all the things I thought I would never have.

"A Descendant," I repeated the word. It didn't sound

familiar. I turned to him, seeing everything through different eyes. "How old are you?"

"Three hundred and sixteen."

"Really?" I asked in amazement.

"No. Not really." He laughed to himself. "I'm ninety-two, but this is going to be a lot of fun."

I felt myself smile. I couldn't help it. *Please don't let this be a dream*, I thought. It certainly seemed like one. There were too many thoughts racing through my head to process anything other than pure joy.

"What did you mean, I was the last healer? Don't you heal too?"

"No, we all have different abilities. Yours is healing."

"Abilities?" I scoffed. "What like super powers?" The question was a joke, but he took it more seriously than I expected.

"Well, kind of. Some abilities are a little too strange to be called a super power. Each family line has the power of their ancestors, which is why we call ourselves Descendants. My dad says you have the power of your mother, descendant of Asclepius, known as the god of healing."

"The god of healing?" I asked in astonishment. A stifled laugh escaped my lips. This had to be a joke.

"We're not gods though," he added. "In fact, neither were any of the gods in Greek mythology. They're our ancestors, and they were just like us. We've been around for a while. Sorry. I'm assuming you don't know any of this, right?"

I laughed. "You've got to be joking. Gods?"

"Correction. *Not* gods."

"Right," I said with raised eyebrows. "You don't really expect me to believe you?" I looked him straight in the eyes, calling his bluff, but he only smiled.

"I figured you wouldn't. It's like trying to tell someone unicorns exist or something. It's hard to believe unless you see for yourself."

"So you can prove it?" The picture was convincing, but I needed more.

"Yes. Tomorrow, okay? I'll make sure you get a complete history lesson."

"Well, can't you tell me now, about the history?"

"I thought you didn't believe me?"

"Well, say hypothetically I did."

"So, if, *hypothetically*, you did believe me, I'd explain that we've had to live in hiding since the exposure of our race in Greece back in B.C. Our ancestors thought they could live in peace with humans so they tried to integrate—"

"Wait," I interrupted, thrown off a bit. "Humans? What are you saying? We're not human?"

From the look on his face, I could tell he hadn't really considered my reaction to that seemingly small detail of his explanation. "Well, yes and no. Obviously we have similarities. In appearance, we're the same, but no, we're not humans, we're Descendants. We're different."

I sighed in place of a response. Not because I didn't believe him, but because it was actually starting to sink in. My whole life, I'd never felt normal, but maybe that wasn't it. Maybe I was normal. I'd just never felt like a normal human, because I wasn't.

"Well coming out of hiding didn't go so well," William continued, talking through my loss for words. "Clearly we're living in secret again, but that's where the myths came from. People embellished the truth. Our ancestors led humans to believe they were gods because of their abilities, and it got out of hand. There was a war between our race and the humans, and we didn't necessarily lose, but we retreated back into hiding. Now, here we are."

His entire story sounded like something completely made up, but I didn't get the feeling he was lying to me. I didn't know what to think. Then there was Kara. *You really don't know anything do you?* Her words had been confusing at the time, but suddenly they made sense. Maybe William was telling the truth.

"What about my father?" I asked, digging deeper.

"Your father had the power of Hephaestus. He could manipulate materials, metal, stone, wood, that kind of thing."

"How do you know so much about me and my family?" I asked, realizing he knew more about my parents than I did.

"My dad," William answered. "He was friends with your parents."

I looked down at the picture of them with so many others.

"How many are there?" I asked, handing him back the photo.

He tucked it into his back pocket and leaned back against the wall. "Over 300 families here in San Francisco, but there are many others elsewhere. There are five mainstream communities in the U.S.—New York, Los Angeles, Dallas, Chicago, and here. Of course there are smaller ones other places, and you can always live on your own if you want, like you did. Living alone is hard, though. There's no support, no safety net. Not many of us choose that."

"I didn't *choose* that," I corrected, "my parents did."

I didn't know why I felt so suddenly defensive and bitter about their choice, probably because I didn't understand it. Why would they pull me out of this life and hide me away like I didn't exist? I wished I knew the reason. I wished they had told me what I was, that I didn't have to dig around for answers like a dog sniffing out game, searching for the broken buried pieces of my life.

"Do you know what made us the way we are? What gave us abilities?" I asked, feeling the place on my leg where the cut should be.

"What made any of us? Evolution, God, the big bang? We're just as lost as everyone else on that one."

"But there's got to be some theology around it, right? I can't imagine the myths are true. Are they?"

"Parts of them are, but nobody really knows where the abilities came from. There are theories. Some say our powers are God-given, and associate the 500-year lifespan with the Bible because people lived hundreds of years back then. Others reject that idea because there really isn't any proof of the connection. We still debate over it, but no one really believes our ancestors were gods. They were just like us."

"What do you believe?"

"I try not to dwell on things I can't be sure of, and just try to live in the moment."

"You aren't even the least bit interested in where you came

from, to know why we're different?"

"Who says we're different? To me, being a Descendant is completely normal. They're the ones who are different."

I never really thought of that. I'd always thought of myself as the only one, the outcast. Now that there were more, lots more, maybe it no longer made sense to see it that way.

"So what's your ability?"

He thought about it, apparently unsure he should tell me. "Persuasion."

I smiled to myself remembering the intense urge I had to kiss him at the end of our date. "Well, I guess the way you acted last night makes more sense now."

He smiled back, a little embarrassed. "Yeah, sorry about that. I got a little carried away."

"And Kara?"

"Occupational hazard," he answered with a shrug. "*She* kissed *me*. I mean, she was in a dominating position. I didn't see it coming. I couldn't have prevented it."

He realized when he looked at me that wasn't what I meant.

"Relax," I said. "So you kissed. Why do I care?" I looked away. If he couldn't see my eyes, maybe he wouldn't see the lie in them. "So, what's her ability?"

He lost himself in thought for a moment, confused by my reaction.

"She reads minds," he finally answered. "She's also a highly trained super killing machine, but that's not really an ability, more of a skill she's picked up over the years."

"So what you're saying is my jewelry box might not of have been very effective," I said, setting my useless weapon down in front of me.

"That was the best you could do, huh?" William asked. "Your plan was to kill her with your little metal box?"

"Yep," I answered, unconcerned with what had already passed. I had questions. "Why does she want to kill me?"

"She doesn't want to kill you," he said, shaking his head. "It's complicated. She's not on our side."

"So, what does she want from me?"

"I think deep down she wants the prophecy to be true. She wants freedom."

"What's the prophecy?"

He looked at me with empathy. "You should get some sleep," he said in place of an answer.

I didn't accept it. "You have to tell me. You said people have been waiting for me, to change things."

"They have."

"Well, I want to know."

"Of course you do, but I can't tell you everything all at once." He stood up, stretching his arms above his head before turning to face me. "There is a lot you wouldn't understand."

He took both of my hands, subtle heat building in his fingertips, and lifted me onto my feet.

"And what is with the hot hands?"

"Tomorrow."

He walked me to my room and watched me pull the covers up around me.

"What *were* you doing here?" I asked, hoping to get even the smallest answer out of him.

"I was spending the night on the fire escape, waiting for

Kara." He shook his head angry at the thought of her. "I knew she'd come."

"Don't you need to sleep?"

"I'll doze off on your little blanket couch. If that's okay," he answered.

I nodded.

"It just makes me feel better if I'm close by."

"Me too."

6.

"WAKE UP, sleep-o-holic," William said with a nudge. "We have class."

"Huh?" my voice grumbled with sleep.

William laughed, clearly amused by my morning grog. "Hey." I must have dozed off again. "Wake up."

I sat upright in bed, realizing if William was here, it must all be true. I hadn't dreamed it.

"Class?" I asked, rubbing my eyes.

"Yeah. Get dressed. I'm taking you to The Institute."

"What's The Institute?"

"It's where I go to school."

As the details from last night began to come back to me, a sense of anticipation had me wide awake. "Are there others there?"

"Descendants? Yeah, that's the idea."

I had no clue what class or The Institute would be like, but I wanted to know more. As I pulled on some Levi's and a blue top, I realized that although not everything was clear to me, the one thing that mattered had never been so closely within grasp. If there were others, love was a possibility, and although my insecurities tried to convince me otherwise, the truth was for once in my favor. I smiled at myself in the bathroom mirror, unable to hold back my happiness.

The way to The Institute was nothing like I expected. There was no elaborate campus or secret road leading to some mysteriously secluded location. In fact, it was quite the opposite. William drove us straight into the heart of downtown San Francisco. I should have known that the bustling city so full of people would be the best place to hide an organization of this kind. A sideways grin settled into his cheek as he watched my curious eyes try and understand where this place could possibly be.

"What?" I finally asked him, a little embarrassed by his excessive interest in me.

"Nothing, you're just . . . fun to watch."

The corners of my mouth gave away the hint of a smile. "Why?"

"It's like you're trying to find Mount Olympus out the window or something. It's cute."

"Well, I don't know," I said, laughing at myself. "I have no idea what to expect."

"What are you imagining?" His eyes stayed forward on the road as he waited for my answer.

"Honestly? I can't stop picturing people walking around wearing togas and olive branch headbands." I smiled, knowing the thought was completely ridiculous, but it was what my mind had conjured up.

He burst into a belly laugh. "You're joking, right?"

"You asked."

"You're way off," he said, still chuckling to himself. "Not even close."

As we pulled into the drive of a gated underground parking structure, William stopped to enter his keycard. The Institute was nothing but an indistinct office building. Nothing drew attention to it. There were no numbers, no signs, nothing suspicious about it whatsoever, tall enough to blend in but not tall enough to stand out. The gray outer walls were neither new nor old, and the windows that sat above the bright clear ones of the first floor were tinted dark as if that part of the building was asleep. Never in a million years would I have guessed it was a center for people with powers.

We parked close to the elevator and took it to the first floor, but as the doors opened, I was suddenly confused. I had expected something unusual, but what I saw was certainly no school of any sort, and there was nothing strange about the place.

The inside of the building was nothing like the bland outside. The floors were a brilliant white marble that reflected sound up from the ground like a drum, as sharp heels click-clacked over the surface. Directly above the pristine floor, the ceiling was just as remarkable, decorated with elaborate scenes from famous Greek myths. Whether on their own or as part of a collaborative image, nearly every figure was depicted. The paintings covered the entire surface with explosive color and technique that reminded me of the Sistine Chapel.

Dramatic crystal chandeliers hung in all four corners of the room surrounding a more grandiose one that dipped low and gleamed like the sun. A gold border of crown molding connected the extravagant ceiling to the sleek walls.

"What is this place?" I whispered. It was noisy enough to talk aloud and keep my words quiet, but I felt intimidated by the purely business setting of the lobby. It was busy with people. Men in suits and ties and women in skirts and heels hurried in crisscross patterns across the floor—a multilane intersection of people taking care of daily business.

"It's San Francisco Headquarters for Descendant Affairs," he said at normal volume.

"I thought this was The Institute."

"That's on the top floor, but we have to get you registered first."

My ears perked up. "Registered for what?" Betsy and I had spent years making sure we stayed anonymous. Registering for something wasn't okay in my mind.

"For classes."

"I don't know if I'm comfortable with that." People rushed past us, irritated that we were standing in their way.

"Trust me. I wasn't either," he empathized, "but my dad said it was necessary. These are your people, Elyse. It's time for you to be a part of this."

It didn't take much to convince me. Things were different, these *were* my people, and I didn't have to worry about hiding who I was or being exposed. We were all in the same boat.

"All right," I said with an eager smile.

We walked toward the front desk dodging the streams of

oncoming people and took our place in line with the rest of the casually dressed citizens.

"Hello, miss, how can I help you?" the young secretary asked the old woman at the front of the line. Her hair was a natural red, tied back in a bun that reminded me of the 1930s. Her features, gentle and pink, reacted calmly to the aggressive tone of the woman she was helping.

"I filed for an extension on my community residence expiration a week ago." The old lady's nasally voice was upset and worried. "It expires today and I haven't heard back."

"All right, ma'am. If you go through that door on the right you can talk to someone in Processing."

"So I waited in this line for nothing?" the woman spat.

"I'll let them know you're on your way," the receptionist said, unfazed. As the woman stomped away, I watched her rickety body wobble with fury. I realized that she must be about 400 years old. I thought a bit about what that woman had been through. That many years of life was bound to make someone a little jaded.

"How can I help you, sir?" Her voice was closer now as we moved through the line.

"Yes. I got my notification for identification renewal. I'm just checking in," said the man in front of us. He looked around forty, which would make him 200 years old or so. His hair was salt and pepper black, and everything about him seemed so normal. That's when I noticed that everyone here was a little too normal. Where were all the crazy powers people were supposed to have? It was all just too boring for a community of mythological Descendants.

"Why isn't anyone using any powers?" I asked William.

"Oh, they are forbidden on this floor. Just a precaution."

"What about the other floors, why not take precaution there?"

"Well you need an ID card to access the elevators, so it's pretty safe."

Suddenly there was nobody in front of us, and we were next.

"Hi," I blurted out, but beyond that I wasn't sure what registration entailed so I let William continue.

"We're here to get her registered. She's new to the community," he explained.

"Name?" I noticed she asked him and not me.

"Elyse Adler," I made a point to answer.

As she typed my name in, I half expected the computer to reject the entry, to shoot off bells and whistles declaring me an imposter. Instead she responded with: "Here we go . . . It looks like most of the information has already been entered. Let me just print out her ID card," she talked to me through William of course. I understood her desire to address him— it was the perfect excuse to admire his jaw-dropping good looks—but I still resented it.

"Really?" I asked confused. "I don't remember filling anything out. How can you be sure that is my file?"

She raised her eyebrows at my apparently ridiculous question.

"The picture," she said, turning her screen to show me my profile. Sure enough my most recent driver's license photo stared back at me from her computer monitor.

"We'd also like to enroll her in school," William added.

"Certainly," she fluttered.

I rolled my eyes, which made him laugh a little under his breath. He was polite, but not flirtatious as he wrapped up the transaction.

"Does that ever get old?" I asked, a little peeved as we walked to the internal elevator.

"What?" he asked obviously playing dumb.

"Oh come on. Having women drool over you like that."

He pretended to think about it for a second. "Nope, never," he joked. "Why, are you jealous?"

It only took a minute before I decided. "Maybe," I said.

He laughed, clearly thinking I was absurd. "You are."

He handed me my new ID, no more complex than a simple library card, and grabbed my free hand as we reached the elevators. Although my attention was strongly aware of the warm skin of William's palm, I watched as each person scanned their card upon entering and did the same. I wondered briefly what would happen if you entered without a card, but let the thought drift away as William gave me an excited look. We rode the lift to the top floor as instructed, stopping every few floors to let out small groups of well-dressed people.

When we finally reached the very last floor, I didn't know what to expect, and as the doors opened up I stood dumbfounded at the unworldly display of activity. We were let off in the middle of the passing hall, and students were making their way to and from class. None of them seemed to notice our arrival. They simply kept on as they would normally, or as was normal for them. But they were no ordinary group of kids. There were plenty of students who, like us, had no outwardly visible ability and walked to class just as we were, but interspersed between the mobs, there were those who stood out amongst the crowd. The closest passerby, a boy who was seemingly feeble and small, carried a girl on each shoulder like it was nothing.

"Show off," William teased him.

"You're just jealous," the boy joked back.

A blurred image of a girl whipped past us at a speed that was incomprehensible, and like a flash of light she was gone. The boy walking next to me grew two feet in less than a second, apparently looking for a friend down the hall, before shrinking back to his regular size. A few people ahead of us, I could see a girl surrounded by what seemed to be a force field that kept people at a distance.

Adding to the whole effect was the stream of airborne objects that ran just above the teeming traffic of the hallway, like a moving river of debris. Desk chairs, scattered paper, books, computer parts, backpacks, a cell phone, were all floating above our heads with a number of other items on their way somewhere.

"How is this happening?" I asked, pointing above my head.

"Mr. Gransky." William smiled at the objects above us. "He is the janitor here. Makes it easier to keep an entire building cleaned and organized when you can move things with your mind. He does favors for people too, interdepartmental mail and things. He's always moving random stuff around."

"Quite a multi-tasker," I added with amazement as the items continued to soar above us.

Aside from the mind-blowing stunts that were passing before my unbelieving eyes, there was nothing elaborate about the place—just the typical features of any school building. White linoleum floors colored with gray flecks and scuff marks reflected the false fluorescent light. Doors with windows lined the single hall that seemed to continue around the corner of each end in a square.

Suddenly, out of nowhere, someone stepped out in front of us, nearly causing me to trip over my own feet.

"Wow," William said, catching me by the arm. "What's with the surprise attack, Professor?"

"Sorry," the old man said with a high, amused voice. "The girl must come with me."

Before I knew it, the professor had me by the wrist, pulling me in the opposite direction of the crowd and away from William. I didn't know what to do. Who was this man, and where was he taking me?

"William?" I called out at him with concern.

"Wait, Iosif," he yelled with a laugh. The professor stopped, giving William the chance to catch up. "We have Origins and History right now. Can't you wait to talk to her?"

"No. Dear, I really must speak with you now. Is that all right?"

To my surprise, he was addressing me not William.

"Um, I guess so," I said full of uncertainty. My eyes looked to William for an escape, but he was simply amused by the old man's insistence.

"Fine, take her," William said with a mischievous look in his eyes, "but you owe me one."

My jaw dropped. He was supposed to be getting me out of this, not bargaining a deal.

"Okay, all right," Iosif agreed eagerly. "A free hall pass, but that's it."

With a nod, we were off again, and William simply waved and smiled, finding amusement in my expression.

"William!" I shrieked. What was he doing, trading me for a hall pass?

"You'll be fine," he yelled back. "The old man won't bite. Not unless you struggle."

William's grin never faded, and I was sure it lasted long after I lost him in the crowd. I promised myself I would get him back for enjoying the sight of me getting dragged off by such a loon, but what could he have done really? Professor Iosif, however odd, clearly had authority over him. Still, as far as I was concerned, William owed *me* one.

7.

THE PROFESSOR WAS extremely old. His white hair had thinned on top, and the rest of it stood out frizzled and wild from the sides of his head like a bald Albert Einstein. He had full circle wire rimmed glasses and a crooked pointy nose to hold them up. His body was hunched over as we trudged down the still busy hallway, making him slightly shorter than me. As we reached his office, he closed the door and smiled widely, unafraid to bare his strangely jumbled mess of teeth. Although he seemed about as crazy as he looked, his overall personality was kind and welcoming.

"I'm so glad you've finally come. I was starting to worry." He seemed to find his own words funny and chuckled to himself.

"Come to The Institute?" I asked, not knowing he'd been expecting me.

"Well, yes."

"I didn't even know this place existed until this morning,"

I answered honestly.

"That's understandable," he said as he fumbled around looking for something. His office was dark. What little light did manage to find its way in seeped through spaces between the high stacks of books piled up against the window. There was a kitchenette and some cupboards to the right and two shelves on the left that housed a collection of items so old one might expect to find them in a museum. I imagined the antiques were actually things he had owned over the past 400 years or so he'd lived. His desk was completely covered in newspapers, open mail and ungraded papers, and I wondered from the look of the place if he considered this a second residence.

"Would you like some tea?" he asked, finally finding what he was searching for.

Not wanting to be rude, I accepted and let my eyes wander some more as he prepared it.

"Why aren't you asking questions?" He set the tea in front of me and sat behind his desk. "I know you have many."

"Oh," I answered. I did have questions, lots of questions. I just wasn't used to someone being willing to answer them.

"Let's start with your ability," he pushed past my lack of response. His eyebrows raised in curiosity. "You are familiar with the process."

I returned his calculating stare with an unnerving look.

"Well, yes and no. I know my blood can heal, but how does it work exactly?" I realized he might know more than I thought. "Can I heal *anybody*?"

"Yes, essentially, and anybody can heal you. You're our cure as much as we are yours. However, there are some specifics you don't seem to be aware of. Only the blood from your right side heals."

"My left side doesn't heal?" I'd always been too scared to experiment with it. Aside from the one time with Anna, William had been the only other person I'd healed.

"Your left side contains a very unique poison. A small amount may only paralyze a victim, but in larger doses, it is lethal."

Poison? The thought made my insides writhe with guilt, and I felt sick. What if Kara's blade had hit me in the left leg? I would have poisoned William.

"I had no idea," I said in disbelief. I thought briefly of the day Anna and I had exchanged blood, and how lucky we had been that she had grabbed my healing hand and not the poisonous one. "I'm assuming the poison has the same effect on . . . humans?" It felt strange to think of Anna as human, as if I was setting myself apart from her. Were we really that different?

His face became uncomfortable. "We aren't allowed to use abilities on humans, Elyse, but yes. Your blood would heal them or hurt them all the same."

It took me a while to register the first part of what he had said. "Why wouldn't I be allowed to heal a human?" I asked, worried about the fact that I already had.

"It's the law. A very rigid law."

I decided to keep that secret to myself, just in case.

"I'm sorry," I said. "I wasn't raised in a community. My parents sort of kept all of this from me. They didn't tell me there were others."

"They did what they had to, for the good of our world, for your own good."

"What does that mean?" I asked frustrated. "William said something about everyone waiting for the last healer. How did he know me? How do any of you know me?"

"He's eager," Iosif answered with a secret smile, "and he's right. We have been waiting for you, and it's very important that you don't let anyone know who you are. No one else has figured it out yet."

I laughed. "Okay, that will be pretty easy since *I* don't even know who I am."

"Well it's time you know. I brought you here for that very reason," he said, settling into a more serious posture, "to tell you the truth about us and about yourself. Over the centuries, our kind has been oppressed. The powers that be have grown accustomed to the amount of control they keep." He spoke with intense eyes and cautious ears. "Before you were born, my wife had a vision of one who would bring an end to it, whose destiny was so deeply intertwined in the fate of the future, that she must be protected. That night, we sought out the parents who would bring this unborn child into the world and told them that they must live apart from the communities and keep their child in the dark about who she truly was. That child is you, and now the time has come."

"I don't understand. The time has come for what?"

"For you to fulfill the prophecy, lead the war, save us from the enemy," he said, his arms gesturing with enthusiasm.

A burst of laughter came rolling out of me. It was the only

reaction I could process. "You can't be serious."

Even through my laughter, his expression didn't falter. "Indeed I am."

"I don't mean to be rude," I said frankly, "but that is the most ridiculous thing I've ever heard."

There was not a million to one chance that I was this prophecy savior. I knew that for sure. There was no way someone as young and emotionally unstable as myself could make such an impact.

"You do not have to accept the prophecy for it to be true."

"You can't possibly believe that I'm going to change your world."

"It is inevitable."

"Maybe for someone else," I disagreed. "I don't know anything about . . . anything. I don't know your world. You have the wrong girl, Professor."

"I assure you, no."

I stared into his crazy blue eyes that seemed to have faded with age. They were honest, believing, sincere, and that scared me. "I wouldn't even know what to do. Besides, I've got nothing against . . . whoever it is you feel is your enemy."

"The Council," he answered, "and you will."

How could I take this crazy looking man so seriously? He had obviously lost his sense of reality years ago. "Look, I've got to get to class," I said, looking for a way out. I stood and headed for the door without being properly excused. "It was really . . . nice talking to you though." What else could I say?

"Remember what I told you," he continued, talking to me through his open door as I slunk away. "Your destiny will find you. Oh, and Origins is in room 22A."

I didn't look back as I charged down the empty hall, and when I found the right door, I let my shoulders relax a little, trying to forget the conversation I'd just endured.

I walked into the classroom over thirty minutes late, right in the middle of a lecture.

". . . we have to be responsible. The choices we make affect more than just ourselves." Despite my tardiness, the professor gave me a look of pleasant surprise. The strange attention made me squirm, and I avoided looking directly at him out of embarrassment. Luckily William was sitting toward the back next to an empty seat, and I dove into it, desperate to avoid curious eyes.

Dr. Nickel was written on the blackboard in elegant cursive. He was a tall, handsome man with clean-cut gray hair and a strong build for his age. His charismatic smile reached the back of the room, clearly expressing his love for teaching, and I recognized him immediately. I knew I'd seen him before, but couldn't think where.

"We have a new student," the professor announced, causing the entire class to zero in on me.

I raised my hand, acknowledging the group, but couldn't find my words.

"I know we're all familiar with our ancestry, but I would like to run through a quick overview for Elyse, just to bring her up to speed with the class." Apparently he knew me as well.

The students redirected their attention to Dr. Nickel, and I slumped lower in my chair.

"What is your first impression of the word Myth? Anybody? The first word that comes to mind?"

"Legend."

"Imaginary."

"A story."

"Yes, a story," Dr. Nickel said through grinning lips. "The Greek word from which we derive the word mythology actually means 'story-telling,' but in truth, mythology is often described as being thought to be true by a particular culture. In the case of Greek mythology, it was true, very true, to the humans who were aware of the existence of our ancestors. The Greek mythology of today arose from a particular point in time when our ancestors were less concerned about the consequences of integrating with human society. Most of what was known to be true at the time has been embellished beyond fact, but there are still parts of it that mark significant events in our history. As we all know, the Trojan War, which has now become more of an interesting fable, was the reason for our decision to become more reclusive. The battle was between us and the humans, not just humans themselves. So, if our people were fully integrated with human society, and for many years lived in peace, what changed? In essence, what caused the war that divided us? If we were to integrate now, what sort of problems would we face? Would they be the same?"

"Human hostility," a redheaded boy yelled, sounding fairly hostile himself.

"Not necessarily," said the girl next to him.

Other voices began to pipe up throughout the room.

"Well, based on the history of our people, human hostility would most definitely be a problem."

"That was ages ago. Times have changed."

"History repeats itself. It would be no different."

Dr. Nickel raised a hand, quieting the class. "Well, let's analyze why we experienced human hostility during that time," he said, trying to focus the discussion.

"We were arrogant," another girl answered. "We tried to pass ourselves off as gods."

"Right," someone else responded. "So if we didn't present ourselves in such a way, if we didn't act superior, maybe human reaction would be different."

"Are you kidding?" a surly girl with a high ponytail jumped in. "Hundreds of Descendants were killed back then. People didn't want us around. They felt threatened. Things are fine the way they are."

"Fine by what standards?" William suddenly spoke up. "Don't pretend you don't know how The Council is. You talk about human hostility? What about our own hostility toward humans?"

"There are arguments for both sides," Dr. Nickel interrupted, "and consequences."

I sat quietly for the next hour, listening and learning as Dr. Nickel worked through pros and cons for exposing the Descendant race to humans. Pros: a better world, freedom, abilities in public, lives would change, less crime, human interaction, the list went on. Cons: human hostility, secret governmental experiments, persecution, another war with the humans, The Council fighting for power. Again, the list went on.

When Dr. Nickel dismissed the class, I expected William to head out with the rest of the students, who were now making use of their abilities, but he grabbed my hand and headed toward the professor.

"Hey, Dad," William said, and then it hit me. I'd seen him in the photograph next to my parents.

"Hello, Elyse," Dr. Nickel greeted me.

"Hi," I answered, getting used to people already knowing me by name.

"Are you adjusting all right?"

I laughed. "I was until some crazy guy tried to tell me I had to save the world."

"I knew he would tell you," William said, slightly irritated. "Did he say anything else?"

"Anything else? What, a crazy prophecy isn't enough for you?"

William threw a secret look to his father. "It's not crazy," William answered.

"We shouldn't talk about this here," Dr. Nickel insisted, glancing at the open classroom door. "Come with me."

I followed the two of them to a well-lit and neatly organized office. William closed the door behind us and took the seat against the wall as I lingered, unsure of what to expect.

"Elyse, why don't you sit down?" Dr. Nickel suggested. "I know this might be a bit hard to process."

I sat without a word. It wasn't as easy to brush off this man's words or take them for nonsense. He was put together, professional, and he had known my parents.

"The oracle can see all things that will be, but only the things that will cause profound change stay in the forefront of her mind, things that will change the course of the future. It's a hard job, knowing what will happen. When things don't play out the way they should, do you watch the sequence of unfavorable events unfold or do you step in and try and change the tide? Not long after you were conceived, she saw you, Elyse. She saw what would happen if she didn't come that night."

"What night?"

"The night your parents left to go into hiding. Think about it. Why would they leave their people?"

My eyes moved back and forth between the two of them as I picked at my cuticles. "What are you saying?" I asked. There was nothing special about me. These people clearly thought I was somebody I wasn't.

"He's saying that Iosif is right," William answered.

I didn't know what to say. What do you tell people who think you are their answer? I wasn't who they thought I was. I wasn't going to save them from anything.

"But how do you know you've got the right girl?"

"I was there the night the prophecy was foretold," Dr. Nickel continued. "Richard and Sarah were hesitant." The names of my parents rolled off of his tongue like he had said them a thousand times. "But they had no choice. The oracle told them that your survival was essential, that when it was time, you would lead us into a new era of existence, and that the corrupt Council would meet its end. Their only option was to go into hiding before you were born, before you could be registered within a community. The Council has many abilities at their fingertips, and they would eventually come to know the significance of your existence. That's why your parents left, and that's why you knew nothing of where you came from."

My lips tightened in anger. I needed to blame someone for my ignorance. "Why didn't you tell me this when we met?" I asked William accusingly.

"Yeah, because you seem to be taking it really well," he answered.

"The future is never certain, Elyse," Dr. Nickel added. "To be honest, there is no guarantee that you will live out this future. There are certain events that must occur in order to set things in motion. Without them, there is no prophecy."

"What events?" William demanded.

"I can't say," his father answered with genuine regret in his eyes. "To tell you would be to alter the course."

William stared at his father with suspicion.

"So, what you're telling me is that this whole thing is a maybe?" I asked.

He nodded. "In a sense, but your protection was a push in the right direction."

"Iosif seems to think it is inevitable."

Dr. Nickel smiled. "He's a bit of an optimist, being married to the oracle and all."

I couldn't believe it. My whole life, I had been shut out, "protected," so I could be a pawn in someone else's game. I never got to choose. I felt the sting of betrayal as I thought about my parents. How could they have kept this from me my whole life? Did everyone know about this prophecy but me? The Nickels, my parents, the world of Descendants, The Council? A sudden rush of fear kick-started my heart. If The Council was truly as corrupt as everyone said, and if I really was their enemy, then wouldn't my death be the perfect solution for them?

"What about The Council? What do they know? Why haven't they tried to . . ."

"Tried to what?" William asked.

The two of them looked at me to answer the question.

"To kill me."

"I wondered that myself," Dr. Nickel answered. "I'm sure they are aware of the prophecy, but quite honestly I'm not sure they realize who you are, Elyse. When they figure it out, the oracle will let us know."

"So what should I do until then?" I asked.

"Go on with business as usual, I suppose."

"Business as usual?" Somehow that seemed easier said than done. "Well, maybe I shouldn't be here, so exposed," I said with uncertainty. I didn't want to leave, but if all of this was true, maybe I was destined for a life of running. "Obviously staying hidden . . ."

"You've been hidden long enough," Dr. Nickel interrupted. "You have to face your future eventually, and it's time to let the prophecy unfold. We need you."

8.

FOR THE NEXT few days, it was easy to pretend like nothing had changed. Denial was a close friend of mine, and William was the perfect distraction. He stuck around while I locked myself up in my apartment, avoiding The Institute with the excuse of having furniture delivered. On the third day without stepping foot outside, he decided to take matters into his own hands.

"That's it," he announced from my new dark purple couch.

"What?" I responded from the floor. I'd been laying on my back staring through the spinning blades of the fan.

"We have to get out of here. Look at you."

I lifted my head briefly, glanced at him, and then let it drop back against the carpet.

"Can't a girl just lie on her own floor if she feels like it?"

"You're so melodramatic," he said, hopping off of the couch. "Get up."

I sighed as I pushed myself to sitting. "It's too late to go anywhere."

"Yeah, for an old lady."

I refused to stand. "Eighty-nine *is* old," I argued.

He narrowed his powerful green eyes. "Don't make me persuade you. I'll do it," he teased.

I smiled. It was hard to say no to him. "Fine. Where do you want to go?"

"I want to introduce you to my friends."

Friends. The idea had only just crossed my mind, and it made me nervous and excited all at once. I could have friends who were just like me. "Okay," I agreed, getting onto my feet.

***

When the ocean came into view, so close I could see the shallow waves crashing onto the shore, I realized why William had told me to dress warm.

"The beach?" I asked, surprise somewhat suppressing the anxiety I was feeling. I didn't have a lot of experience meeting new people.

"Yeah. It's open and abandoned at night, so everyone can use their abilities here."

"You're not afraid it's too exposed?"

"Nics takes care of that," he said naturally. "Ready?"

"Yeah," I said, beginning to chew on the skin around my nails.

William helped me into my coat, and we set out for the sand. Silver light sparkled atop the deep navy blue surface of the calm water, but the radiance was pale against William's bright eyes.

"Don't be nervous," he said sensing my anxiety. "You've got nothing to worry about."

"I know. I just haven't had to be social in a while."

He stopped and stepped in front of me, taking my hands and weaving his fingers in and out of mine, something I still wasn't used to. The warmth that grew between our palms felt good in the cold. With so much else on my mind, I'd almost forgotten about it.

"Why do our hands get warm like this?" I asked. "Does it happen to all Descendants?"

"No. Just us." His face glowed under the soft light of the night sky like some unearthly being sculpted by the hand of perfection. His features stood out intense and magnificent against his gleaming skin. His lips, a brilliant blood red, caught my eye as they settled into the mesmerizing smile that always made my stomach flip.

"So, what does it mean?"

"Obviously it means you've got the hots for me."

"Come on. Really," I probed.

"What? You don't?"

"Seriously?"

"I told you. It protects us. As long as we are touching, our abilities are magnified. We're stronger when we're together."

We walked the long stretch of beach, taking our time to get to wherever the mysterious hang out spot was. I walked cautiously, taunting the tide by staying just out of reach of the creeping waves. William walked slightly ahead, kicking and splashing through the water.

"Come on, Elyse, live a little," he teased.

I smiled at his boyish behavior. I was happy he could be himself around me, and that he felt comfortable enough to be as wild as he pleased.

"I don't want to get wet," I explained.

He shook his head. "Bad excuse."

"How is that a bad excuse?"

"Who cares if you get wet," he answered wryly.

"Um, I do. I don't want to be cold."

"So what if you're cold."

"Well, it's not very pleasant," I said, thinking I'd closed the argument.

He laughed out loud, low and hearty.

"So, are you just going to live in your little shell because it's comfortable?" He turned to face the open water gesturing to the breathtaking scene. "Think of all the fun you'll miss. You've got to step out of the box and learn to *love* the cold. I mean if you . . ." but before he could finish his sentence, I reached down and batted a handful of ice-cold ocean water at his back.

He froze. Immediately I worried he was mad, that I had crossed a line and ruined the night. When he finally spun around, his expression was unreadable, and I didn't know what to think.

"All right, that's it," he said, a sinister smirk appearing on his face. Out of nowhere he sprang toward me, and I let out an instinctive scream as he chased me down the abandoned shore. I ran carelessly through the water, disregarding my wet feet and jeans. William's laugh was close behind me as he tossed splashes my way.

I felt free, like a little kid again, breaking the unspoken rules of adulthood, and the laughter poured out of me uncontrollably. The carelessness gave me courage, and I turned to challenge my pursuer. I assumed a low crouching position and he mimicked—a standoff.

"You're going to get it," he threatened with a magnificent smile.

"We'll see," I returned, and the splashing frenzy began.

When our rolling laughter became too much, we fell onto the sand and sprawled out on our backs. Our bodies were drenched and tired as we let our heavy breath flow freely.

"You cold?" he asked through his breathing.

"Yeah," I admitted.

"Worth it?"

I smiled. "Definitely." The cold was chilling to the bone and made my body shake, but I didn't care. William was right. Life was better when lived outside of my comfort zone.

"You still want to meet up with everyone?" he asked, turning to face me on the ground. His wet hair was dark and stuck to his face.

"Sure, let's go," I said with a new sense of encouragement.

"All right, it's just up the beach. You won't be able to see them until we pass through Nics's shield, though," he said getting up.

"Her shield?" I asked as he pulled me off the ground with impressive strength. "What exactly is her ability?"

"She's descendant of Nyx, goddess of darkness or night. Really her power has more to do with manipulating light, though, which sometimes creates the illusion of darkness.

That's where the misconception comes from. It's really useful when we want to hang out here."

"Interesting," I said, pondering the mechanics behind it. "Well, come on."

"Also, just so you know," he warned, "it's a little strange passing through it. The shield, I mean. She creates a wall by extracting the light, and the blackness can be a little disorienting if you aren't expecting it."

"Isn't a black wall kind of obvious to people we want to hide from?"

"Well, it's invisible until you step through it."

"So, how is it a shield if we can see through it?" I asked confused.

He laughed at my persistent interest, but answered my question.

"You can see what Nics wants you to see through it. She tells the light what to reflect through the shield, and what she doesn't want others to see, like us, she tells the light not to reflect."

"Sounds like a complicated ability."

He smiled. "Yeah, but not to her."

As we got closer to the invisible place we were seeking, I could hear voices in the distance, a mix of laughter and low garbled speech.

"So, it's not sound proof then," I realized.

"No," he answered, "but we are pretty far out, nobody ever comes here."

"They're here," I heard an unseen girl's voice say as I stumbled into the pitch black. I inhaled sharply at the abruptness of it.

"You okay?" William asked from next to me. I could see nothing but solid black emptiness, not even myself.

"I think so," I managed.

"Just keep walking straight. Here." I felt his hand searching, and I let it find mine.

"Okay, how far is it?" I wondered aloud.

"Not far, about twenty feet."

I walked slowly and carefully, trying not to trip over the sand. My eyes were closed as I let my focus drift to William's warm sandy hand instead of the black abyss ahead of me. When we reached the edge of the wall, my eyes were still pinched tight, and William's voice was the only indication that it was over.

"Okay, Elyse," he chuckled, "open your eyes."

As I did, I saw a girl coming to greet us. Her white smile was bright against her coffee black skin. She was beautiful, with a sporty physique and shoulder length dreadlocks that suited her well.

"Hi," she said waving. "I'm Nicole, but everyone calls me Nics." Her expression turned suddenly curious. "What happened?"

William and I looked at each other searching for the answer to her random question.

"Did you fall in?" she guessed, laughing at us.

"Oh," William said as he realized we were soaking wet and covered in sand. "No we were just . . . she started it."

"Hey," said a tall, handsome guy approaching. His short blond hair was tousled, and his expressive face wore a wide smile.

"Sam?" I asked, remembering him as the one taking inventory back at the coffee shop.

"Yeah," he said reaching his large hand to shake mine, his face full of energy and excitement. "Nice to finally meet you, Elyse."

I blushed a little as he spoke my name, wondering if William had told him about me.

"You too," I added.

I could see two other figures standing close to each other in the orange glow of a distant bonfire that had been burning wildly in the background. I wondered why they hadn't come to meet us, but before I could ask, the two of them lifted off the ground floating in mid air. With the blink of an eye, the girl vanished, shrinking into a multicolored stream of shimmering light that zipped like a hummingbird in circular patterns around the guy—a moving rainbow. Despite his best efforts to catch the gleaming light in his hand, she continued to dart back and forth just out of reach. As she moved farther away from him, he took off soaring through the air to chase her, the two of them flying in spiral formation toward us.

"You can see why we need the shield," William noted. I was glad to know that I wasn't the only one blatantly staring at the couple.

As the rainbow stream drew nearer, she snapped back into her bodily form to land. The wavy locks of her blonde wind-whipped hair fell over her shoulders. She had a short voluptuous body that was thicker than most, but the curves were sexy and added to her classical beauty. The boy, who descended softly beside her, had a cap of black hair shaved close to his head and a short sturdy body that surpassed her in height just slightly.

"Elyse, this is Paul and Rachel," William introduced them.

"Hi," I said, a little timid. "Sorry for staring, but I've just never seen anything like that."

"It's fine," Rachel's face lit up as she spoke. "Come over by the fire, you guys must be freezing." She gave us an interested look, obviously wondering why we were wet, before grabbing my arm and leading the way. Paul kept up, walking on the other side of me while William, Nics, and Sam followed close behind.

"What bloodline are you?" Paul asked as we walked. The question seemed as natural to him as asking for my occupation.

"Bloodline?" I asked, honestly not understanding.

He shot William a glance as he realized I didn't know much about what I was.

"Who are you descendant of?" William clarified.

"Oh. Asclepius," I returned, hoping that was the answer he was looking for. It sounded so strange to claim relation to a Greek god. I almost expected him to laugh at me.

"Isn't that healing, though?" He thought about it for a second. "I thought that was really rare."

Rachel looked at Paul. "Yeah, like prophecy rare."

"Oh, come on," William interrupted, giving me a look. "All that healer stuff is just a rumor."

Suddenly I remembered what Iosif had said about not letting anyone know who I was.

"What's your ability, Paul?" I asked quickly, trying to get the focus off of me.

"I'm of Hermes," he answered, but I still felt curious eyes on me. "It's pretty prevalent. Rachel has a rare one though. She's of Iris. We're both messengers." He took a seat on the sand and reached his hands for the warm flames. The heat of the fire felt good against the dampness of my clothes, so I sat as close as I could.

"I'm faster though," Rachel chimed in with a proud grin.

"It must be hard to resist when you're in public," I said.

"So hard." She looked at Paul who agreed with a nod. "At least we can fly at The Institute, though."

"All right, my turn." I heard William's voice from behind me.

I turned around eagerly to meet his gaze.

"William," Rachel whined. "We just met her. You get to see her all the time."

I could tell from her tone that she was of a pouty spoiled nature, but her puppy dog eyes didn't faze William in the slightest.

"Too bad," he said matter-of-factly, and Rachel rocketed into the air, irritated and unsatisfied.

Paul rolled his eyes and gave me an apologetic look before he took off after the runaway ball of light.

"Much better," William said, sitting beside me.

"What was that about?" I asked. "I thought you wanted me to meet your friends?"

"Well, you met them, and now I want you for myself," he explained.

I blushed at his candid words.

"Where did Sam and Nics go?"

"Oh they're fighting down by the water. They do that."

"Hey, you guys want to help Nics and I build a sand castle?" Sam yelled running toward us.

"Not really," William answered.

"Me either," he confessed. "She's making me."

"How is she making you?" I asked.

"She said she would extract the light around my head if I refused." He pressed his fingers to his forehead. "That's psychotic, right?"

I couldn't suppress the laughter.

"Just give her a little buzz and she'll calm down," William suggested.

"Buzz?" I asked. "Can you shock people or something?"

"I wish," Sam laughed. "You didn't tell her my lame excuse for an ability, William, or what?"

"Can you believe it?" he answered. "We actually have more interesting things to talk about."

Sam ignored him and continued. "I'm of Dionysus, god of wine and theater. Basically I can turn any liquid into wine," he said rolling his eyes.

"Including the liquid in your body," William added. "He can make you a little tipsy or cause you to black out completely with no recollection of the insane party you'll think you attended. Impressive, huh?"

"Sounds like a great ability to me," I said.

"I don't know. When compared to that." He pointed to the airborne pair flitting about high above the flickering flames like some sort of light show.

"Sam," Nics yelled from a distance.

"I wouldn't keep Nics waiting," William advised. "Give her a little buzz like I said, and she'll probably let you off the hook."

"Yeah right," he scoffed. "I'd like to see you mess with her. I'm just going to stay here. At least if she hurts me, Elyse can repair the damage." He nudged my shoulder with a fake punch and sat down next to me.

"I don't know," I said unsure. I wasn't exactly a seasoned healer, and the expectation made me tense. "Is she violent or something?"

"No," William laughed. "He's being ridiculous. Nics is great."

"Ha!" Sam clearly disagreed.

"Have you ever heard of the phrase 'third wheel?'" William hinted at Sam.

"Sorry, buddy, third wheel or not, she's crazy, and I'm not going anywhere."

William glanced at me subtly, trying to let me in on something secret, before meeting his friend's eyes with intense concentration. Suddenly Sam seemed hypnotized, his expression soft and besotted. The moment was brief, but I realized what he was trying to do—influence Sam with his ability. William laughed as he dropped his gaze and ended the connection.

"Come on, Will. I told you not to do that. I can't believe you . . . so ridiculous . . ." Sam mumbled as he stalked off toward Nics.

"That's one way to get rid of him," William chuckled.

Out of nowhere the multicolored light glowed in front of

us, and Rachel snapped into her physical self in seconds.

"Someone's coming," she warned. Her expression was serious and afraid.

"How many? More than one?" William asked immediately.

"Three guys and a girl," Paul answered as he approached with the other two. "They're young. Teenagers."

"What should I do?" Nics asked. "Should I drop the shield?"

"No," Sam insisted, signaling all of us to lower our voices. "If you drop the shield, we'll appear out of nowhere to them. You'd expose your ability."

"They're slowing down," William said, before the four of them stopped short of Nics's invisible black wall.

"Rick," the girl giggled with the hint of a warning in her voice.

"What? You like it."

"Yeah," another jeered with laughter.

"Hey," she yelled as the third pulled her close, trying to kiss her. "What are you doing? Stop, Steve. Stop."

"We should do something," I said, uncomfortable watching her struggle.

"We can't," Rachel answered, eying the rest of the group.

"We don't have to use abilities," William added.

The piercing scream that carried through the walls of Nics's shield made everyone's heads turn at once. One of the aggressors threw the girl to the ground. "Please don't do this," she pleaded.

"I have to do something," William said, heading off toward the fight.

"William," Sam said catching his arm. "You can't. You'll expose Nics's ability."

The young girl scrambled to her feet, and screamed again, as two of the guys, clawed and ripped at her clothes.

"We have to do *something*," I said severely.

Sam gave Nics a regretful look before becoming suddenly focused on the aggressive men. His eyes became fixated, strong and sharp, like an animal catching sight of prey.

"Sam," Nics warned.

"I don't feel so good . . ." one of the men said before falling forward onto his knees, face first into the sand.

"Sam don't," Nics demanded, moving toward him.

William grabbed her. "It's too late." She struggled as the other two men fumbled and collapsed in a heap next to their victim. The girl's panicked, tear-filled eyes looked around for the source of their unconsciousness, but found nothing. Frantic and eager to escape, she grabbed her purse and kicked the blond one in the stomach before fleeing the scene.

When William let Nics go, she flew forward pushing Sam to the ground. "You idiot," she yelled with tears in her eyes. "Why? Why did you do that? And for what? If they find out, you know what they'll do."

We all went silent with a sort of fearful tension that was laced with uncertainty. A line had been crossed, the forbidden tampered with. No eyes met, but the atmosphere was thick with dread. I could feel it.

"Will?" I looked up at Sam as he spoke. His eyes were wide and worried as he turned to William for affirmation. They filled me with fear. "I couldn't just watch her . . . she wouldn't know anything," he stammered. "It'll be okay, right?"

"Yeah," William said too quickly for it to be true. "You know
. . . it's . . . she didn't see anything . . ." But he was thrown, and
it was clear nobody felt certain of the consequences.

"Should we just leave them?" Rachel asked to no one in
particular.

"Yes," William answered, taking charge of the situation.
"We need to go." He looked around at everyone and nodded
decisively. "Meet at Cearno's."

We all departed without a word, too shaken to speak about
it.

9.

CEARNO'S WAS QUIET. Only a few lonely patrons sipped teas and coffees behind their books or newspapers. A couple spoke softly to each other in a dimly lit corner, and then there was Cearno himself, cleaning behind the counter.

From what William had told me, Cearno could never escape the hordes of customers that would always find him. His ability was too enjoyable for it to be kept to himself. Everything he prepared turned out irresistibly delicious. He was a master of taste. Even the simple passion fruit iced tea I was slowly savoring filled my mouth with such magnificent sweet and tangy flavor I felt like each sip was an experience.

Paul had opted to go with Sam and Nics, claiming someone had to act as mediator between the two, so William, Rachel and I waited in a corner booth for them to show up. Nobody spoke a word as we sat there, and as time passed, tension and silence held us captive. I finally had to break the ice.

"Is he going to get arrested?" I blurted out. I couldn't contain the frustration in my voice. Why weren't they talking about it? If something was going to happen to him, wasn't there anything we could do? It was like watching herds of sheep scatter aimlessly, afraid of the wolf, but making themselves more vulnerable in the hunt. "What's going to happen?"

"I don't know," William answered without confidence.

"Well, what's the situation here?" I prodded. His lack of assurance made me nervous. "What's the worst thing that *could* happen to him?"

"They could kill him," Rachel answered with disgust. "Isn't that their fix-all solution?" The sarcasm was obvious as she spoke, even through her ever-cheery disposition, but I had to make sure she wasn't serious.

"They wouldn't *kill* him, right?"

"No," William answered for her. "They wouldn't kill him." But even he seemed unconvinced of his own words, like it was something he was hoping for rather than something he knew for sure.

Rachel huffed and went back to concentrating on her straw, an apparent sign of her skepticism. Nobody really knew what would happen. Would they kill off one of their own kind for something as trivial as this? My heart began to jump in awkward patterns again.

"How did this happen?" I mumbled to myself.

"What?" asked Rachel, her curiosity piqued.

"This, The Council . . . who are they? I mean, did you elect these people into office or . . ."

"*Elect?*" Rachel said with a chuckle, combing her golden locks out of her eyes. "Where did you hear that? The Council is far from the elect."

"I guess I had just assumed the communities were a democracy."

It was hard to believe that a group of people capable of such miraculous abilities would ever be ruled unwillingly.

"The Council has claimed they are the rightful heirs for thousands of years. It's like a royal family. You don't really get to vote anyone in or out. You just hope that the next generation straightens things out, which clearly, they haven't."

William was preoccupied, his eyes busy finding each person in the coffee house and evaluating their every move. I wondered if his paranoia was as obvious to Rachel as it was to me.

"You guys shouldn't talk about this here." His tight lips and hunkered brow added to his serious tone, but he was too handsome for it to have any affect.

"Hasn't anyone tried to overthrow them?" I asked.

There was a long pause while Rachel offered William the opportunity to answer, but he looked away, and she gladly kept on.

"They're Descendants of first generation Olympians," said Rachel, enjoying the heat of the conversation. "It's not possible."

William threw her an ice cold look that said more than I understood. I took it as an overreaction, a symptom of his worry.

"First generation? Like Zeus?" I pushed on.

"Exactly. There are six of them." She paused, reassessing a bit. There was a brief moment as she flickered her eyes toward

William, finding the same cold look as before, only this time I picked up on the hesitant tension between them before she continued. "Five, actually. They are descendant of Zeus, Hera, Hades, Demeter, and Hestia, and their abilities are nothing to sneeze at if you know what I mean."

William quit trying after his several subliminal attempts to steer the conversation. Instead, he listened as Rachel explained things to me, things that as a culture, they were not proud of.

It was hard for me to see him worry. I could almost feel the gut-wrenching ache I knew he had in his stomach just by reading the tight lines on his face. It made it difficult for me to concentrate when he looked like that, but I wanted to know.

"Christoph is the worst of them all," she continued. "He has Zeus's bloodline, so he thinks he should be the most powerful. He is more eager to punish than the others."

"So what can he do? Throw thunderbolts or what?"

"The whole bolt thing was an alias. There is a bloodline that can manipulate electricity, but Zeus only used him as a cover. It was actually pretty smart. It kept him protected. The ability of Zeus's bloodline is as good as it gets. He can take your power away like it was nothing with a single glance, or if it is in his favor, he can amplify it ten-fold."

"Only for men though," William corrected, giving in a little to our conversation. "Adrianna is his counterpart. She's of Hera, and she can do the same but only for women. Nature's way of balancing the scale, I suppose."

"Unless they're both corrupt," I added.

"They are," he said with shame in his voice. "The truth is, if that girl at the beach remembers anything, and somehow they find out, none of the consequences are good."

"Christoph could take away his ability. Antec, who is descendant of Hades," Rachel added, "could send him to the underworld for who knows how long—"

"Wait, underworld?" I asked surprised. "You're telling me that is real?"

"It's a prison for our kind," William answered. "Antec controls it, and if that is your sentence, he can make you disappear right on the spot."

"What's it like?" I asked, picturing a fire-filled hellhole.

"Nobody really knows," Rachel said. "One second you're here, the next you're gone."

There was obviously another punishment, one I was pretty sure I could guess at. Nevertheless, the details came as a shock to me.

William sighed with remorse. "Dimitri is another unhappy scenario. He's descendant of Demeter."

"Goddess of the harvest?" I asked. It was hard to imagine the goddess of the harvest causing any harm, but then again, nothing had turned out like the Greek myths I was familiar with.

"Yes," William answered, "but the ability passed down through her bloodline is much more lethal than you would think."

"Dimitri can make any living thing grow and flourish, or die. Including us," Rachel explained.

"For plants, the ability isn't much, but growth for us means that he can make us age, take away centuries of life even."

"Or, he can just kill you with a touch of his hand," said

Sam's voice as he approached the table.

We all jumped. He had snuck up on us so easily, and I wondered how much he had heard. Was he listening from a distance as we discussed the possibilities of his potentially dismal fate?

"You okay?" William asked.

"He's going to be fine, bro," Paul said, slapping a guff hand to Sam's back. "Nobody saw anything."

"What's with the decade dialect, *bro*?" Nics asked mockingly as she walked up beside him.

They all seemed much more light-hearted about the situation than we were.

"Times are changing. You've got to roll with the punches, dude," Paul continued with a grin. Rachel rolled her eyes and shook her head, but an endearing smile flashed quickly across her face. "Seriously though, he's going to be fine."

"He's right," Nics agreed. "Those guys were probably drunk before Sam ever got to them. Even if they did wake up and remember suddenly passing out, people would just think they drank too much."

"Besides," Sam added, trying to convince himself and the rest of us he'd be fine. "The girl didn't really *see* anything either. She wouldn't have much to tell. Three drunk guys passed out before assaulting her—not very incriminating on my part, right?"

I was afraid to ask. Everyone was so optimistic, but the troublesome question burned in my mind.

"Does The Council have ways to tell if a Descendant uses their ability on someone?"

"Only if an agent is in the vicinity," Nics answered with confidence. "Most Descendant abilities only work within a short distant range, so they'd have to be close, I'd imagine."

Suddenly I felt the guilt of his choice on my conscience. If an agent had seen him, it would all be my fault. Kara *had* been following me.

"Yeah, and we were pretty secluded," Sam contributed. He seemed so hopeful. I couldn't bring myself to say anything about Kara.

So far, everything seemed to have turned out all right, although none of us could deny the lingering unease that plagued the night. It was something only time would tell.

"Well, I'm getting some food before Cearno closes up shop," Paul said, casually moving away from the topic. "You guys want anything?"

After our order, Cearno cleaned up and got ready to head home. "Just lock up when you leave," he said trustingly to William before heading out the door. We were out later than I expected, but none of us would be able to sleep anyway. All we could do was wait. To pass the time, we did the only thing we could—hope that it would all be fine.

The six of us had the place to ourselves. Paul and Rachel claimed the dartboard and went off into their own little world where everything was safe and good. Now and again I caught a glimpse of explosive color or the two of them casually hovering far above the ground, a site I couldn't imagine ever getting used to.

Sam took advantage of his ability. Without ever taking a drink, he was noticeably tipsy, even through his attempt to hide it. He was clinging to Nics, and although she usually liked to provoke him, she was quiet and understanding tonight, reciprocating his need for her. They had commandeered the jukebox, dancing a drunken waltz to every song, no matter what the count.

William and I stayed at our table, nibbling on leftover pastries and sipping Cearno's famous late night lattes.

"Why didn't you tell me any of this, William? About The Council?" I asked through the music.

He looked at me, a mix of guilt and surrender in his eyes. His gaze didn't falter. It was honest and pointed, like a place with mirrored walls where you can't escape yourself.

"There *are* six first generation Olympians. Rachel left one of them out."

"She left out Poseidon," I said with a nod. "I noticed that." I picked a blueberry out of one of the muffins and popped it into my mouth, savoring the flavor.

"Only, Poseidon was never a first generation Olympian. The sixth was Ares. Sort of the same scenario as with Zeus, Poseidon was his alias."

"So, what's his ability?" I asked, expecting it to be worse than death.

"He can mimic any ability. Being god of war, he can challenge anyone as an equal using their own power."

"Okay," I said, not picking up on the significance. It didn't seem any more threatening than the other abilities of The Council. "Why would Rachel leave that out?"

He took a deep breath before he answered. "My dad's bloodline is Ares."

"Your dad?" I asked in amazement.

"Yeah. I don't take after him," he said.

"He's part of The Council?"

"Well, yes and no." He rubbed the back of his neck, sliding his fingers through his hair. A nervous habit I had picked up on. His face didn't let on any hesitation in answering my question, but it was there.

"You don't have to explain," I said with disappointment. He didn't feel comfortable enough to confide in me. Why would he? It hadn't been that long since we'd met, though it felt much longer.

"I know I don't *have* to," he agreed. I lost him in thought for a while. He took his time in remembering the details, or maybe he was just reluctant in telling me.

"My dad only told me his side of the story once," he continued, "but even if he hadn't, I would have learned about it in school. Not too long ago, one of the biggest civil wars amongst our people broke out. My dad . . . he started it."

He looked up at me with worried eyes, searching for a reaction that wasn't there.

"What happened?" I asked, hoping my voice didn't betray my surprise.

"My dad spent most of his life with them. He was part of The Council just as much as Christoph. After a while, though, he started picking up on things. Christoph sort of stepped into the lead role without anyone realizing how it had happened. He has a way about him. He's articulate and convincing. My dad says he could persuade you to cut off your own hand and make you believe it was for the greater good.

He manipulates—justifies bad things with good reasons."

I could see the hatred billowing up inside him like a thick black smoke, dark and threatening. I'd never seen that look in his eyes before, and it made the hatred infectious. I found it easy to loath anyone who had hurt him enough to evoke such feelings.

"When things started to go really wrong," he kept on, "my dad went to Lilia. Her ability is the most vital of them all. She is descendant of Hestia, and without her, the goddess of hearth and home, none of their abilities work. If she's not in the vicinity of at least two of The Council members, all their powers simply cease to be. She was on the fence about Christoph, and my dad's plan was to convince her to leave, that it was the right thing to do, the only way to put them in their place and establish a true democracy. Well, Christoph had seen it coming and already had Lilia convinced to see things his way. He told her it was her duty to stay and that without them it would be chaos, that Descendants couldn't handle democracy. The Council is what they've always known."

"So, did Christoph kick him out?" I asked.

"No," William answered. "He left. His only other option was to try and overthrow them. There were a lot of people on my dad's side, and they fought for years. A lot of people died, Descendants and humans, but when they got too close, defeating some of Christoph's greatest men, it was all for nothing. He threatened that every day the war continued he would murder humans in massive attacks that he claimed could be blamed on the humans themselves. Christoph knew my dad was a good man, so his plan was to terrorize the human race until my dad gave in. Well it worked—he failed. All of that death and blood on his hands for nothing."

"No, not for nothing," I rallied against his bitterness. "Is that why you didn't tell me, because you were ashamed? Because it's not too late to—"

"No, that's not why," he interrupted. "I know he fought for a good cause. I just didn't want you getting any ideas."

"*Ideas?*" I asked, shocked and confused by his accusation. What kind of ideas could he possibly think I would come up with? I knew he believed I was meant to fulfill the prophecy, but did he imagine I would storm the gates, sword in hand, ready to fight? I couldn't help but laugh. "That's ridiculous."

"I know," he confessed immediately. We both sipped our lattes, completely ignoring everything around us. "I just keep having this dream. We are downtown, lurking in the dark corners of bars, trying to keep from being seen. Someone is after us, so we have to keep moving, and you're really scared, but you won't tell me why they are coming for you. Then we start running. A man chases us, and eventually he grabs my jacket, but when he turns me around, the man is my father. He says, 'we need her to fight,' and as soon as you see him, you leave me there and go with him willingly. And that's it. I lose you to his war, and I can't ever find you."

"It's just a dream, William," I reassured him with a shake of my head.

"I know," he said, dropping his gaze to his shoes.

His eyes stayed down, his lashes, thick and long, hid them from me. He was embarrassed or ashamed of his admission, but I cherished the thought that he wanted to protect me from the very idea of losing each other. It was in these moments that he stood out to me like the moon on water—a captivating light that draws the eye. The muscles in his jaw pulsed as he clenched his teeth unknowingly, his soft lips relaxed into a gentle pout. His eyebrows sank down on his brow, and I put a finger to his hard chin and lifted his face toward mine.

"Just a dream," I said. I smiled at his little fit of worry over such a silly idea. After all that had happened with Sam, I couldn't believe this was what was getting him down.

His lips so full and perfect, touched mine gently, smooth as rose petals. They barely met at first, as if he was afraid the full pressure of his kiss would crush me. I could feel the yearning in his touch as his fingertips found my cheek. This kiss was more than desire, more than just because we could. It was a desperate kiss that spoke the words, "I need you."

"Get a room," Sam yelled drunkenly from across the place.

Our shy eyes found each other, both blushing and embarrassed, and we laughed.

"Oh shut it, you drunken sailor," William yelled back.

"Is that a challenge?"

"No," William laughed. It was nice to see him smiling again.

"Only one way to settle it," said Sam grabbing a couple of pool cues.

"You wanna play?" William asked me with a grin.

"I'm tired," I confessed. "Go ahead. I'm going to bed."

He pushed his chair away from the table. "I'll come with you."

"You don't have to. I'm just upstairs. I'll be fine."

"Yeah, she'll be fine," Sam slurred, before tripping over a chair and fumbling to the floor.

"I think you should stay," I said, watching Nics double over in drunken laughter.

"I probably should keep an eye on these two," William agreed. "You sure you'll be fine?"

I nodded. "Positive."

He smiled and gave me a quick peck on the cheek before accepting Sam's challenge. "You're on."

10.

WHEN I LEFT Cearno's in a state of half sleep, I found the door to my apartment ajar. I grabbed the knob and pushed it open with caution, assuming I had forgotten to close it all the way.

"Hello?" I asked, just in case.

No answer. I shut the door behind me.

It wasn't until I reached the top of the stairs that I felt something wet on my palm and realized I had blood on my hand. I made my way to the sink, looking for where I'd cut myself when I heard her.

"It's not your blood," Kara said from behind me, making me jump a foot in the air.

"What are you doing here, Kara?" I asked, callous and guarded. The last time I'd seen her, she'd stabbed me in the leg.

She was slumped down in the corner, sitting on the floor of my kitchen, a bloody mess.

My face registered with shock. "What happened to you?"

I waited for an answer, but she only glanced at me briefly, annoyed by the question, and continued staring off into the distance.

"Are you hurt?"

If she wasn't going to talk to me I would find out for myself. I knelt down in front of her, looking over her blood stained hands, arms and face. She seemed fine.

"It's not my blood either," she said, her eyes finally meeting mine.

"Who's is it, Kara?"

"It doesn't matter."

"It does matter," I said anxiously. "Are they okay?"

She shook her head. "No. She's dead."

"Who's dead?" I coaxed.

"The girl you all thought you saved tonight. Why did you *have* to meddle?"

My stomach pulled in at the thought of her. She was maybe eighteen years old, so young.

"Why is she dead, Kara?"

"Why do you think? I had to kill her. He made me."

"Oh my god," I said in shock, taking a seat on the floor next to her. I didn't know who *he* was, but if Kara was being forced to kill people, something was very wrong. An uneasy feeling settled in my chest.

I forgot she could read my thoughts until she answered my question. "*He* is Ryder, my boss."

"Why did he make you kill her?"

"You and your friends. That's why. We can't use abilities

on humans."

Her words hurt. Sam was only trying to help.

"But she didn't see him. She couldn't know anything."

"That's not the point," she hissed. "It's not allowed."

I shook my head in anger. It wasn't the girl's fault. She was the victim.

"What about the boys?" I asked.

"Dead. Ryder took care of them."

We sat in silence for a few minutes as I took in the morbid reality. I stared at the dried stains that had dyed her hands and arms red.

"Here," I said, standing to wet a rag at the sink. "You should clean yourself up. You can use the shower if you want."

She looked at me with blank empty eyes. "You shouldn't be nice to me."

I handed her the towel. "Why not?"

"Because when they find out who you really are, they'll make me come for you too, and I won't have a choice."

The thought was disturbing, and I tried to pretend it wasn't true.

"There is always a choice."

"Not for me."

I didn't think Kara would hurt me, not unless she had to, and if that was the case, I wanted to make sure it would never come to that. I hoped William would have a plan.

Kara laughed to herself as she got to her feet.

"What?" I asked.

"What sort of plan do you think he has? Make everyone fall in love with him?"

"What are you talking about?"

"His bloodline." She waited for it to click. "He didn't tell you."

"What?"

"His bloodline is Aphrodite," she smirked. "Goddess of love. That's his ability. He can make people fall in love with him. Let me just say, I hope you have a better plan than that."

As she headed for the shower, my stomach began to tie itself in knots. I felt sick and humiliated. Was I just his toy, his little puppet dancing around as he pulled the strings?

"Oh, and Elyse," Kara said, shaking me out of my enraged internal rant. "Ryder knows about Anna." She dropped her gaze. "I'm sorry." With that, she closed the door to the bathroom, and the pipes groaned as she turned on the water.

Time seemed to stop, or maybe it was just my heart that ceased to continue. My body shook with fear. What did she mean Ryder knew about Anna? I needed answers.

I ran to the bathroom. "Hey!" I yelled. "I need to talk to you."

No answer.

"Kara," I screamed, getting more and more frantic as the seconds passed. "What do you mean he knows?" I wriggled the handle, but it was locked.

"What?" she called from inside. "Whatever you're saying, I can't hear you." Her mocking tone sent me over the edge.

"Get out!" I banged on the door with hard fists. "Get out! I need to know if she's okay."

The sudden urge to get to Anna came over me. I couldn't wait for Kara. I needed to leave. No matter what she said, I couldn't trust that it was true anyway. I had to make sure, to see for myself.

I ran down the steps and out my front door. If this guy Ryder knew about Anna, and he was the one who had the girl killed, I couldn't take any chances. Once I was on the street, I hesitated as I passed Cearno's, remembering William.

Another surge of betrayal convinced me to keep walking. I had to get away from him anyway. Why wouldn't he have told me he had the power of Aphrodite if he wasn't using it on me? I sped up slightly, and by the time I rounded the corner, I was running at full speed. I wasn't sure whether or not he would come looking for me. I knew he'd be worried, but I didn't care.

As I ran, I felt nothing but the aching and the brutal cold through my clothes, both sensations unrelenting and unbearable. My whole body was rigid in response to the chilling night air. My muscles pulled my skin tight, and propelled me on and away from the source of my troubles, as if I could out-run them all. I didn't remember when the tears had started, but I could feel them now, stinging my cheeks as the wind whipped past my face.

In the dark streets of the city, I was thankful for the splashes of light the street lamps offered. The cold was biting on the skin of my arms and legs, and I wished I had brought a jacket.

When I came to the train station, I could have kissed the pavement. I sat exhausted on a bench, trying to convince myself everything would be all right. Although I had no idea how I would handle it if Anna was hurt, or worse. I had to call her.

Each ring of the phone was agony as I waited for her to pick up. *Please be there. Please pick up*, I pleaded in my head, but it went straight to voicemail. I tried again and again without success, and eventually had to give up. I told myself she was just sleeping. It was late.

The waiting made it all worse, as if sitting there helpless allowed everything to catch up and slam into me. The protective walls I had spent my life building came crumbling down, and I sat bare and broken, letting my rocking sobs flow freely out of me. I didn't care if people stared. Things were safe when I was hiding, things were easy. Now, everything was breaking apart.

On top of my worry for Anna, I couldn't stop myself from thinking about William. I kept watch for him out of the corner of my eye, wondering if he'd show. He didn't, but I practiced what I'd say to him. Why? How could you lie to me? Was it all just a game? I rifled through my thoughts for the answers, a reason, a clue. What did he stand to gain from luring me into his life? Was *everything* a lie? Was it my fault for not seeing it? I wiped my wet cheeks and runny nose with my sleeve and tried to call Anna again. No answer.

The lights of the MUNI lifted me only slightly out of my overwhelmed frenzy. Thankful I still had my bag slung around my body, I dug up the change and stepped onto the N train, worried and angry.

Inside, it was quiet and fairly vacant with only a few faceless passengers coming and going every few stops. I sat in the back corner, choosing to bury myself deep into my mobile refuge. A few unsteady lights flickered on and off sporadically, and I immediately related to the feeling. After all, wasn't that William's game, to turn me off and on again at his leisure, completely out of my control? It was cruel to make me a slave to my own heart—a heart that had been manipulated and deceived. He was callous, and I hated that I still had feelings for him even now. Maybe if I was far enough away, I would stop feeling like I was unraveling.

With my head to the window, I watched the passing city rush by my dazed and bloodshot eyes. I glanced at the time every minute or so, anxious to get to Anna's. The close-fitting walls of the train were my only comfort, as I condemned myself for putting my friend and her daughter in danger.

As I barreled on in her direction, I stared at her number on my cell phone, still calling every few minutes. I hadn't known being her friend would put her at risk. How could I? I had seen her so many times in the past, though, and she had never been approached or endangered. Were things different now? Surely I wouldn't be expected to never see her again. I wouldn't accept that. I couldn't. She and her daughter Chloe were all I had left, the only thing that even came close to family.

It was a ways to her house, a thirty minute ride including a transfer to the BART, but it seemed like hours had passed. I thought maybe the trip would allow me to think, to pull myself together, but I was even more anxious when I got there. All that had happened tonight was weighing on me, making me an emotional wreck.

As long as Anna is okay, I'll be fine, I comforted myself. As far as William was concerned, I would just have to get over him. People had to deal with these sorts of things every day. Well, maybe not exactly this. Being betrayed by the love powers of your mythological crush wasn't all that common, but people felt heartbreak and pain and managed to move on. That's what I would have to do, move on.

My feelings were erratic, darting back and forth between confidence and complete devastation, even as I entered the complex where Anna lived. I wandered through the town houses looking for 32B, exhausted to the core. Fear was my only source of energy, the only thing keeping me going. Every part of me was begging for sleep.

After I'd found it, I weighed my options. What if this put her in more danger? What if someone had followed me and saw me go into her house? I looked around cautiously, knowing I probably wouldn't have seen them anyway. I couldn't believe I had endangered the last two people on earth that I *truly* loved. As I stared at her front door, I decided it was best not to talk to her.

I did my best to stay quiet as I crept to the front window, stepping awkwardly around overgrown hedges. If I could just see inside, see that she was safe, it would make me feel better. I cupped my hands between my eyes and the glass, and saw her, sitting unharmed in a recliner. My shoulders relaxed, and I felt the fear dissipate. She was fine.

I turned to leave, satisfied with seeing her alive and uninjured, and tripped over the hedge behind me. I let out a startled scream and tumbled backward.

I heard the door open before I even had time to scramble to my feet. "Elyse?" Anna said in alarm. "What are you doing out here?" She laughed at the sight of me in her bushes. "Are you spying on me?"

It made my heart settle to see her familiar face. She had the same button nose covered in freckles, and silky flat hair turned slightly silver over the years. Her eyes squinted tightly behind her lifted cheeks as she smiled.

"I swear, every time I see you, I'm—"

I jumped to my feet. "Shhh," I snapped, grabbing her hand and rushing her inside.

"What's going on?" she asked in a hushed voice.

"Why haven't you been answering your phone?"

"I don't know. It's probably on silent. What's wrong with you?"

"Everything," I said, closing my eyes, trying to wish it all back to the way it was. "I might have been followed. Maybe not though. You have to be careful." All the worries I'd been toiling over were spilling out in one long breath. "Make sure you lock the door, and . . ."

"Elyse?"

My heart began to pound with anxiety.

"Is everything all right?"

"No," I answered, and fell into her arms for comfort. I noticed how thin and frail she was as I wept into her shoulder, too thin.

After a few minutes of long awaited consoling, she led me to the couch. The place was small and more cluttered than I remembered. Shoes were lined up by the door, DVD's piled next to the TV, and books stacked everywhere there was space, but it was as tidy as she could make it.

I took a seat on the worn out toffee-colored sofa. Anna brought me a blanket and hot cinnamon tea, still waiting for me to be ready to talk. How could I tell her she and Chloe were in danger and that it was my fault? I was thankful she was giving me time to settle down, to process the fact that everything was fine. She was fine. Her presence was comforting, and so nostalgic that I hardly noticed her aging eyes. As I looked past her into the girl I remembered, reminiscence dredged up inside of me.

The memory of our quiet town, which fell asleep at sundown every evening without fail, was like a forgotten dream that I could suddenly recall. It was a safe place, so Anna and I were allowed to venture off to the pair of swings behind our old brick school every night after dinner. We'd peel the loose fencing back and climb into the closed off space unnoticed, free to do as we pleased.

"I'm going to get out of here, Elyse," she'd say. "I'm not going to let this place suck *me* in like it has everyone else."

The wind whipped past our ears as we launched ourselves into the fading light of the dusky sky. I loved the feeling, diving head first into a pool of sweet summer air as the horizon turned the color of rainbow sherbet with the setting sun.

"I don't know. It's not so bad." I never understood why she wanted to 'get out.' The place was heaven to me. It had everything I always wanted—school, friends, a normal life—but Anna wanted more than that. She wanted to really live.

"*Not so bad?* Elyse, there is a whole world out there. Don't you want to see it?" We whooshed past each other, our legs pumping us higher. "I swear, when I'm eighteen, I'm going to find the biggest city there is and live right in the middle of it. I want to fall asleep to buzzing street sounds and go to dinner at one in the morning. Maybe I'll be on Broadway or travel with a band or something."

"Your mom's going to love that," I said, my hair trailing behind me like ribbons in the wind.

"I don't care. I'm not going to just marry Charlie Stanton from down the street and iron his shirts and cook him food."

I laughed at the disgust in her voice as she damned the future plans her mother had mapped out for her.

"Well if you do, remember to send me the wedding photo. *That* I'd have to see."

"Are you kidding? If I marry Charlie Stanton, you're marrying Billy Casey, which means we'd probably be neighbors, in which case I'd be over at your house complaining every day."

"I'm not marrying Billy Casey. He smells like jerky."

"I know," she laughed. "But, *if* I do get married, it's going to be to a singer or guitar player anyway. Not Charlie Stanton."

"I don't think I'll get married," I said as though it were a decision I'd made, not a reality I was forced to face.

"Yeah. Me either. Let's just move to LA and live in an apartment together."

"That sounds like fun," I agreed, but I had my doubts about that sort of thing. When she was eighteen, I'd still look like I should be in junior high. I gripped the metal chains of my swing tighter. "Do you think we'll still be friends by then?"

"Why wouldn't we be? We're best friends, and we're going to be best friends until we're both eighty and playing bingo for money on Tuesdays."

Sitting there in her living room, in a reality so far from what she'd dreamed, returned the memory, fleeting as it was, to the back of my mind.

"I don't know how I got myself into this," I confessed to her. "I guess I would have found out eventually, but . . ."

"What?"

"You're not going to believe me."

She shook her head in disagreement. "After the way you've aged, I would believe you if you said you were Wonder Woman."

"Well, I'm not Wonder Woman," I said, "but I do finally know what I am." If I was going to warn her about what was out there, about the threat posed by The Council, I'd have to start from the beginning. I didn't see any way around it. She needed to know, so she could protect herself and Chloe.

Her eyes widened. "How?"

I sipped my tea and tucked my feet under the blanket. "There are others. Here, in San Francisco."

"You're kidding." She paused, waiting for me to continue. "Well, spit it out already. What did they say?"

"You can't tell anyone," I said firmly.

"Hey, blood sisters for life, right?" A satisfied smile crawled up her cheeks. "I'm proud to say I've kept that secret buried deep." She had. Not even Chloe knew about the day I healed Anna.

"When I told you I was being followed, about William and Kara . . ."

"They're like you," she guessed.

I nodded. "They call themselves Descendants. Each of them has an ability and lives as long as I do. They say we're descendants of Greek gods, only Greek gods were never really gods at all. They were just people like me, who were misunderstood, taken to be gods because of their powers and their aging."

"You're a Greek god?" she asked, eyes alight with amazement.

I laughed. "No, I'm not, but I guess that period of time had some effect on their . . . my people, because they still use the names. William said I'm descendant of Asclepius, god of healing."

She laughed. "No shit, Sherlock."

"Yeah, I guess we sort of knew about the healing, but get this. My left side does the opposite. The blood's poison."

"Yeah right," she said, not sure if I was joking. "Seriously?"

"Well, I don't really have proof of that, but I'm not sure I want to test it." I was glad I'd made the decision never to try the healing again after the blood sisters incident. I could have easily killed someone.

"So, are you going to be all right?" she asked, taking another sip of her tea. "You're not in trouble with them are you?"

Trouble was one way of putting it.

"Yes," I answered honestly. "I think I am. I think we all are."

I told Anna about all of it. How the entire society of Descendants had an elaborate system and way of life, completely unknown to most of the world, and that it was forbidden to expose anything to humans. She was in danger because of that. I told her about the events of the night, how one innocent decision to save a human being had resulted in her death and the death of her attackers. How they all thought I'd be the one to save them from the corruption and evil that ruled their secret race and ultimately threatened her. Lastly, I told her about William and the crushing disappointment I'd felt when I learned my growing love for him wasn't even real.

"If I'm really in danger," she objected, "why hasn't anyone come to hunt me down, huh? How do you know Kara even really killed the girl? She could be acting out this whole thing because she's jealous. I'm not worried about it," Anna said with finality. "Tell me more about this guy."

"He's . . . just a guy," I said, laughing a little through my words. I cupped my tea in both hands, letting the heat warm my palms. The feeling reminded me of William's touch. "I mean, I've never allowed myself to have feelings for anyone, and then, when I finally do, I find out it's not genuine."

"Look at the bright side, though," she pointed out. "Now, there *are* other fish in the sea. You actually can be with someone, even if it's not him."

"You're right," I said, starting to feel better.

Chloe's bedroom door opened, and she peeped her head out with tired eyes and messy hair. She was looking more like her mother every time I saw her. It was like opening a window to the past. She was the childhood Anna I remembered and longed for in the days I spent alone with Betsy after I left. Her chocolate eyes and straight black hair were Anna's. Her lips and cheeks might have belonged to someone else, but the rest I recognized.

"Hey, Chlo bug," I said with a cheery smile.

"We being too loud?" Anna asked.

She walked out in striped flannel pajamas and snuggled into me on the couch. "Why aren't you sleeping?" she asked her mom.

"I'm keeping her awake," I answered.

Chloe looked me up and down, then smiled when she found my eyes. "I'm catching up to you."

"Don't remind me," I said, shoving her with my shoulder. "In my mind you'll always be three."

"I'm fourteen."

"Jeez," I said, looking at Anna. "When she looks older than me, I'm going to lose it."

"Me too," Anna agreed with a nod.

Chloe looked at her in a way that communicated something I wasn't a part of, some silent worry between them that I hadn't been let in on.

"What?" I asked, picking up on it.

"Nothing," Anna said, brushing it off. "We should all get back to bed."

My body was giving out to fatigue quickly and against my will. "Sounds good to me. I'm exhausted."

"All right, will you be okay here on the couch?"

"Yeah. It's perfect."

"Okay, I'll see you in the morning," she said after grabbing a pillow and extra blanket from the closet.

"Goodnight, Chlo bug," I said as Chloe slipped back into her room.

11.

I DIDN'T REMEMBER falling asleep, so it must have happened immediately after Anna climbed the stairs to her room. Like most nights since she'd died, I dreamed of Betsy, reliving that part of my life and longing for her comfort.

"Honey, can you open your eyes?" she spoke calmly in my dream, not a hint of worry in her words. I heard her, but I didn't dare move. I was disoriented, like waking up after a deep sleep and forgetting where you are. I tried to drift back into the coddling blackness, subconsciously aware of the horror I would have to face when I did open my eyes, but their conversation grabbed my attention, and I was suddenly alert.

"She's been in and out for the last few days. I'm sure she'll be fine, but maybe you could come by tomorrow instead?" she said making her words into a question.

"Oh no. I'm sure she's in good hands. We just wanted to come by and see how she was doing."

"That's very sweet of you."

I took my chances and let my eyelids lift just enough to make out the man standing in the hallway. He was thin and tall, wearing a wool gray coat. I couldn't see his face, but there was a boy at his side, maybe nine or ten, who looked curiously through the open door of my room. His eyes were sad as he watched me, not knowing I was peeking at him.

"Not to be insensitive, but do you plan to put her in foster care?" the man asked.

"Actually, I was planning on taking her in," the woman said matter-of-factly.

"That's good. She'll be better off here." He sounded relieved at the arrangement, and pulled the boy back out of view.

"Exactly my thinking, too," she said.

"Have a nice day, miss."

The woman was hidden from my sight, but when she peered around the corner, I saw the reflection of my anxious face in her eyes.

"*Now* you're awake," she teased. "You hungry?" Without an answer, she headed to the kitchen to rummage through the fridge. She acted as if my being there was the most normal thing in the world. Her hair was a light dusty brown, tied back in a braid. She was middle aged and looked tired, but it didn't take away from the sort of raw beauty about her.

"I'm Betsy," she said as she re-entered the room holding a turkey sandwich. "I set a few books out for you to read if you get bored, no TV though." She set the sandwich on the dresser giving me the opportunity to respond. I didn't. "I'll be in the living room if you need me."

"I'm Elyse," I choked out. "Ellie." It was all I could bring myself to say. I didn't dare ask the questions that clung so desperately to the edge of my subconscious.

"What a pretty name," she said as she smiled and left.

At that point I realized that I was in a bedroom that seemed to be set up for me. A few sets of clothes were hanging in the open closet, and atop the pink dresser in the corner were some books and a set of dolls propped up against the wall, their joyful faces mocking my buried devastation. There was a lamp on my bedside table, appropriately pink to match the dresser. The bedspread, also pink, seemed new, and the truth of it all sank in. It was apparent that Betsy had made this *my* room.

Days passed, and I couldn't muster the will to speak. The police came and went, and the funeral for my parents passed by me in a blur that made me numb. I mostly kept to myself, closing the door to my new room and submerging myself in the dark shadowy grief that I found around every corner. My life consisted of losing myself in books and sleeping. My father's words kept echoing in my head—*People like us could not live a normal life if we were exposed.* Despite my behavior, Betsy kept on living in her usual way. She was a nurse, and she went to work regularly, leaving me to my moping, checking in only to let me know that she was home. Tonight, I didn't anticipate a change in our routine when Betsy peered her head in, so her words caught me off guard.

"Hi, Elyse." She paused. "Do you feel like coming out and reading in the living room tonight?"

I could not meet her eyes. My mind was buzzing, and I wasn't sure what to say or how to feel. I'd been raised to avoid this, to break bonds before they were formed.

"Okay," she said as she closed the door. My internal conflict must have gone on too long.

Her presence was a constant reminder of the absence of my family, and the emptiness was paralyzing. It bore deep down into my bones, and there wasn't a moment I didn't feel the hurt. This was all my parents could give me now, this emptiness—an emptiness I would have to learn to live with and grow accustomed to, because if I were to let myself love someone else, this loss would happen all over again.

Despite the pain I felt, Betsy had been kind to me, and I didn't want to seem ungrateful. I slipped out the door and found myself a cozy spot by the fire. She gave me a pleased look and then continued knitting on the couch completely absorbed in her radio program. The new atmosphere hit me hard, and all of a sudden I was scared, confused, and nervous. I felt the salty tears in my mouth, and I realized this was the first time I had cried over it all. Wondering if she'd noticed, I looked up and caught her gaze. Her arms were open and I crawled into their loving warmth letting loose an ocean of grief.

"How did I get here?" I asked after a while. It was like breaking through the fog. Finally I could see things coming into view. I had so many questions.

"A nice man and his son brought you to me. They stopped when they saw the accident. I was the closest house. You're lucky he happened to be heading home when the snow storm hit." She read my expression and hugged me closer. I didn't feel *lucky* at all. The guilt was painful and constant in my chest.

"It was out of your hands, Elyse," she said, letting me consider the thought for a while.

"What about all of my things, the house . . . my parents' things?"

"Now don't worry about all that stuff. You just let me be the grown up, okay? I've talked to the Sheriff about sorting all that out. The house is yours, and everything in it. I'll drive you there whenever you want."

It felt good to be comforted, to be told that everything would be all right. I knew that maybe it wouldn't be all right in the end, and things were bound to change once she knew my secret—that I was, in fact, older than her. For now, I liked being ten, and I was glad I fit in her lap.

"My turn to ask a question," she said after a while. "How is it that a ten-year-old likes to read Shakespeare?"

I glanced at the copy of *Romeo and Juliet* I held clutched to my chest and smiled a little inside before answering. "I'm just an old soul, I guess."

It surprised me how oddly comfortable we felt together, like she'd been written into my life from early on. I knew I wasn't supposed to love her, but I could tell I already did—and love is not something you can undo.

"An old soul, huh? So how old does that make you, thirty-seven?" she asked jokingly. *Not too far off*, I thought.

"Ten," I answered too quickly. "Just ten."

"So that's what . . . fifth grade?"

"I don't know. We never did grades for homeschool."

"Homeschool?" she asked mostly to herself. "That might be

a little hard for me, honey. I have to work. What do you think about going to the elementary school?"

I was confronted with a mix of feelings as she spoke. School had never been an option for me. Things could go wrong. What would happen when I didn't age? I couldn't tell Betsy. What would she think? She would think I was crazy. I knew I'd be taking a risk, but my delayed growth, my secret, none of it was an immediate concern, so I agreed.

"Fifth grade will be fun," I said, somewhat uncertain. The excitement was real, and I couldn't help but feel the anticipation of the new experience. People changed schools all the time. Saying goodbye to friends was normal when you were young, right? I would tell Betsy in time. I would have to. For now, maybe this would help pull me out of the stabbing anguish that marked the loss of my parents.

Things were perfect for the next three years—too perfect. I remembered the day it ended, the day Betsy started in on what would be a life changing conversation.

"Elyse, I need to talk to you about something," she began from her seat at the dinner table. She didn't wait for my response. "Over the last couple of months, I have been getting calls from your school. Your teacher, the principal, even concerned parents have called me."

I was shocked. Why would they call? I had good grades, friends, a good attitude, but Betsy answered my thoughts.

"It's your weight, sweetie." She glanced at my plate of half-eaten chicken, peas, and potatoes. "Well, your size, really. I think it might be time for you to get a real check up at the hospital. I wasn't worried about the calls. I know you are a healthy girl. I feed you. I give you checkups. You've never even had so much as a cold. I mean, I'm a nurse. I think I know how healthy my own daughter is. The nerve of these people."

I could tell she was blaming herself for this, thinking she had done something wrong. The frustration in her voice wavered with the sound of holding back tears.

She set her fork down and buried her head in her hands. "Yesterday, Social Services came to check on you, Elyse, when you were at Anna's. I don't know what to do."

She waited. Whether it was for comfort, advice, or an explanation, I didn't know, but I knew I had to tell her. I couldn't believe this moment had come. It had only been three years. I hadn't expected it so soon. Was I really so small? I dreaded the consequences of my words. They were a death sentence that would destroy the life I knew like a dream upon waking.

"Mom," I said. It was the first time I had ever called her mom. Her eyes lifted in a way that made everything seem okay for the moment, but what I had to say shattered any hope of that. I moved my peas around on my plate. I couldn't look at her. "It's not your fault. I've been keeping something from you. I should have told you a long time ago . . ." Her eyebrows pulled together, forming a deep crease. "Something my parents told me about myself."

Her worry turned to concern. "What is it?" she asked.

What if she didn't believe me? Was I about to lose her, too? Either way, I had no choice. Her reaction was something I couldn't control, and I had to tell her. It was time.

"I know why I'm so small. It's genetic, but not in the way

you think. I'm different. I age slower than most, a lot slower. My parents did, too."

"Why wouldn't you tell me you had a medical condition, Ellie? We should have been seeing a doctor."

"No," I said with force. "It's not like that. People like us could not live a normal life if we were exposed."

"People like *us*?"

"It's what my dad used to tell me."

"What are you talking about, sweetie? I'm not sure I understand."

"You'll think I'm crazy, but it's the truth, I promise. When my parents died, they were nearly 200 years old."

She laughed uncomfortably, hoping I was making a joke out of all of this, but my face stayed controlled as I waited for it to register.

"Elyse, are you okay? You know that is impossible, honey. I know losing your parents was hard for you, but this is just a little . . ."

"Crazy," I finished for her. I was going to lose her. She didn't believe me. I began fidgeting with my fingernails. What was I expecting? I would have to run. She would try and take me to a doctor and it would all be over. I loved Betsy, but I wasn't about to spend the rest of my life being poked and prodded by mad scientists looking for a new anti-aging formula. Tonight, I would run.

"All right, Elyse, I know you have a wild imagination, but this is enough. If you have a serious medical condition, you are going to see a doctor about it, and that's final," she said firmly.

Her words stung. I felt betrayed and alone. I hated being trapped in this young body with no proof of the years I'd lived. Nobody ever believed a child. I tried sifting through memories to think of something I'd seen or heard over the years that would prove I was around, but they were just memories that only I had witnessed. Then it hit me like a break in the storm.

"Take me to the house," I requested with a pleading look. "Take me to the house first, and if you still don't believe me, then I will go to the doctor."

The thirty-minute drive out to the still desolate town of Chilcoot was a silent one. Betsy's focus was locked on the road, and her pinched brow never softened. I scanned the open fields littered with sagebrush allowing my mind to wander, slightly on edge at the thought of seeing the house again.

"Turn here," I reminded her.

We turned in to the nearly invisible driveway that was now overgrown and abandoned. The road was a mile long. It snaked around the uneven surface of the earth following the natural crevices that already scarred the land until the bowl shaped valley emerged. Betsy had been here before, but I doubted the image made her stomach pull in as it did mine. The house was in the center of the valley, as though it had slid to the lowest point it could manage. It would be hard for anyone else to make it out. Trees shot up on all sides protectively as the perfect camouflage.

As we pulled up to the front of the house, Betsy heaved a sigh. I could almost hear her thoughts, they were so clearly visible on her face.

"Do you need me to go inside?" she asked.

"No."

"Then you have fifteen minutes, and you're grounded."

Being grounded was the least of my worries at this point.

"Fine," I shot back at her as I shut the car door.

I walked quickly, climbing the porch stairs and making my way through the front door before I could give myself time to think. I wasn't here to reminisce. I had to focus. I pushed on past the kitchen table, resisting the urge to just sit and be home, and headed for my parents' room.

The door was closed. I had made sure to leave it that way. Being in their room was like putting salt in a wound, and I never went in there unless I had to. The bed was still left unmade and makeup was scattered across my mother's vanity. Everything was left untouched like the scene of a crime, my proof that they were here. But the place had started to collect dust, which proved in contrast that they weren't coming back. I allowed myself time to take it in, to smell my mother's floral perfume and examine things they had left behind. Even their old dusty towels seemed so valuable to me now.

Remembering I only had fifteen minutes, I knelt down beside the bed and ran my hand along the floorboards beneath the mattress. My fingers felt around for the lifted plank and pulled it loose, revealing the golden box that would explain everything. Without looking inside, I grabbed it and closed the bedroom door behind me.

After seeing that I did in fact come back with something, Betsy could not hold back her interest.

"Well?" she asked, forgetting she was supposed to be angry. "Are you going to show me what's in the box?" Betsy could never stay mad for long.

Her curiosity was not surprising. The box was a beautiful dusty gold color with carved floral patterns running along its surface. It was closed securely with an elaborate latch that held it shut like a treasure chest. A box like this was bound to hold answers to buried family secrets.

The contents seemed ordinary enough—a stack of pictures, love letters my parents had written each other over the years, some jewelry, and old coins.

"Here," I said handing her the box. "There are pictures in here of me as a baby. I was born in 1923. The images aren't great, but you can tell it's me."

She thumbed through the pictures with a blank expression, and it was unnerving not to be able to guess her reaction.

"See this one," I continued reaching into the box on her lap. "*Elyse Ellen Adler Summer 1939*," I read off the back. "I look three here, but I was sixteen." I grabbed another one. "This one is me and mother down by the creek. I used to play there all the time. *July 1953*," I read again. "I look six, but I was thirty."

I grabbed another and another, reading the backs of the photos that proved my story. When I stopped, Betsy collected the photos, returning them to the box, her mind lost in thought.

"I don't know what to say, Ellie." She looked at me directly, paying more attention to the person she saw. "This is . . ." Her voice retreated into the silence of her own thoughts.

Fear began to pump through my veins. I felt hot and dizzy. Was it a mistake to tell her, to love her? Trust, it was too deceitful. It was the one thing I had counted on, and it would be the weakness that brought me down.

"We'll have to leave," she said certain of the decision. "We can't stay here. It's too dangerous. We'll move from place to place every few years. It'll be fine."

The relief of her words poured over me like cool water putting out the heat. I was a fool to think she would betray me. Fear, I quickly realized, was the true deceiver.

"Okay," I whimpered not noticing my tears.

"Don't be scared, honey," she comforted. "Everything is going to be okay." I felt the soft skin of her hand wipe the wetness from my cheek. "I love you, Elyse. We'll get through this."

I scooted as close as I could to her on the bench seat of the Chrysler, folding myself into the crook of her arm, and I wept.

***

I woke up with tears in my eyes, but was quickly pulled back to the present by the sound of Anna in the kitchen and the wonderful smell of breakfast. I dried my wet cheeks and pulled myself together.

"I made your favorite," she said as I made my way to the table. "Pancakes and eggs."

"Thanks." I couldn't remember the last time I had a real breakfast. Since I'd come to the city, I'd been relying on pop-tarts, bagels, cereal, Cearno's, anything easy. "Smells good."

"So, I was thinking last night about William. Did you even let him explain himself?" she asked nonchalantly as she flipped the pancakes.

Anna never was one to beat around the bush. Always straight to the point, she never changed.

I would have liked to pretend that a good night's sleep left me with a clear and refreshed mind, that all thoughts of Kara, Ryder, and William had vaporized with the early morning fog, but that was far from the truth.

"He's just not who I thought he was," I said, trying to hide the disappointment in my voice.

"Yeah," she accepted, but I realized that I hadn't really answered the question.

"He betrayed me . . . and manipulated me," I continued. "I don't need an explanation."

". . . but you still have feelings for him," she tagged to the end of my sentence. Of course she was right. It was probably written all over my face.

"Well, that's not really something I can control."

"Maybe it is though. What if you have your own feelings for him, aside from what he is doing?"

"That doesn't really matter. I don't want to love someone who would try and do this to me."

"So, you never asked him why he did what he did?" she persisted.

"No. I actually haven't talked to him about any of it yet. I just kind of left."

"And you're supposed to be the mature one," she laughed. "You're eighty-nine years old. How are you still so naïve?"

"I've never had feelings for anyone before," I defended myself. "I'm new at this, but I'm still smart enough to know when someone is trying to take advantage of me."

"I'm just saying, what if there was a good reason for it? Did you think of that?" she asked, handing me my plate and sitting down to eat.

"I know the reason for it," I said through a bite of eggs. "It's not a good one as far as I'm concerned."

"Regardless, it is important to let him explain himself."

She was quiet for a while, letting me consider her point of view as she ate her pancakes. She did make a good case for him, something I was open to. I didn't want to be right. Then again, she could just be trying to make me feel better.

"You know," she said breaking the silence, "you can borrow some of Chloe's clothes if you want to take a shower and get cleaned up."

I looked down at what I was wearing. Somehow I'd ended up with the young girl's blood on my shirt and jeans.

"Where *is* Chloe?" I asked, trying to push thoughts of Kara out of my mind.

"School." She reached for the green pillbox in the center of the table and opened the compartment for today.

"Shoot. I wanted to say goodbye," I said, noticing the mouthful of pills Anna had swallowed. One gulp of water washed them down like they were nothing.

"It's okay. You'll see her at Thanksgiving. You're coming over, right?" Her voice was overly enthusiastic as she tried to keep my focus off the pillbox.

"Yeah, sure." I didn't let the question distract me. "Since

when are you taking so many pills?" I asked. Straight to the point, that's how she was with me.

"I'm old, Elyse. What do you expect?" She tried laughing it off, but I saw through it and waited for an honest answer.

She looked me in the eyes, her brow lifting slightly, as if to tell me without words, *That's life*.

"What's wrong?" I demanded.

The question prompted more than I was ready for, and as she tried to bring herself to answer, I watched the strong walls of her built up defenses crumble.

"I have cancer." Her confession was like a frost, blanketing everything in cold devastation.

"Well, is it . . ." I didn't know how to finish. I couldn't bring myself to say the word, to even think it could be terminal.

"It's stage four breast cancer," she admitted with tears in her eyes, despite her best efforts to keep them at bay.

"Does Chloe know?"

"Yeah. She knows," she answered with a defeated sigh.

"It'll be okay," I said hopelessly. "Right? I mean, people survive cancer all the time." My attempt to console her seemed to do the opposite, revealing the dismal truth of it all, and she couldn't hold back the sobs as they came. "What does the doctor say? Isn't there a chance?"

Her eyes answered before she spoke. "We've tried, but it's progressed so much. There is nothing else they can really do."

I couldn't speak. What could I say? There were no comforting words, because nothing could make it better.

"I'm just so angry at myself. If I'd have just gone in earlier . . ."

"This is not your fault," I reacted with shock.

"It is," she cried. "I failed her. Chloe is just a girl. How can I leave her?"

"This isn't a choice, Anna, it's . . . unfair. It's not . . ."

"Does it matter?" she said through angry tears. "Her father left, and when I go, she'll be alone."

"I'll be here," I said desperately, trying to give her some peace of mind.

She smiled through her sadness. "That's sweet, Elyse, but she needs her mother. Nobody can ever fill a mother's shoes. Nobody will ever love her like I do."

The familiar pain I felt in my heart as she made her final point had been buried deep throughout the years, but the loss of a mother never leaves you. She was right. Nobody could ever fill those shoes. Betsy had been a friend and a parent, but by no means did she ever fill the hole that was formed in me when I lost my mother. Nobody could bring her back. Suddenly that ache was alive in me. I couldn't bear it, couldn't stand the thought of Chloe reliving my worst nightmare. Anna looked me in the eyes, apparently seeing my refusal to let it be.

"Some things you can't heal, Ellie," she concluded with a need to move on. "Well, I'll go get those clothes and find you a new toothbrush. You need to get cleaned up before you go find him, and I've got a doctor's appointment so . . ."

I caught her hand as she walked past me.

"It'll be okay," I promised.

"I know," she lied.

"I'll find a way," I said, hoping my ability could be the cure.

"How much time do I have?"

She paused, and I felt sick. "There's time," she said, not taking my promise to heart. She squeezed my hand, asking for its release, and went up the stairs to find the clothes.

I let the shower run scalding hot, trying to prove to myself that I wasn't numb. The water felt good, like I was washing all the hopelessness from my life, and I stayed in a lot longer than I should. William's gorgeous smile still burned in my mind, but I tried to push it out. The look in Anna's eyes had given me new purpose, and I wouldn't let her down. Maybe healing was what I was meant to do.

I didn't want to go back. I didn't want to see William. The mere idea of him left a heart-wrenching void in my chest, but I wasn't going to let his childish game deter me. No matter what happened, I was determined to heal her. I'd find a way.

I slipped into Chloe's tight fitting Levis and a hot pink shirt with rhinestone hearts on the front, brushed my teeth and combed my hair. My skin was chapped and dry from a night of crying salty tears. I looked around for some lotion, but came across Anna's collection of wrinkle creams and anti-aging eye serums instead. I suddenly felt a twinge of guilt at the sight of my reflection. My eighty-nine-year-old cheeks were firm and rosy, my hair, saturated with vibrant shades of brown, hadn't grayed in the slightest. I was a perfect picture of health.

"You almost ready?" Anna called from outside the door.

"Yeah. I'll be right out," I answered. I placed the fancy jars back in their place on the counter, trying to remember their exact position. "Okay. I'm ready. Sorry, for taking so long, the shower felt nice. Do you need to go to your appointment?"

"In about ten minutes," she said leading the way down the stairs.

"I should go with you," I proposed.

"No, you should go home. Find William, and hear him out. If you don't like what he has to say, then give him a piece of your mind and be done with it."

"I think I should stay."

She rolled her eyes. "You can't. I'm officially kicking you out. This is a big deal, Elyse. There are others like you. It's a new world. You need to go be a part of it."

I stuffed my dirty clothes into my bag and followed her to the front door. "I guess you're right," I answered, but my reasoning was different. It was the only way I could learn how to heal her.

"Damn right," she said. "You can't run away from your problems, Ellie."

"Are you going to be all right going by yourself, though? You have to be careful. If someone is following you, you have to call me."

She gave me a stubborn look. "I'm a grown woman, Elyse. I'll be fine."

"At least keep your phone on."

I hugged her goodbye wondering how long I really had to help her. She squeezed me as tightly as her fragile body could, unafraid to overstep boundaries. We were as close as we ever were, no awkward moments or empty conversation, just genuine friendship. Blood sisters for life.

12.

THE RIDE HOME was lengthy, and I couldn't help but notice I'd only added more weight to my mental baggage. Although my visit with Anna was comforting and helped clear things up in terms of William, her sickness added to my worries, and the farther I was away from her, the more helpless I felt. *One thing at a time*, I reminded myself. Going home was the answer to Anna's health problems, the only way to find out what I needed to do to heal her.

The part of me that longed for William never let up. I willed the train to go faster because of it. It was irrational and backward, but it urged me on just as fervently as it had driven me away. I knew that seeing him played a part in healing Anna, that maybe he could tell me what I needed to know, but I couldn't escape the fact that I *wanted* to see him. No matter how hard I tried to push him out, the yearning had tangled its roots around my sense of reason and remained, ever-present.

After I got off at my stop, I nearly ran the few blocks between the station and my place. When I finally turned the last corner, something in me expected to see him, and I ached with relief as he came into view like the rising sun. Sitting on the stoop of my front door, hands folded across his knees, he was waiting. His head turned at the sound of my shuffling feet, his face tired and defeated. There was no uplifting smile to admire. Our eyes locked, his communicating worry, mine unassailable surrender.

"How long have you been sitting here?" I tried to make my words calm and steady.

"All night," he said, still seated.

"You slept out here?"

"Didn't sleep much, no."

I couldn't figure him out. This wasn't the behavior of someone trying to manipulate me, and if he was, this was taking it a little far.

"Why?" I asked, pleading. I needed answers.

"I was worried. Kara told me about the girl. Why did you run away, Ellie?"

I gave him a perplexed look. Was he playing more games? Wasn't it obvious why I'd run?

"What happened?" He rose as he spoke, his brow pinching together with concern.

I couldn't tell him about Anna, but the more I thought about his lie, the more frustration began to build. Conflicting emotions raged and I wanted so badly to be strong and give him the piece of my mind I had been practicing.

"You made a fool of me," I returned, my voice cracking as

the tears came. I tried to compose myself, but the rest came out as a jumbled mess of questions. "Why are you here? Why are you doing this to me? Why did you wait here? Why . . ."

"How did I make a fool of you?" he asked. He was closer to me now, baring his striking features like fierce weapons, each one fighting my will to confront him. "What did I do?"

His ruby lips were within reach, moist and ready. I craved them and remembered so clearly and simply what he had done. "You lied," I snapped. "You tricked me into loving you."

Overwhelmed and distraught, I turned to escape down the street, but hesitated remembering Anna's words. *You can't run away from your problems, Ellie.*

A pair of finely sculpted arms wrapped around me quieting my shaking shoulders. I felt his face bury into the back of my hair, his body pressing tight against my back. I sighed deeply, unable to deny myself the pleasure of his touch.

"Is that what you think?" His chest shook as he laughed.

"It's not funny," I said pulling away reluctantly. "Why are you laughing?" I swung around to face him.

"You love me," he beamed.

"Only because you're manipulating my heart and my feelings or whatever you do. Kara told me your bloodline was Aphrodite. You know, it's cruel to play with people's emotions."

"Elyse, my power doesn't work like that," he said, still smiling ear to ear.

"What do you mean? Like what?"

"I mean, I have to be in the presence of the person for it to be effective. Besides I only tried it on you that once, and it's not a permanent thing."

I was still skeptical. Maybe I was just in denial, because it was all too good to be true. I crossed my arms protectively across my chest. How could I be sure this wasn't just part of his game?

"I don't know," I said with a doubtful expression.

"So stubborn," he smirked. His green eyes became sharp and suddenly the familiar euphoric sensation began to spread. I couldn't speak. The feeling was strong, like butterflies without the nerves, and was more suggestive of infatuation than love. It was almost impossible to think of anything but his brilliance. I was a victim to it, a slave to his very existence. Something compelled me to please him, and I knew, without a question in my mind, I would do anything he asked. After a moment, his eyes snapped shut, moving down and away as he waited for me to recover.

"Oh," I gasped, flushing with embarrassment as the feeling dissipated. I was instantly horrified at my absurd behavior, but also completely relieved to know that William wasn't the villain I had made him out to be.

". . . which means," he continued, "that you love me, like you said."

I stood mortified at my confession.

"Well, how was I supposed to know?" I asked, a little embarrassed.

"You could have just asked."

That probably would have been the more rational response. "I'm sorry," I mumbled.

William seemed back to his normal self, satisfied with

my sad excuse for an apology. I didn't know what to say, but he needed no words. He pulled me closer, our faces almost touching. He reached for my face and held my head with both hands as he pushed his mouth into mine. His lips were pillow soft and delicate, moving in perfect rhythm with my own. His breath was warm and tasted of spearmint, and with each brush of his lips my pulse quickened sending hot blood through my body. When his lips left my mouth, they did not pull away, but lingered close, and traveled up my cheek to my ear.

"I love you too, Ellie," he whispered.

I melted at the sound of his low growling voice, but doubt had me questioning him again.

"How do you know for sure you do?"

"Well, I am kind of an expert," he teased.

"Shut up." I laughed. "So I guess after waiting all night at my door, you might want to come inside?"

"No, actually I was thinking I'd just sit out here for a few more hours."

I rolled my eyes and cracked a smile.

"Yes, I'm coming inside," he said reassuringly.

"Good, because I need to pick your brain. I have questions," I said unlocking the door.

"I have some questions too, actually," he added, suddenly more serious. "Where did you go?"

"A motel," I lied as we climbed the stairs to my apartment.

"Nice shirt," he added suspiciously. "I didn't think you liked rhinestones."

"Oh, yeah. Well, Kara got blood on my clothes, so I . . .

picked these up at a thrift store nearby. It was all I could find."
I threw my purse onto the couch. "I'll be right back. I want
to get into some of my own stuff." Guilt instantly set in as
I regretted the lie, but I needed some time to consider the
situation with Anna. I was sure William wouldn't approve of
what I had planned.

The weather was sunny and perfect since yesterday, so I
threw on some cutoff jean shorts and a plain blue tank top. I
ran my fingers through my flat hair and pinched my cheeks
trying to bring color to my face.

"You dressed?" William asked from behind the door.

"Yeah," I answered, and he peeked his head in, his hair
falling into his eyes the way I liked.

"So what did you want to pick my brain about?" he asked,
kicking his flip-flops off and climbing onto my queen size
bed.

"Oh." I wondered how I to phrase my question. I couldn't
very well ask him, *So, how do I cure my human friend with
cancer?* Especially not after last night's episode. "I was just
curious if you knew more about my ability. I'm not sure how
to heal something that isn't an open wound."

"Like what?" he asked.

"Like . . . a black eye," I improvised.

He nodded his head, wondering to himself. "To be honest,
I don't know. The only reason I knew how to heal your leg was
because of Kara. I'm not sure how she knew, but the night she
stabbed you with that blade, she told me how to heal the cut."

I sat backwards in my desk chair to face him. "I don't
remember that."

"You wouldn't. Part of her ability is that she can speak to others telepathically."

"So, she told you with her mind?"

"Yeah," he answered casually. "You should ask Iosif, though. He would know."

I watched him curiously from across the room, noticing the little things that made him so uniquely beautiful. He scanned the row of books I had lined up on my night stand for easy access.

"*Romeo and Juliet?*" he observed, taking it off of the table. "If love's rough with you, be rough with love, prick love for pricking and you beat love down." He flashed a heart-stopping glance at me. "That's my favorite line." He took his time thumbing through the pages.

Everything about him seemed no less than perfect. How his thick hair, the color of golden honey, always seemed to reflect the light as he combed his fingers through it. How the green color of his eyes fought with the brown pressing it to the distant edge. How his lips, shaped for the perfect kiss, slid over his teeth in a smile that nearly blinded me. It was a contagious smile that filled the room and drew immediate attention. His body was sturdy and hard, and the rustic subtleties of his face gave him the look of a man, not a boy. I felt as though I could spend hours or even days examining every detail, every imperfection, every fleck of color in his skin.

"Are you sure your ability doesn't . . ."

"What?" he asked, eager to hear the end of my sentence.

"Have lasting effects?"

He laughed. "You tell me."

My cheeks flushed as I remembered my embarrassing confession on the front steps. "I'd rather not."

"No," he answered. "Nobody has ever experienced lasting effects."

"Not even Kara?" I hadn't even realized the thought had been bothering me. I had buried it deep, hoping I'd never have to ask it, but I had to know.

He sighed and looked away. "I was worried about that," he admitted.

"So there is something between you two."

"No," he assured me. "Kara . . . she has issues."

"I sort of figured that," I said, moving to sit with him on the bed.

He scooted back to lean against the headboard, and I nestled in beside him.

"We used to be best friends when we were kids. Before the war, we saw each other every day. She was like a sister, really. You know, she'd come over and we'd play cops and robbers, hide from our parents for hours just to make them crazy, beg to stay the night at each other's houses. We were pretty inseparable."

I turned toward him, my eyes drifting to the muscle flexing in his cheek. "What happened?"

"The war. When it started, Kara and I were in our fifties, just kids. It's not an easy thing to make friends in a war, especially when your dad is leading the rebellion. Kara was the only one I had. When The Council found out that she was descendant of Prometheus, they wanted her. They wanted the ability to read thoughts. So they took her."

I felt my lips part in surprise. "So, why is she still with them, William? The war is over, right? Why doesn't she get out?"

"There's no getting out, Elyse. She has no choice."

"Why?"

He placed the book he'd been flipping through back on my nightstand and turned back to me. The answer was obvious to him.

"They'll kill her. They'll kill her family."

Everything seemed so hopeless. Did they really expect me to stand up against such a ruthless enemy? I felt myself begin to fold under the surmounting pressure. I pulled my knees into my chest.

"What am I supposed to do, William? I'm no leader. I can't . . . how am I supposed to defeat The Council? It's not possible."

"Can I be honest?" he asked, tilting his head to find my downcast eyes. "I don't want you to."

"What?"

"It's like my dad said, nothing is certain. What if you're right? You know, I thought I'd be okay with it, with you taking them on, I just didn't expect . . ."

"Didn't expect what?"

"That my love for you would get in the way." He'd said it earlier, the word love, but I didn't believe him. This time, it sunk in, and my guard was suddenly and abruptly down. "What if you got hurt or killed? I would never forgive myself."

I wanted to switch the subject. It was too overwhelming to think about.

"Why did you lie?" I asked, forcing him to talk about something else. "About your ability."

He thought about it. "I didn't lie. Technically," he added.

"Okay, so why didn't you tell me about your bloodline?"

"I don't know. It was stupid," he said shaking his head. "I didn't want to you to doubt your feelings. I didn't want you to second guess whether or not you really felt the way you did or whether I was forcing you to feel that way. You know it's real, right?"

"I know," I accepted. It was more real than anything I had ever experienced, and to be honest, I wasn't quite sure how to handle a reality that so closely resembled my dreams.

"Look," he said, his hand reaching for the back of his neck. "There's something else I need to tell you."

I could feel the apprehensive expression form on my face. After everything I'd learned since I met him, I couldn't imagine there was more. "What?" I said, dreading the news.

"I thought Iosif might have told you, but I guess he thought I should be the one."

"Is it bad?"

He laughed. "That depends. I don't think it's bad."

He sat up on the bed and took my hands. "Feel the warmth?" The familiar heat pulsed between our palms.

"Yes," I answered, waiting for the truth.

I could tell he was starting to get nervous. He swallowed before he continued. "It happens every five hundred years to two people."

"I knew it," I said, squeezing my knuckles tightly around his. "I knew it meant something."

He smiled. "It helps us find each other, so that when we do, we know for sure."

"Know what?" I urged impatiently.

"That we'll be the new mother and father, the parents of the next generation oracle."

He waited for my reaction, not knowing for sure if it would be good or bad. "I don't understand," I said, trying to make sense of what he was saying. "We're supposed to have a baby? When?" My breathing started to quicken. "Now?"

He laughed, sensing my oncoming hysteria. "No," he reassured me. "Not now. It just means whether you like me or not, you're stuck with me. Destiny sort of has a way of making sure we stay together, like soul mates." He kissed my hand, calming me. "When we're ready, somewhere way out there in the future, yes, we're supposed to have a baby."

"How could we be the parents of an oracle?" I asked, still questioning the possibility of such a theory. "That ability isn't either one of our bloodlines."

"The oracle isn't really a bloodline. It's a phenomenon that happens every half a millennium to a different couple, regardless of their ancestry. This time it's us."

I knew William thought of this as a good thing, and maybe I did too, but it scared me that so much of my future had been planned out for me. So many people were relying on me, had expectations of what I would do and who I would be. This was just one more thing I wasn't sure I'd be able to deliver. But I liked the idea of William as my soul mate, of being destined to be in love. It was what I always wanted.

"You okay?" he laughed, throwing a painfully gorgeous

smile at me. "You're kind of quiet."

"Sorry," I staggered. "I think I'm still getting over the shock of it all."

"Yeah, not exactly something you hear every day."

The warmth continued to emanate between our palms, a reminder that we belonged together.

"But you were right," I said, reassuring him. "It's not a bad thing." I leaned in to kiss his gentle lips, enjoying the moment, but he pulled away long before I wanted him to.

"So what you're saying is, you *do* love me," he teased.

"Do I have a choice?"

He couldn't hold back his smile. "Nope."

"So now what?" I asked, settling back into reality.

"Feel like hanging out downstairs with me?" He glanced at the clock. "It's my shift."

13.

FROM THE MOMENT William and I walked into Cearno's I knew something was wrong. Rachel, Paul, and Nics were all at a table, and all three of their heads turned in anxious anticipation as the door chimed.

William's smile dropped. "Where's Sam?" he asked, unable to hide his worry.

"We were hoping you would know," Paul answered as Nics shoved her chair away and headed for the bathroom, clearly upset.

I empathized with her. If she knew what I knew, I could see why she'd need to leave. My stomach started to tighten into knots making me want to throw up. I'd forgotten about Sam. Kara had been forced to kill the girl, but she hadn't mentioned Sam.

"His phone probably died," I added, hoping it would be true. "Right?"

"I don't know," Rachel said, her eyes falling to the table. "It just keeps ringing, and nobody's at his house."

I looked at William, knowing that Kara had told him about what happened, and saw little confidence in his eyes.

"He's supposed to work today," William said, trying to put everyone at ease. "He'll be here."

"If The Council—" I started to ask, but William gave me a sharp look that silenced me instantly. Rachel's head nodded toward a young college girl studying at a table across from us, and mouthed the word "human." I hadn't realized we needed to take such precautions in this place, but apparently, I needed to catch on quickly.

"I should get back there," William said, planting a soft kiss on my cheek.

Rachel's lips pulled into a tight smile as he left.

"So you guys are really hitting it off, huh?"

"Yeah, I guess we are," I answered, hoping the conversation would get my mind off of Sam.

"Has he, you know, *persuaded* you to rub his feet or make him breakfast yet?"

I laughed at her and sat in one of the empty chairs at their table. "Not yet. He did try and make me kiss him though."

"Creep," she teased.

"It was just for a second. He didn't actually do it."

"Uh-huh." She acted as if she didn't believe it.

I was starting to blush. "Should we go check on Nics?" I asked.

"She doesn't like being checked on," Paul answered. "She gets mean."

Just as I was about to insist we go anyway, the bathroom

door swung open, and she stormed out, heading back to her seat.

"I'm going to kill him," she announced. "If he's made me this worried over nothing, I'm going to kill him."

"Relax, he's fine," Paul insisted.

"Shut up, Paul," Nics snapped.

"Told you," he said to me.

The more Nics worried, the more I was sure something had happened to Sam, and it was my fault. If I hadn't been there, maybe Kara wouldn't have followed them. I had to say something. I just didn't know how.

"Has anyone seen Kara?" I asked.

The three of them went silent. "Why?" Nics questioned.

Before I had the chance to answer, the door chimed.

"It's her," Rachel whispered. I could sense the fear coming off of her. "And Ryder."

I followed the others, keeping my eyes down, despite my urge to turn and get a glimpse at the infamous Ryder who'd made Kara murder an innocent girl. The thought made me scared. Why was he here?

"Sam?" I heard Nics say softly. I had to look.

My eyes found Ryder first. He was older, in his fifties in human terms, with rough graying stubble on his angry face. He wore a black leather jacket and a gold chain around his neck like some mafia thug, and dragged our friend behind him by the shirt, beaten and haggard. Something about Sam looked different, and I couldn't decide if it was just the abuse or if it was what everyone had feared—they'd aged him.

Keeping hold of Sam's collar, Ryder made his way over to

the human girl. "Leave," he demanded, and she darted out of the café, abandoning her books. "You four." He nodded at a group of familiar customers, Descendants, and pointed toward the door. They obeyed, looking back at us with remorse.

As soon as we were alone, Ryder threw Sam forcefully against a wall. His body absorbed the impact and fell limp to the ground.

"Hey!" Nics yelled, causing us all to rise to our feet.

"Shut it, or you're next," Ryder barked at her.

William rushed out from the back, but Kara must have convinced him to stop where he was behind the counter. Her eyes were locked on him, and he didn't move.

Sam let out a groan of pain as Ryder gave him a swift kick to the stomach. Impulsively, I tried to reach for him, but I couldn't move. My body was stuck, frozen where I stood, without even the ability to speak. I tried to take a step, move my fingers and toes, turn my head, but Ryder's ability, whatever it was, had rendered me motionless.

"Today you all are going to learn a little restraint," Ryder cackled to himself as he picked Sam off of the floor by his hair. "If you think it's okay to break our laws, think again." His fist cracked against the side of Sam's face, causing blood to ooze from his nose. I couldn't turn my head to look away, and realized, neither could anyone else. Ryder had us all frozen still, and every one of us was forced to watch helplessly as Sam was pummeled by this crazed madman. "Let this be a warning to you. There are always consequences." Another fist hit Sam in the mouth, splitting his lower lip, but he was already unconscious.

I felt tears drip down my cheeks, knowing it was all my fault. If my body would have been allowed to move, I was sure I'd be trying to control my rocking sobs.

Ryder's violent eyes turned to me. "And *you*." My heart began to hammer within my still chest. I had no defense, no way to escape. Whatever pain he intended for me would have to be endured. His thick, rough hand grabbed my jaw, pinching my cheeks with his strong fingers. "I'm not sure what you're trying to pull or how you managed to get you and those humans flagged, but I'll be watching." His fist slammed against my face before I saw it coming. Only able to breath, I inhaled deeply and waited for the next blow. It came from the other side, and I could feel blood sliding down the side of my cheek. When the third came, the sweet relief of unconsciousness saved me.

Faint voices brought me back. I listened for a while before I had the courage to open my eyes.

"What's his bloodline?"

"I don't know. Maybe Sophrosyne?"

"It's getting bad."

"Reminds me of the war."

"What do you think he meant by her managing to get flagged?"

"No idea."

I felt a hand on my cheek. "Hey," William said, noticing I was awake.

I tried lifting my lids, but they were swollen, and didn't open all the way.

"You okay?"

I nodded, but didn't speak. Out of the corner of my eye, I saw Sam lying next to me. We were in my bed, and the voices of Rachel, Nics, and Paul were coming from the living room of my apartment.

"Is he?" I asked quietly.

"He's pretty bad."

I sat up slowly, and my head began to throb. My whole face felt like a balloon as I examined it with my hands.

"Here," William said, taking a kitchen knife from off my bedside table. He cut the pad of his thumb as he'd done before and waited for it to bleed.

"I'm starting to make this a habit, aren't I?"

"Yeah, knock it off will ya?" he teased.

He dabbed the blood from his thumb with another finger and applied it to my left eyebrow, easing only a fraction of the pain.

"Why are you doing it like that?" I asked. "Your thumb won't heal."

"Left is poison," he reminded me, and then he placed his cut thumb over another gash on the right side of my lip, healing us both.

Our eyes locked for a moment as his hand lingered, and he moved his face slowly closer to mine. His kiss was its own kind of relief. Everything would be all right. His soft mouth was hard to pull away from after such an ordeal, and I let myself get carried away.

"Gross," Sam moaned.

"Nothing to see here," William said using his hand as a privacy screen. "Just stay unconscious a little longer."

"Sure," Sam groaned, "don't mind me."

"You all right?" William asked, all jokes aside. I wasn't sure what I looked like, but I was hoping it was nothing like Sam. His eyes were already black, and one was swollen shut. Small cuts were scattered here and there, but the majority of his injuries were bruises from being kicked and beaten. His whole face was a swollen mess, and on top of it all, I was right. He'd gone from looking eighteen to thirty in a single day. I wondered exactly how many years they had taken from him, if he even knew the number.

Sam sighed. "Yeah I'm all right. How do I look? Any gray hairs?"

"Don't worry, Nics will still think you're hot," William said with a smile.

"Shut up," he said, trying not to laugh. "Is she here?"

"Thanks for telling me he's awake," Nics said, rushing through the bedroom door, Paul and Rachel following behind her.

Sam didn't try to sit up, or even move, but his gaze stayed locked on Nics. "You owe me," he said, trying to smirk through his puffy upper lip.

She shook her head, holding back a smile. "I told you not to do it."

"You still owe me."

"You're an idiot."

"How is the pain, from one to ten?" Rachel asked.

He winced as he shifted. "Somewhere between 10 and 500."

I smiled, glad to know he was still in good spirits. "I can

fix the cuts," I offered, "but I don't know how to heal the swelling."

"I'll take what I can get."

The four of them left, giving me space to treat Sam without the pressure of a crowd.

"I'm sorry I can't do more," I told him, healing the last cut on his face. The swelling was still pretty hard to look at, but I wasn't sure how I was supposed to heal those kinds of wounds. I kicked myself for not asking Iosif when I had the chance. I needed to find out.

"Are you kidding? It feels so much better already," he said, closing his eyes.

My guilty conscience set in. In my mind, I had done this to him. "This is my fault, Sam," I confessed. His eyes opened and he was looking at me again. "Kara was following *me*. If I wouldn't have come—"

"No. I won't let you take the blame for them," he insisted. "They did this to me, not you."

It felt good to hear him release me of the guilt, and although I still considered myself somewhat responsible, at least I wasn't holding it inside wondering who would hate me for it.

"You'll probably feel even better if you wash all this dried blood off of your face," I suggested. "Do you want me to run some warm water in the sink for you?"

"Ladies first," he said. "You didn't get off too easy yourself." He closed his eyes again, desperate for sleep, or maybe desperate to escape what had happened. "I'm just going to rest for a second." I couldn't imagine how tired he was, what he had been through.

"Sure." I slid off the bed and headed for the bathroom. My heart felt lighter, like it was easier to breath now that I had Sam's forgiveness. "Thanks," I said, looking back at him, "for not blaming me."

"No prob, bob," he answered with closed eyes.

The warm water turned pink as I scooped it up into my face. It was soothing against my sore cheeks, and I dreaded seeing what they must look like. After my skin was rinsed clean, I faced the mirror. There was already a purple bruise forming below my left eye, and the right side of my face was noticeably bigger than the other.

I'd never been beaten up before, but it made me feel stronger, tough even. I survived, and maybe next time, I would know what was coming. Having felt the pain, maybe my instincts would kick in, and I would be able to fight back.

I moved my face closer to the mirror, examining my war wounds. I couldn't believe he hit me. A heavy feeling settled into the pit of my stomach as I thought of Anna. I hated the fact that Ryder knew about her, but if he hadn't taken me, punished me like Sam, being flagged must mean we were safe.

"What do you think he meant when he said I was flagged?" I asked William as he came to the bathroom door.

"I don't know," he answered, taking the wash cloth and dabbing the spots I missed, "but it might have saved your life."

His touch felt good, and I stayed quiet as he examined my face.

"You think he would have killed me?" I asked when he was finished.

"Depends on what you did," he said with a look of interest. "Feel like telling me?"

I thought of Anna. All my life I'd been her secret. Now she was mine.

I shook my head. "No."

The rest of the day was spent watching movies with everyone on my new TV. It felt like the only thing we could do to distance ourselves from what had happened. Sam and I got the recliner sides of the couch while the others sprawled out on the floor. It was nice to be with everyone, with friends, but I couldn't take my mind off of Anna.

"Just be careful, okay?" I said, sneaking a phone call to her in my room.

"It was never a problem before, Elyse," she answered. "I'm sure nothing will happen."

"Anna. Promise me," I demanded.

She sighed into the phone. "I promise."

When everybody left, William insisted on staying. I didn't protest. He'd been sleeping in my living room every night since Kara's break-in anyway.

"William, how is it that I ended up living above Cearno's?" I asked when we were alone.

"What do you mean?"

"Of all the places? All the cities?" I mused while snuggling against him in my bed. "I think Betsy knew."

"She did," he confessed.

I looked at him in shock. "How?"

"We've known Betsy ever since the crash. My dad and I were the ones who took you to her house after it happened."

The memory came rushing back, the pain of it suddenly fresh in my mind. I remembered the image of the crumpled car I'd tried to erase thousands of times, those first days with Betsy, the hollow aching that consumed me then. But for the first time, something about the memory was different.

"You were the boy," I said, making the connection. I didn't need to ask. I knew it was him. He had those same sad eyes as he looked at me now.

He nodded. "We were on our way to visit you for the first time since your parents left. My dad said the blizzard would be good cover. When we saw the crash, we stopped. We didn't know it was your car. There was nothing we could do about your parents, but you were still alive."

I didn't wipe the tears as they streamed freely down my cheeks, but this time they weren't solely tears of grief. There was another feeling that accompanied the sadness. William had been there all along. The thought was comforting.

"I had no idea," I said.

"I sat with you in the back seat on the way. You were out cold, but it was the first time I felt my skin burn against yours."

I noticed the warmth of his arm against mine and smiled. I was getting used to it.

"We came to visit you a lot after that. My dad would always say, 'Time to go see the girl you're going to marry.'"

"I never saw you," I said, too shy to respond to the last part of his sentence.

"You weren't supposed to."

I couldn't believe Betsy had kept that kind of a secret from me, but I knew she felt it was for my own good, my protection.

What would she think now, knowing I was smack dab in the center of it all? I felt sleep beckoning me as I thought of her. At least she came to visit in my dreams.

"Thanks," I said, closing my tired eyes.

"For what?" he asked.

"Saving me."

We hadn't planned on sleeping together in my bed, but that's where we ended up. *Why not?* I told myself as I drifted off, using his chest as a pillow.

14.

WAKING UP NEXT to William was both a thrilling realization and a horrifyingly embarrassing experience. I opened my eyes in the dim light of the morning to find him gazing gently back at me. I couldn't dredge up a more pleasing image to grace the first moments of my day, but how long had he been watching me? I smiled back at him warily, taking note of my sprawled out legs and cowlicked hair. Smiling made my cheeks hurt, and I remembered my face. I must look like a train wreck.

"Hi," I managed as I sat up pulling my knees into my chest.

"Hi," he chuckled back. "How are you feeling?"

"Better," I answered, feeling the sore spots with my hands. "Does it look bad?"

He shrugged. "Purple's not a bad color on you."

I laughed. "Great."

"The good news is the rest of your body seems to be working perfectly." I gave him a strange look. "Bit of a bed hog, huh?"

"Really?" I moaned. How humiliating. What was I thinking having him sleep in my bed?

"Actually, it's fine. You're a lot less shy in your sleep." He sat up as he spoke, propping himself against the headboard.

"How so?" I shot out anxiously.

"'Snuggly' might be a bit of an understatement," he said with an overly-satisfied grin.

I laughed uneasily as I tried to hide my bruised and battered face behind my still untamed hair. The thought of my body quickly succumbing to William's innate allure as soon as my conscious mind was out of the picture was unnerving. Who knew what deeply buried subconscious desires would make themselves known in the night. He was lucky I didn't suffocate him. Suddenly, the image of a child squeezing its beloved new pet beyond its capacity accompanied my thoughts.

"You should have moved to the couch." I hoped I hadn't kept him up all night.

"Are you kidding? The more Elyse the better."

"But what if I snuggle you to death or something?" I asked half teasing, half considering the possibility of such a thing.

"Well, *if* that were to happen, I couldn't think of a better way to go. 'Come, death, and welcome. Elyse wills it so.'"

"All right, Romeo," I smiled at his witty reference, "but you do realize he dies at the end right?"

"A risk I'm willing to take."

I glanced at the clock with regret. 11:26. "I guess we should get up," I said without enthusiasm.

"Yeah, we have class soon."

As soon as William headed for the bathroom, I let myself

sprawl out again, burying my face into the gathered bed-sheets which had captured his lingering scent.

Then, out of nowhere, there was a knock at the door. I hopped down the stairs in my pajamas, expecting Rachel or Nics.

"Let me in," Kara demanded, pushing me aside as I answered the door.

"Wow," I said as she charged past me up the stairs.

"Who is it?" William asked.

"Me," she answered.

I found the two of them in the living room and kept my distance.

"What are you doing here?" he said without welcome.

"Nice to see you, too."

"What's going on?" I asked with an angry voice. I hadn't exactly forgiven her for standing back and watching while Sam and I got beaten to a pulp.

"Nice face," Kara snickered.

"That's it," William said, grabbing her by the wrist and dragging her toward the door. "Get out of here."

She yanked her arm free. "This is the thanks I get for saving your little girlfriend from torment?"

William looked at me, then back at her. "Explain," he demanded.

"Elyse is the one who needs to explain. Do you want to tell him your little secret or should I?"

I shook my head. I wasn't ready to tell William about Anna.

"Elyse, what is it?" he asked urgently. His eyes were fixed on me as if I were holding a grenade about to explode.

"My best friend is human," I admitted. "She lives in Oakland."

"She stayed the night there," Kara added.

He brushed his fingers through his hair, pinning it back and out of his face. "So that's where you went when you didn't come home?"

I nodded. "I didn't know about any of this when I met her. I've known her for half of my life. She and her daughter are as good as family."

"What does she know?" William asked.

"Everything," Kara answered for me.

He shook his head. "What about the daughter? What does she know?"

Kara watched me out of the corner of her eye as she spoke. "Not as much."

His face was pained and full of furious concern as he thought about what to say. He sat on the couch, eyes dropped to the floor. "Why hasn't Ryder killed them?" he asked perplexed.

Kara shrugged. "They're flagged."

"What does that mean?" I asked, moving closer now that I could see she wasn't a threat.

"It means they've been granted amnesty. They're untouchable. I don't get it. I've never heard of a human being flagged before. It doesn't happen."

"Untouchable? According to your pal Ryder, Elyse is flagged. Didn't seem to matter much to him."

"It was the best I could do, okay?" Kara spat.

"What's that supposed to mean?" he asked, getting frustrated with her.

"He was going to kill Elyse," she shouted. "I didn't have any other option."

He stood quickly, nervous. "Kara, what did you do?"

Her eyes were apologetic. "I had to tell them, William."

"What?" I begged. "Tell who what?"

"We've got to go," William insisted. "Now." He grabbed my coat off of the hanger and threw it at me.

"Why?" I asked confused.

"She told them who you are, Elyse," William yelled.

"I had to," she fought back. "I knew they wouldn't touch her if they knew she was the new mother, but that's it. That's all I told them."

"You know they'll be investigating her now. What happens when they make the connection to the prophecy?" William asked with an edge to his voice.

"I don't know," she answered with remorse.

William grabbed my shoulder bag and nearly dragged me out the door, leaving Kara standing alone in my living room.

"I can't believe it," William murmured to himself as he drove like a maniac in the direction of The Institute. "After all these years of keeping you a secret, she goes and blabs."

"She had to," I defended her. "Would you rather he killed me?"

His face stayed hard and angry as we drove, but I could tell he was just as grateful for Kara as I was. "No."

"I can't believe he was just going to kill me," I thought out loud.

"I can't believe he *hasn't* killed your friends."

The thought was paralyzing. Anna and Chloe were in

danger because of me. The idea that they would be killed simply for knowing me seemed too insane to be true.

"How do they get away with it, killing so many innocent people?"

"They say it's for the greater good," he answered honestly.

I sat dumbfounded for a few moments, gazing out the car window at the passing streets. The silence prompted him to speak.

"It's completely backwards, I know," he admitted, "but they get away with it because they claim it's for our protection, that there is no other way."

"Doesn't everyone see the injustice?" It made me sick to think about it.

"We know it's wrong, but what can anyone do about it?"

Only one answer seemed the appropriate response.

"Fight back," I returned, but he shook his head.

"We tried fighting back. It didn't work," he answered, pulling into a parking spot. "And according to the prophecy, it won't work without you."

I heaved a sigh and shot out of the car slamming the door behind me. "What am I supposed to do?"

"I don't know," he said to me over the roof of the car, "and I don't want it to be true any more than you, but that's the reason nobody has stood up to them. That's the truth."

We walked in silence for a few minutes, but I was too frustrated to keep quiet. I felt William's eyes fall on me, watching and waiting for me to say something.

"Well, that's crazy," I retaliated. "Isn't it?"

How long had things been like this? It was one thing to withhold abilities for the safety of the communities, but to kill off innocent people? And what did everyone expect me to do about it? He stopped me in the middle of the maze of parked cars to answer me straight to my face.

"No, crazy is putting the ones you love at risk to challenge a force that will undoubtedly come raining down on you with an iron fist to destroy the very memory of your existence. That's crazy. Why would anyone risk that when they know about the prophecy?"

"What if the prophecy isn't even real? What if Christoph just made it up to keep people waiting for someone who will never come?"

"The prophecy is true, Elyse. My dad heard it from the oracle herself."

"If it's true, why doesn't Christoph just kill me and get it over with? Why not take out the enemy before it all starts?"

"That's what I'm afraid of."

15.

OUR CONVERSATION HAD generated a whole world of emotions I wasn't ready for. There was no way of knowing what to expect. If I was truly in danger, what would happen if they did come for me? All I could control were my own actions, my own choices, and right now, I needed to figure out what to do about Anna before it was too late.

Sympathy shined through William's soft expression as we stepped into the elevator. Only one man joined us, and when I looked at him I immediately began to smell lavender. The floral fragrance made me instantly relax, and for a moment, I let go of my worries. I felt like I was getting an ambush aromatherapy treatment. When the man stepped out, he winked a blue eye at me and took the scent with him.

"Thanks, Henry," William said as the door closed.

"What was that about?" I asked as we rode the elevator to the top floor.

"I don't know. Normally he makes it smell like chocolate. I

guess he thought you looked stressed."

"I am," I said, as we stepped into the flowing mass of Descendant students. Those who passed stared at my swollen face. "I need to find Iosif."

"Okay, let's go," William said decidedly. Obviously he assumed I needed advice on how to deal with The Council's new knowledge, and maybe I would ask about that, but my main concern was Anna.

"I think I should go alone," I said, stopping him in his tracks.

He looked at me, and I could tell he thought I was upset with him about our conversation.

"Sure," he answered, and he let go of my hand.

I thought about explaining, but there was nothing I could say. He couldn't know about my plans for Anna. I knew he would try and stop me, so I let him think I was mad and turned to find the door to Iosif's office without a word.

The professor answered before I knocked.

"Please, come in," he welcomed me with a mangled toothy smile.

"Hi," I said, as he closed the door behind me.

"I thought you might be back." He seemed pleased with himself, and took a seat behind his desk leaning forward with interest. "You must have more against The Council than you'd originally thought." His eyes strayed away from mine as he took notice of the bruises on my face. "How can I help you, my dear?"

Although the answer to his question popped into my head immediately, I thought carefully about how to word it.

"Well, I thought maybe you could tell me more about my ability," I explained, sitting down to face him. He didn't need to know more than that.

His expression became curious. "Ahh, but there is another reason. A specific goal you seek to accomplish, and this is why you hope to learn of your ability. Am I right?"

He was more than right. He was dead on. My heart began to thud. Did he know what I was planning? Was it a crime to even *think* of healing a human? I should have expected this. I was in a school for people with special abilities, and here I was trying to pry information out of one of the eldest professors. I felt stupid for not considering the fact that he might be able to decipher my plan. I bit the inside of my upper lip. This was a bad idea.

"I assure you I am on your side, child," he continued. "Destiny has chosen you to do its bidding and appointed me to assist you in the process. Whatever it is you don't want me to know is safe with me."

I didn't like that he could come so close to my thoughts of Anna. Even if he was trying to help me, it was best for him to do so in the dark.

"So what is *your* ability?" I asked changing the subject.

"Intuition." The source of the deep lines in his face became clear as he smiled widely. "My bloodline is of Metis. I do not know your thoughts, but I can sense the essence of them. Do not let this frighten you. I am here to help."

His face still held a kind smile, making it hard to not trust him, but as soon as he spoke again, the lightheartedness fell from his expression.

"This goal, I am supposed to ensure you accomplish it. Whatever it is you need to know, I am here to provide the answers." The sincerity of his tone was nothing to be questioned.

"Why would you do that? You don't even know what it is."

"My wife told me to." He seemed to find humor in these words as well. "But as you know, my wife is no ordinary woman."

Although he spoke of the oracle lightly, I picked up on the reference instantly. She was still meddling, still pulling strings, trying to control the outcome of my future.

"She is here to help you and is putting herself at great risk to aid in the success of your destiny."

"My destiny." The idea of someone plotting out my future for me was unsettling, especially when I had my own plans. To think this woman had seen something in my future worth risking her safety for didn't help either. "I wanted to talk to you about that actually."

"I know you struggle with the truth, but it will unfold before you."

"Even if I have other plans?"

"I imagine so. No matter what path you take, it will lead you where you need to be."

"What if the path I take involves breaking Descendant law?"

He scratched his chin, and his lips pulled together in a tight apprehensive line. "Your choices will dictate the course, but in the end, it will play out as foretold."

"I know how my ability works if I apply my blood directly

to a wound," I said getting to the point.

"Yes. Obviously, the larger the wound, the more blood you'll be forced to sacrifice."

I knew that in order to heal I would have to inflict pain upon myself, but thinking about it still made my stomach churn. I dreaded the answer to my next question.

"What if what I want to heal is not a wound but a body?"

Picking up on the essence of my thought, Iosif gave me an understanding nod. "That is something that comes with great risk to you." His eyes focused on me intently, gauging my reaction.

"All right," I accepted, sitting up straight in my chair. I knew there would be consequences, but I was willing to pay the price.

"In the case of a sick body, the person would need to ingest the blood like medicine, but depending on the severity of the illness . . . the amount you would have to give could kill you."

My heart nearly stopped. *Kill* me? I had to make sure.

"To cure a body of progressed cancer for instance . . ."

"Would be a sacrifice," he finished.

I had assumed I would have to run away, hide, fight back against The Council, but I never expected the act alone to kill me. I needed a second to digest it. I looked down at my thumb which had nearly been picked raw and forced myself to stop. He couldn't be right. My body was meant to heal. How could it be so weak? There had to be some other way, a loophole, a trick.

"Couldn't I just draw a little at a time? Save it until I have enough?"

"As the blood is preserved outside of your body, it loses effect. The only way is to do an immediate transfer to the injured being."

My one shred of hope was put out like a match on a windy day. My sacrifice, or more appropriately, my death, was the cost of healing Anna.

"I know that must be difficult to hear, not what you expected," he sympathized.

"It's not what I expected," I admitted, "but if it's the only way . . . Turns out I'm not your prophecy girl after all, Professor."

"Prophecies are not to be interpreted or arranged. They unfold as they please, taking us all by surprise. Your sacrifice could be what causes the war that brings an end to The Council. There is no way to tell."

If what he said was true, only one of two things would happen. Anna would die, or I would. The thought was devastating. I felt sick and numb and hollow, like my very being had been sucked dry from my still standing body.

"I think I just assisted you in something that will very possibly cause your own death."

"Yes," I answered decidedly. "I think you did."

When Iosif excused me from our meeting, I found William waiting for me in the hall expecting answers. I was grateful in that moment that his eyes, which carried all the beauty of the earth and infinite sky, could not bear witness to the crumbled wreckage of my love-sick heart. If Iosif was right, and I chose to save Anna in place of my own life, it would break him, and as I thought of losing him, I felt my throat tighten. I couldn't allow myself to cry.

Seeing him had me questioning a decision that I had considered already made. Suddenly, I didn't know if I could go through with it. After all these years, I'd finally found love. It wasn't fair that it should be taken away so soon. Before William, I would have died for Anna without a second thought, but as he looked at me, I could see the love in his eyes. He needed me, too. Maybe it was selfish, but there had to be another way.

"Well?" he asked.

Well what? I wondered in my head. Had he heard something he wasn't supposed to? I wasn't ready to face him about my choice. He wouldn't understand. I couldn't look him in the eyes. How could I, knowing how deeply I would break his heart if I chose Anna over him? But a broken heart would heal, and Anna, if left untreated, would undoubtedly die. My chest felt heavy.

"What did he say?"

I tried to steady my voice, act myself, and smile back when he hit me with one of his intoxicating looks.

"He said things will play out the way they were foretold no matter what I do."

He threw his hands up. "That's it? What are we supposed to do? Run? Fight? I need to talk to him."

"No," I insisted, grabbing his hand before he could walk away. "William, come on. He just means what your dad said, 'business as usual.' Iosif said no matter what path I take, it will lead to the same place. We just have to wait and see what happens."

He sighed heavily as the classroom doors began to open, and students poured out into the sterile hallway. "Wait and see?"

"Yeah," I said, coaxing him along with a tug of my hand.

We walked to the car without a word. The more I thought about it, the more conflicted I felt. If it was really her or me, how could I live with myself knowing that I had the power to save her and didn't, that I held the cure, but denied her of it? Tears began to well up in my eyes as we left the elevator. I casually dabbed the corners where they had started to pool, catching the drops before they could fall. I tried to tell myself that I had time, time to figure out what to do.

"They could be wrong about me, William," I mused once we were in the privacy of my apartment. In truth, it didn't matter whether they were right or wrong. My main focus was Anna, and whether or not healing her led to fulfilling the prophecy was of little concern to me.

"They're not," he said. I could read the uncertainty in his eyes. They were lukewarm, undecided, worried. Thoughts were happening behind them that I couldn't decipher, but he was sorting through them more intently than listening to me.

"What are you thinking?" I asked.

Our eyes met, both searching each other for different answers.

"Even if they don't know about the prophecy, they know you're the new mother. And who knows what Christoph has planned?"

"If they come for me, I'll fight back. If I'm supposed to bring them down, maybe this is how it starts. I'll do what I have to," I said, my eyes pleading for him to understand the deeper meaning, but how could he?

"And what is that, Elyse? Do you even know what you'll have to do? Because I haven't got a clue."

I didn't answer. I couldn't tell him. I wasn't sure I was ready to admit it to myself yet, but he would never let me go through with it. He could never know.

"William, nothing's even happened yet."

"Yet," he pointed out. He paced back and forth in front of the couch, running his fingers through the back of his hair every few minutes. "You're right. Nothing's happened, and I'm not going to let it happen. I don't care about some ridiculous prophecy. I'll do whatever I have to. I'll keep them away from you."

"What will you do if they come, William, make them fall in love with you?"

"Funny." He raised his eyebrows. "But don't underestimate the power of infatuation. Once I've got a hold, I can make anyone do whatever I want. Hand over their weapon, take a bullet for me, or jump off a cliff to save my imaginary dog." The muscles in his jaw tightened.

I had never really considered William's ability in that way, as a weapon. The idea made me worry for him, and I began to peel the skin around my thumb. Would he try and fight when I was gone? I didn't ever want it to come to that.

"You won't need to. We have time," I said quietly, hoping it to myself.

"Elyse," he said, kneeling down in front of me and taking my hands in his. "You could *die*. Every moment you're in danger. Every day is a day I could lose you." He tucked a loose strand of hair behind my ear. "You'll never be safe as long as you oppose them."

It was hard to see his face, so stunningly handsome, twisted with anguish. I didn't want to die. I didn't want to lose him, but it seemed like no matter what I decided, there would be consequences.

"Well, what am I supposed to do?" I asked. "I can't change what they said. I didn't ask for this."

"I know. It's just, how am I supposed to protect you if I don't know what's coming and when?"

"You can't think like that, William. All we have is now, this moment. If you live in the future, you'll miss things, right here, right now, and you'll regret it later."

I tried to listen to my own words, take my own advice. I couldn't help but think about time.

"How can you be so calm about all this?" he asked, finally sitting down beside me on the couch.

I wasn't calm. I was falling to pieces. The only thing keeping me together was him, but my fear wasn't going to turn back the clocks. Dwelling on the future wouldn't make it better, and letting William see how truly fragile I was wouldn't help.

"Worrying won't change anything," I answered.

He sighed. "Maybe you're right."

"Promise me you won't let this ruin everything. Your dad said the future is never certain, so until this prophecy becomes a reality, let's just enjoy the time we have." If I couldn't find another way to heal Anna, I wanted whatever time I had left to be the best it could be.

"Look, I'll try, but you can't expect me to just pretend like none of this happened."

To be honest, that's exactly what I was hoping he would do. "Why not?"

"Because it *did* happen."

His persistence was flattering, but I wished he didn't care so much. It would make my choice easier, less heartbreaking for the both of us if I did have to go through with it.

"All right," I conceded, "but I don't want to talk about it anymore."

"Too bad," he argued. "We need be prepared, have a plan or something."

"A plan?" I laughed. "Like what? Are you going to stand guard at my door all night?"

"Maybe."

"Every night? Come on, William, be rational."

He sank deeper into the couch with a sigh, realizing that he was a one man army. I wondered to myself if this was a losing battle he so fervently sought to fight.

William continued to stay every night after that. At first he refused to sleep in my bed with me, claiming that wasn't why he was there, that it was too much of a distraction if anything happened. After the second night, he gave in. Sleeping in separate rooms felt as unnatural as fighting the urge to breathe, but not even he could keep away the daunting thoughts that crept through my mind once I closed my eyes.

As much as I denied it, I was scared, scared of the future, The Council, of losing Anna, of leaving William, but mostly of death. It kept me awake. I couldn't avoid it. It haunted me like a nightmare I could never wake up from. The end, my end, it would be over. No matter how many ways I wrapped my mind around it, I always came back to the same conclusion. There was no way out of it. It took a while before those thoughts sank deep into the back of my mind, only emerging now and again to seize me by the throat and cut off my air. When they did, I had to remind myself that I wasn't in it alone. No one gets out of this world alive, and it was good that I could choose the way I'd go, that I could help people when I did. It wouldn't be a waste. I would be fulfilling my destiny. Then again, maybe William was my true destiny, the prophecy and the world of Descendants. How could I abandon everything, my people? The two sides of my conscience fought for peace, desperate to accept my fate one way or the other.

I did my best to sneak calls to Anna. I wanted to see her more than anything, but William wasn't letting me out of his sight.

"How are you?" It was always the first thing I asked, and she knew it was more than just a casual greeting.

"Good today," she said, but her voice lacked truth. It was too cheerful.

"What did the doctor say?"

"I didn't go," she sighed.

"Why?" I tried to keep my tone even, but I heard it waiver with disbelief and anxiety.

"There's nothing they can do, Elyse," she answered candidly. "I had a realistic talk with Dr. Mendez over the phone."

"Well, what did he say?"

My heart was skipping around like a Mexican jumping bean trying to wriggle its way out of my chest.

"He said they could try another round of chemo, but . . ." her sentence dropped off hopelessly. "I just can't go through it if it won't work."

"Maybe it would."

"It's everywhere, Ellie, too far gone." She took a deep breath. "The cancer has metastasized to my bones and lungs. It's stage four. Who knows if *you'll* even be able to help?"

"No," I said encouragingly, ignoring the nausea churning in my stomach. "I will. We'll figure something out."

16.

NOTHING HAPPENED IN the week after Kara divulged our secret. Things were too quiet, and I hoped it wasn't the calm before the storm. William held me tight when we slept, like if he didn't cling to me, I would fall away from him. I did my best to get through the days without looking over my shoulder. In the past weeks I'd known about The Institute, I only managed to attend two classes, Origins & Human Evasion. There was just too much on my mind to care about any sort of schooling, but William was desperate to cheer me up, and promised this class would be different.

When I walked into Abilities Defense for the first time, every head turned my way, like I was back in the fifth grade again. The classroom must have been three times the size of an ordinary one. There were no chairs or desks, just open space with comfortable beanbags and sitting areas along the walls. Light streamed in through the tinted windows of the top story, and the building block pattern of the city stood out like a backdrop on a stage.

I noticed the absence of William's hand in mine as he stepped in beside me, and I held back the impulse to grab it.

"All right, begin paired exercises," said the woman addressing the class, unable to hide the eagerness in her voice.

With just a hint of a smile, William joined the group, leaving me with the teacher.

She beckoned for me to follow her to her desk. It was in the corner, free from the commotion that had broken out amongst her students. Laughter, discussion, along with cracks, bangs, pops, and a variety of other unexpected sounds filled the atmosphere as the kids practiced their skills.

I took a seat facing her with my back to the chaos, waiting for her to speak. She had short red hair that stopped at her chin, but from the age in her eyes, I could tell that if not for the dye job, it would be slightly gray. She looked at me affectionately through her delicate silver glasses before finally letting on.

"You look so much like your mother."

Her words caught my attention, and I stopped fidgeting with my nails. I had closed the door on that chapter of my life, expecting it to fade like smoke, but here the embers continued to burn.

"How did you know my mother?"

"I guess I should have known she wouldn't have mentioned me," she said, pausing to recollect. "I'm Helen. We were best friends."

Curiosity swelled in me like rice in water. Maybe she knew something that would help fill the hole that was left in me when they died.

With the flick of her wrist the classroom froze, not only the ticking clock and the pendulum that swung in rhythm on her desk, but the students as well. Everything was still, left motionless as it was in that moment, like a snapshot taken of time.

"Sorry to stop time on you like that. I know it's a little strange for people at first, but it's my only hiding place here at school for valuable things. Kids and their abilities, you just never know."

She reached her hand deep into the back of the bottom drawer of her desk as I stared wide-eyed at the unmoving scene around me. It was surreal. I wanted to go touch something just to prove to myself I wasn't imagining it.

"Kind of fun, huh?" she said with a smile as she found what she'd been looking for.

"Amazing." I returned the smile.

"I've been saving something for you," she said, revealing the hidden trinket. "It's a bracelet. It was your mother's. She gave it to me before she left. She said she wouldn't be needing it anymore."

The bracelet was a solid gold ring. It was too small to slip over my hand, but it unclasped on one side and hinged on the other. It fit perfectly, and sat snug against my skin.

"It's beautiful," I said as I examined the intricacies.

It was finely carved so that a design was visible along its surface—the rod of Asclepius. The etched carving of the serpent wrapped itself around the imprinted staff.

"Your father made it for her," she added. "He was really

talented with that sort of thing."

I smiled, remembering how he liked to tinker in his shop behind our house. Even after a long day's work in the field, he would come in for dinner smelling of metal and wood. Nearly every piece of furniture we owned had been hand-crafted by him.

"I never understood why she gave it to me," said Helen referring to the bracelet, "but I'm glad she did. It will help you when you need it most."

She took my hand gently in hers to examine the bracelet already on my wrist.

"See here?" She pointed to the two raised nodules that played a part in the pattern. "Push them at the same time."

As I did, something sharp stabbed the delicate skin below my palm with a quick jab, and I let out an involuntary cry of pain.

"Ouch. What was that?" I asked accusingly.

She laughed at my reaction.

"You've got to get a thicker skin."

She continued to hold my hand firm with the palm down, and quickly grabbed a tissue to catch the droplets of blood that fell from the small hole at the base of the bracelet.

"This is a tool," she said. "Wear it every day."

She unclasped the bracelet and stuck her own thumb with a pushpin to heal our wounds.

"You didn't have to do that," I said as I watched what looked like a snakebite magically heal on the underside of my wrist.

"I did it for your mom all the time. It's no big deal."

"Did she do a lot of healing?" I asked.

"Well, she healed me plenty of times," she answered. "To be honest, we were a little reckless in our day. With me being able to stop time and her ability to heal, well, we always pushed our limits to the edge."

"How so?" I asked, smiling at the thought of my mother's sweet and gentle demeanor giving in to reckless fun.

"Back then it was different. There weren't really any planes to jump out of or anything, but we were always seeing who could ride the fastest horse, climb the tallest tree. We definitely saw our fair share of black eyes and broken bones."

I looked down at the bracelet and imagined my mother wearing it, pushing the raised gold buttons that would draw out her power. She would have known what it meant to have this ability. I wondered if she ever had to struggle with the sacrifice I faced, if she ever felt her purpose was more than just to heal cuts and scrapes. What would she tell me if she were here? If it were her, would she be strong and stand up for what she believed in? But I didn't know what she believed. I was on my own in this.

"What about humans?" I asked with hesitation. "Did she ever heal any humans?"

"You know that isn't allowed. Don't you, Elyse?" Her tone was emphatic, but something was off about her expression, insincere.

"Yes," I answered plainly, unsure of her feelings on the subject. "I was just curious."

The classroom came back to life just as quickly as it had frozen still, with a flick of her hand. Some students remained comfortably seated and quiet on couches, their eyes closed in concentration. Others sat in beanbags facing a classmate, trying to evoke some internal reaction in their partner. Meanwhile, the students with more visually obvious abilities were erupting into chaos. Rachel and her boyfriend flew around the room like flies trapped in a box, a girl with frizzy brown hair knocked objects over with a pulse of invisible force, blue streams of electricity crackled as a boy pulled energy from a light socket on the wall.

"Hey," William said, stealing my focus. "Can I take her, Helen?"

"Sure," she said with a knowing grin. "Have fun."

"This just can't be real," I said, continuing to dwell over the scene, but William ignored the busy room and pulled me to one of the beanbag setups.

"You'll get used to it." A smile curled up into his cheeks. "I told you this would cheer you up." We sat cross-legged facing each other and scooted close enough that our knees were touching.

"So, what am I supposed to do for this paired exercise? See how much I can bleed before I pass out?" I laughed. This *was* cheering me up.

I pulled back the bracelet, which had now emptied the remaining blood into the tissue, and saw my flesh clean and new.

"I have a bruise on my arm you could try," he offered.

"A bruise?" I laughed. "Oh come on. I think you can handle that."

The deceivingly elegant bracelet looked out of place against my ordinary clothes. The sharp jab was still fresh in my memory, the skin still tender, although it had healed. "I'm not drawing blood for a bruise."

"Wuss," he teased with a smirk.

He was right though. I would have to get used to it. I couldn't avoid my ability.

"How about I practice on you?" he suggested.

"It's working," I joked.

"I didn't even start yet."

"I know."

The rest of the class went well. It was even fun. William made my infatuation grow uncontrollably, which I found amusing, since I thought I was already overly infatuated. Nics convinced me to heal a cut she had on her leg from kicking the sharp edge of a table, and Sam got us all drunk and sobered up within a ten minute time span.

I even found myself anxious to attend the following week, but to think every class would be so free-form and mellow was naïve. After all, the title of the course was Abilities Defense. How could I not expect some sort of violence?

On Thursday, I walked into class with ease, comfortable and eager to attend. Things started out the same. Students made themselves at home on the beanbags around the room, while others were practicing their abilities, either in pairs or on their own.

William was beside me when Helen approached, and we both greeted her with a smile.

"Hey, Ms. Stanzic," William beamed, happy to point out that I had decided to come back.

"I'm so glad you enjoy the class, Elyse. I have the most

amazing idea for today's lesson," she announced.

"What is it?" I asked, taking the bait.

"Well, as long as you're here, you'll just have to wait and see."

I laughed it off, thinking nothing of her plans, and followed William over to the corner where Nics and Sam were quietly bickering.

"What's going on?" William asked, inferring a little more than a greeting.

"Nothing," Sam spat.

Nics looked at us reluctantly and rolled her eyes. "He's mad because I told him not to go up against me when we duel. I don't want to make him look bad."

"I should challenge you, just to prove you wrong," Sam said defensively.

"Wait, when we duel?" William asked the question just as I was thinking it, but before they could answer, Ms. Stanzic began to address the class.

"All right everyone," she asserted with a raised voice that got our attention. "Class is starting." Everyone stayed where they were, but each head was turned her way, earnestly awaiting instructions. "As you know, we are not allowed to conduct a duel without the presence of a healer. Until now, it has never been an option. I am excited to say that today it is. So today we duel."

Her eyes met mine as soon as she finished, and I knew she recognized the panic in them. Was she crazy? What if someone really got hurt and I couldn't heal them? It would be my fault. The idea was terrifying. These kids had incredibly strong abilities, and if something went wrong, was she really relying on me to fix it? I had no experience with my power to heal, and I wasn't sure I wanted to test it on live people who might truly need help. I caught her gaze and shook my head subtly, hoping she would get the message.

In that instant she waved her hand with a flick that stopped all motion and left us the only two not locked in that moment in time.

"Try not to move too much," she said immediately. "They'll notice I stopped time if anything is different, and I don't want them to know."

"Why not?"

"They can't think you're not comfortable doing this, or they'll have second thoughts."

"Well, I'm not comfortable doing this."

"I know, but you have to start somewhere," she urged. "Elyse, you have to get used to using your ability so that when it comes time for you to act, when it's life or death, you don't hesitate."

I bit the inside of my cheek as she waited for my response. Did she know about the prophecy? I knew she didn't know about my plans for Anna, but her words struck a chord nonetheless. If I couldn't do this, how did I expect to have the courage to do what I needed to for my friend?

"Fine," I agreed, "but you have to tell them to take it easy. If someone is injured beyond a certain point, I won't be able to heal them without—"

"I know how it works," she answered. "I won't let it get that far, but these kids need to learn how to defend themselves.

Things are going to happen, and it's my responsibility to teach them well, to get them ready for it."

"For what?" I asked. Maybe I knew the answer, but I was testing her.

"For war," she answered simply, before setting the world in motion around me once again. "Who wants to go first?"

William looked at me with suspicion, and I wondered if he'd noticed the brief interruption of time.

"Are you okay with this?" he questioned with disapproval.

"Yeah," I answered, trying to seem confident. "I could use the practice."

I got the feeling he didn't completely buy it, but he didn't argue. Instead, he stared at Ms. Stanzic looking for my reprieve, but her face was serious and unyielding.

Everyone was quiet, hesitant to be the first to go, but out of the corner of my eye I saw Sam give Nics a challenging look before he stood.

"I'll go Ms. Stanzic," he volunteered. I was surprised to see he wasn't more self-conscious about being in front of everyone since he'd been aged, but even more surprised that no one was talking about it. The class seemed to accept it as simply unfortunate, and nothing more was said.

"Thank you, Samuel. Who else? We need someone to go up against him."

Sam's gaze was locked on Nics expectantly, but she turned away from him and rolled her eyes at William and I, giving her head a subtle shake that meant "no." He glowered at her, but she only smiled back at him in amusement.

"I don't want to embarrass him," she whispered into my

ear.

"How about you, Bianca?" Ms. Stanzic asked a thick haired brunette who was smacking her gum. I recognized her as the girl who had been moving things with bursts of force last class.

"Sure," she said, standing with confidence. She smiled eagerly as she made her way to the center of the classroom.

Although Sam looked ten years older with his newly matured face, her cocky attitude made me worried for him.

"Is he going to be all right?" I asked William under my breath.

"I hope so," William answered. "He owes me ten bucks."

I scoffed at his joke. "I'm serious."

"Me too," he laughed.

"All right. Here are the rules," Ms. Stanzic declared. "Don't use full force. We're not trying to kill each other here. Try to keep the classroom intact. If you break a window . . . well, that's on you, and by all means is no one to interfere. If you get out of hand, I will be glad to un-enroll you from my class. If a winner is not obvious, I'll decide, and if you've had enough and give up, yell forfeit. Got it?"

Sam and Bianca gave a nod and went to opposing sides of the room.

"Ready?" Ms. Stanzic asked. "Begin."

Bianca shot off a burst of force so quickly it took my breath away, and I wasn't the only one. I heard a collective intake of breath from the surrounding crowd as well. The invisible surge moved fast through the air like waves of heat, blurring my vision, and I grabbed William's hand as it hit Sam full on. He stumbled backwards with surprise, his face pinched in pain, but he scrambled to his feet in time to miss the next blast.

"Come on, Sam!" Nics yelled, and when he heard her voice, he became suddenly determined.

Bianca must have known she only had the first minute or so to attack before Sam's power took hold, so she let off a series of blasts, trying to overwhelm him. He did his best to dodge them, catching the edge of a few that hit him like a slug to the shoulder, but I could tell he was focusing. The girl started to waver. She blinked her eyes hard and slow, trying to clear up her apparently impaired vision, but she didn't give up.

"That all you got?" she mumbled foolishly before shooting off another blast, but it was so off target it hit the light and sent shattered glass in all directions.

Once Sam had her fully intoxicated, he didn't need to move much. He just stood still and focused while her blasts hit most anywhere but him. Within minutes, Bianca looked at Sam wide-eyed and dizzy before running to the trash can in the corner to hurl.

"Man, she can really hold her liquor," Sam said to the crowd, and we all roared with laughter. Even Bianca gave a smile as she stood up, freshly sober, and heading to take a seat.

"I'll go next," Nics announced without the teacher needing to ask. Sam gave her an irritated look.

"Me too," said a slightly overweight boy with curly brown hair.

"What's his bloodline?" I asked William with a hushed voice.

"Cronos. Sleep. Nics will win," he answered confidently.

Their duel was brief. Nics was quick to block out his vision, as she so often threatened Sam, by creating a void of light around his head. The boy stumbled around blindly, inflicting his ability on whoever was in his unpredictable line of sight. Half the class passed out cold before Ms. Stanzic called it off.

"All right, Nics," Ms. Stanzic laughed. "I think Stan has had enough. Lift the shield."

Just as she did, Stan's gaze found her reactively. He had just wanted to see where she had been standing, but the effects of his ability were still active in his defense, and as soon as he looked at her, she was knocked out.

"Shoot," Stan yelled as she began to fall.

It all happened so quickly. He tried to wake her, but by the time her eyes snapped open, her face was already inches from the floor, and we all gasped as she hit with the full force of her body weight. The side of her head smacked hard against the linoleum, and we all heard the sound of skull hitting ground before we saw the blood.

She was silent at first, even as blood poured freely from the split skin on her eye, but after the shock wore off, she began to groan in pain.

"Stan," the teacher said assertively. "Knock her out."

He looked at her confused, but as the blood continued to seep out onto the floor in a puddle, he realized what she was asking. There was too much blood for it to be coming from the cut on her eye, but I couldn't move. I stood dumbfounded as I watched her. Nics, so strong and reassured, lay there helpless and injured on the floor.

"Elyse!" Ms. Stanzic yelled, snapping me out of my daze. I

wasn't the only one astounded. The whole class seemed to be frozen as if Ms. Stanzic had stopped time again. Even William sat unmoving, his face still with fear. I jumped to my feet without thinking. There was so much blood. Was I too late? Had I waited too long? How long had it been?

I rushed to her side, apparently the only one willing to address the situation. I wondered if they would all just sit and watch while she died before stepping in to help.

I pulled her blood-matted hair back exposing the cut on her eye and saw how it spidered up her forehead into a split in her skull. I wondered why Ms. Stanzic hadn't stopped time. She could have prevented this. *She could stop time now*, I thought, *so I could help Nics*, but she didn't. In real time, I pressed the gold buttons on my new bracelet and jumped at the feel of the pain in my wrist. I started with the split on her scalp, where the injury was worst. There was so much blood, hers and mine, I couldn't tell if it was working, but as more drops fell over the broken flesh of her forehead and eye, I could see the skin start to seal up. Her wounds were healing, and I couldn't believe I was the one doing it.

"I think it worked," I said, looking for reassurance in Ms. Stanzic.

"I'm sure it did," she agreed, with a satisfied smile. "Stan, go ahead and wake her up to see how she's feeling."

We all stared on with nervous eyes as she began to stir. She looked at me first.

"Are you okay?" I asked unsure.

"Yeah," she answered, a little shaken up. "Thanks."

Class ended soon after that. All of us were more than

discouraged from continuing the dueling, so Ms. Stanzic let us have free time to practice. Just as we were about to leave, everything froze, and I found myself trapped once again in a moment in time with her.

"Do you think I'm horrible?" she asked, moving around the still bodies toward me.

I sighed. "No," I lied. I couldn't help but resent her lack of effort in stopping the incident. So many times she could have helped, and I knew she didn't on purpose.

"Yes you do," she said, acknowledging my lackluster response. "But that's okay. I don't need you to like me. I need you to learn. I need you to do what you were meant to—for all of us."

17.

I TRIED NOT to dwell on her words throughout the week, and by the next class, we were back to paired exercises. Anna seemed to be doing well, which meant I still had time to come up with a plan. There had been no sign of Ryder or The Council. Not even Kara had been around to cause my still waters to ripple.

Ms. Stanzic was making her rounds, evaluating techniques and suggesting ideas while William and I were testing Nics on light manipulation. I would call out objects and Nics would make each one disappear. It was a fun game, but we were shortly interrupted by the sound of my name being announced over the intercom.

"Elyse Adler, please report to the fifth floor," a woman's voice droned through the building.

"What do you think they want?" I asked, hoping one of them would know.

"Fifth floor is administration," Nics answered. "They

probably just need you to fill out a form or something."

I wanted to believe her, but I had a bad feeling in my stomach as William and I headed for the elevator.

The fifth floor was nothing like The Institute. It had a completely different layout. The entire level was one big room with a winding maze of cubicles surrounded by office doors and a front counter.

"I'm Elyse," I said to the gray-haired receptionist whose lips pulled into a frown. "You paged me."

The corners of her mouth continued to sag as she passed me a letter. "Report to testing," she croaked and pointed to the right corner office.

"What does it say?" William asked as we worked our way through the cubicles.

"Something about a Human Evasion Test."

He grabbed the letter from my hand without asking. "You're kidding?"

"What?"

"I can't believe they're making you do this."

I grabbed the letter back. "Why? What is it?"

"It's a test we all have to take when we turn fifty. They put you in a situation, and you have to get out without exposing your ability or age."

"Is it hard?"

We stopped just outside of the testing office, and the muscles in his jaw tightened as he remembered. "It was one of the hardest things I've ever had to do in my life."

The expression on his face told me this wasn't a simple sit down exam.

"What did they make you do?"

"I had to watch a guy get mugged in the street without helping. The mugger had a gun, so I couldn't just jump in. I had to let it happen without persuading him to stop. The guy was almost beaten to death. It was horrible."

The thought made my chest hurt. "Why didn't you just help him? Who cares about some stupid test?"

"They kill any humans who know about us, Elyse. If you fail, they die."

"That's . . . disgusting," I said, appalled. "You were just a kid."

"We've all had to take it. It's their way of indoctrinating us. So we don't expose our abilities."

"Forget this," I decided out loud. "I'm not taking a test like that."

As I turned around, ready to charge my way to the elevator, my body froze, and I found myself face to face with Ryder.

"Going somewhere?" A snide smirk crawled up his cheeks as I struggled to break free of his invisible chains. "I'm here to escort you to your exam."

I could smell his foul breath as he moved close to me and grabbed my jaw with one hand. I expected him to hit me like he had before, but instead, his rough fingers pinched tight, forcing my mouth open. He flaunted a tiny blue pill in his other hand before shoving it down my throat, and in a matter of seconds, I was out.

I heard the commotion before I opened my eyes. The sounds were disorienting, unfamiliar. The last thing I remembered was choking on Ryder's thick fingers, and then blackness. As

I lifted my lids, things were blurry. I was groggy from the mystery pill. I didn't know where I was.

When my eyes began to focus, and my brain finally registered the sound of cries for help and terrified screams, I nearly stopped breathing. My fingers dug into the warm asphalt that lay beneath my back as I tried to make out my surroundings. I didn't know what happened or how it happened. The crumpled wreckage of a city bus lay sideways in the street, and smoke was billowing from somewhere inside it. Bodies were strewn across the pavement and blood was everywhere, painted on people's fearful faces and pooling beneath the wounded. The chaos overwhelmed me, sending me into an internal frenzy, and my chest began to rise and fall with panic.

An older man with glasses knelt down beside me, his brown hair wet with blood.

"No," I gasped. "I can't help you." It was for his own good.

"Are you all right?" he yelled over the cries.

I didn't notice the pain until he asked. Suddenly I realized why my right leg felt cold. My jeans had been died a deep scarlet from a laceration that ran across my thigh. I pushed myself up to sitting trying to remember how it had gotten there. I had no memory of the accident.

"Get away," I screamed, not knowing what else to do. I couldn't walk. "Get away!"

The man looked at me with resentment and jogged off to help another.

"Please!" a woman yelled from a few feet away. She cradled her daughter closely and rocked her back and forth, trying to soothe her own grief. The girl lay limp in her lap, blood seeping through her shirt. I doubted she would make it without help.

I looked at my bracelet and threw myself back on the pavement with my eyes closed tight. If I healed anyone, Ryder would kill them all. No matter what my decision, the little girl was going to die. There was nothing I could do. I thought of the day my parents crashed, the day they died. Here I was again, unable to save them, useless, helpless. The woman's cry was gut wrenching, and I couldn't escape it. I leaned forward, unable to control myself and retched onto the blacktop.

My heart ached and burned with anger. Why would they do this? What purpose did it serve?

"Please!" the woman yelled. I tried not to hear her, to ignore her sobs and my own tears that dripped into my ears as I lay there. *Focus on the pain*, I told myself. My leg was throbbing, and the cold was spreading. How was I supposed to get out of here like this?

It wasn't until I heard the sirens wailing from a distance, growing louder as they approached, that I felt dread swarming in around me. I was losing a lot of blood. What if they took me to a hospital? Would they do a blood transfusion? The dizziness was starting to hinder my thinking, and my heart beat wildly trying to keep up with my hemorrhaging wound.

The fire trucks arrived, followed by ambulances and police cars, all before I could get myself out of sight. As a last resort, I attempted to stand and walk, dragging my useless leg behind me, but the world began to spin.

"Over here," I heard a voice call as I collapsed against the hard ground.

"No," I protested, but it was little more than a whisper. I hadn't realized how weak I was.

I felt the gurney beneath me and saw the clouds move by as I was carried away. Part of me was glad to be rid of all the chaos as I was rolled into the ambulance. I needed to escape the weeping woman.

The doors were latched shut leaving me with a lady in a navy blue jump suit and a low ponytail. I felt her hands on my leg and heard her speaking comforting words, but none of them registered. I had to make sure I never made it to the hospital. How many people would they kill if my ability was discovered in a public place like that? With my last ounces of energy I sat up and heaved my body toward the ambulance door. I had to get out, by any means necessary.

"Whoa," the woman said, trying to restrain me.

"Stop the truck," I demanded. "Let me out."

"Calm down, you're all right—"

"Please," I begged, struggling with what strength I had left. "Just let me go."

My heart stopped at the moment I caught sight of a syringe in her hand. This was it. My last chance before the situation would be out of my hands. She attempted to restrain me with one arm and prepared the needle with the other, as I squirmed and pleaded for release. It wasn't enough to hold me down, and just as she was about to stick me with what was surely a sedative, I broke free, flinging the needle into the air. The woman reached for her radio, but before she could call, the syringe landed at my feet. I grabbed it and plunged it into her neck.

Her eyes widened, and she looked at me in shock. When she slumped to the floor, I shuffled my way to the rear door and waited for my moment. At first I thought I'd have to jump out of the back at full speed. I imagined how I would do it, trying to convince myself that I wouldn't die on impact or get run over by another car, but for once, luck was on my side. In San Francisco, rolling hills and innumerable cars caused the vehicle to slow for traffic, and I made the jump without killing myself.

I hobbled on one leg to the sidewalk. Drivers and pedestrians all turned their heads. Somewhere along the way my adrenaline must have kicked in, because as soon as I rested my body against the wall of a nearby building, I couldn't imagine where I'd found the will to get out of that truck.

I prayed that nobody would call 911 after seeing me jump out of a moving ambulance and told myself I would have to move to a safer place. I just needed five minutes to rest, a few seconds to close my eyes.

Focusing on the sounds of the city kept me lucid. People talked and walked past me without pausing. I heard footsteps come closer and then fade away, but when someone stopped next to me, my eyes snapped open.

"It's me," William said, quieting my alarm. He knelt down next to me, brushing my hair away from my face. I let my eyes close again as he slid his arms under my body. "You'll be all right." His lips met my forehead as I snuggled into his chest. Only then did I allow myself to fully submit to unconsciousness.

18.

MY BODY WAS rigid with fear as I sat unmoving on an unfamiliar couch in an unfamiliar living room. William was next to me, but that only made me more afraid. He might not survive this, and his presence made me afraid for two. I tried to understand where I was from my fixed position on the sofa, but the windows were pitch-black with night. I felt trapped and anxious as we awaited the impending doom, as if the quiet lonely room was taunting me. Behind the black wall of night, I was aware of the war taking place. I wanted it to take place—I was their leader.

The blare of the city's alarm shook my bones. This would be an attempt against us, to breed fear amidst the masses. The alarm kept on, urging me to leave the house, to escape, but I couldn't. I wouldn't. Suddenly the faceless image of the wispy gray oracle came into view. She had a message for me.

"Wake up, Elyse," she yelled.

My eyes snapped open, all my senses abruptly confronted

with shards of light. It was all a dream. My heart relaxed, and I began to return to reality. Nothing around me was familiar, nothing but William.

His smile brought me back. "Is it just me or are you prone to passing out?" He'd been waiting patiently at the foot of a navy blue couch for me to come to, and was pleased to see me awake.

I stretched my feet out over his legs and moaned into the pillow beneath my head. "You try getting punched in the face or losing half of your blood. See how you turn out."

I rubbed my eyes, still trying to get my bearings. I was in someone's family room. The air smelled of sweet almonds, and the eggshell colored walls and cream carpet were comforting.

"What about my leg?" I asked, peeking under the throw blanket that was draped over me.

"My mom took care of it," William answered.

"Hi, honey," said a high and cheerful voice from the kitchen. A countertop bar with three stools was all that separated us from her. She had a kind face and the heavy-set body that belongs to most moms.

"Hi," I returned.

William reached under the blanket and warmed my cold bare toes with his hands, our skin building heat on contact.

"I tried to help," he said, "but she used her mom powers to fight me off."

"I'm Sofia," she introduced herself, making her way to my side. Her hair was the same honey color as William's, and her eyes wrinkled around the edges as she smiled at me. "How are you feeling?"

I flexed my feet and felt the muscles tighten in my thighs.

"Okay, I guess." There was little strength in my right leg, but I could move it. "Thank you for healing me."

"I was able to close up the skin, but you lost a lot. You might still feel some pain and be a bit weak," she explained. "Just let me know if you need anything, all right? I'll leave you two alone."

When she left us to ourselves, William moved to sit on the floor facing me.

"What the hell happened?" I let out, finally facing the incident I had hoped wasn't real. "One minute I'm at Headquarters, the next I wake up in a war zone."

"Ryder obviously planned the whole thing."

"Why?"

"You're flagged. I think this was the only way he could get to you, through official channels."

I sighed. This guy was going to be a problem. "I hate him."

"Well, at least you passed. His plan sort of backfired."

I shook my head in disgust. "People died, William."

He traced his fingers along the skin of my arm. "I know. Ryder made me watch the whole thing."

"How?" I asked, mortified.

"He had me frozen in one of the buildings near the crash. We were watching from a window."

I couldn't believe any of it had happened. It was too horrific to be real.

"I don't remember even getting on that bus. I don't remember any of it."

"That's how it was for me, too."

"How did you find me?" I asked, looking into his eyes. I felt so grateful. He had saved me.

"We were watching the ambulance on monitors, and once you got out, Ryder let me go. I recognized where you were, so I just ran for that intersection."

"I don't know what I would have done."

He leaned forward and kissed my shoulder. "It doesn't matter. You're here now, and safe."

"Have I been out for a long time?"

"A few hours. Woke up in time for dinner, though," he said. "Feeling up to eating with my parents?"

With everything weighing so heavily on my mind, including Anna's condition, I hardly wanted to have to put on a happy face for anyone. I felt more eager to cure her than ever after what I had been put through. Even if that eagerness was fueled by hate, I welcomed it. Nevertheless, I was starving, and couldn't deny myself a home cooked meal.

William helped me to the dinner table, insisting I shouldn't walk on my own. I exchanged pleasantries with his parents as Mrs. Nickel doled out portions of pork stew and homemade bread. The smell reminded me of my mother's cooking, which I hadn't had in nearly fifty years. I waited eagerly to taste it.

"So," Dr. Nickel said, braving conversation once we'd been served. "Have you thought about the prophecy?"

Spoons clanked against porcelain bowls in the silence.

"There's an ice breaker for you," William said, shaking his head. "You just had to bring it up."

"I think it's relevant given her circumstances. Maybe the test has changed her mind."

All three of them looked at me for a response, but what could I tell them?

"Iosif says whatever I do doesn't matter. The prophecy will play out how it is supposed to."

"Great advice, huh?" William added. "Now we know exactly what to do."

"It's true, son," Dr. Nickel said with a nod. "Don't take his words so lightly. It will happen."

William stirred his food, avoiding his father's eyes. "What if I don't want it to?"

Dr. Nickel looked at me before he answered. "It's not your choice."

"Does *she* even get a choice? What if she doesn't want this?"

"She will in time."

Mrs. Nickel and I stayed quiet while the two of them talked as though I wasn't in the room.

"She doesn't have time," William argued. "They know she's the new mother which means they'll figure out the rest soon enough. What if they come after her?"

"How do they know?" Mrs. Nickel jumped in.

He shook his head. "Kara told them."

Mrs. Nickel's brow furrowed. "Why would she do that?"

"She was trying to help me," I said, unable to keep quiet any longer. "It doesn't matter anyway. They won't come after me. I'm flagged."

"Elyse, that isn't . . ." He closed his eyes briefly, gathering his thoughts. "We don't know why, for how long, who flagged you. It isn't a safety net. We can't rely on that."

The Nickels, still shocked by the news, didn't say a word.

"After what they put her through today, I think we should leave," William continued.

"We can't." I reacted without thinking. I couldn't leave Anna.

William looked at me with surprise. "Why? Who knows when they'll make a move?"

I thought quickly, searching for another reason to stay. "If I'm supposed to fulfill this prophecy, it won't do any good to run. I've been running for too long—my whole life."

Dr. Nickel smiled brightly. "I like the way you think."

William looked at me, angry and defeated, and I wondered if he could see through to the real reason I needed to stay. We ate the rest of the meal in silence, and when we were finished, I followed William out of the dining room.

"You want to see my room?" he asked. "I don't want to stay down here."

The upstairs hallway was typical of any family. Collage-like framed photos filled every blank wall with captured images of the three of them. There was a young girl as well. I hadn't known about her.

"Who's this?" I asked, pointing to a younger version of William's mother. "You have a sister?"

"Yeah, Edith. She's at a friend's house."

I noticed that the photos were recent, or at least within the last few years. There were no baby pictures or classic wedding snapshots.

"So, she has your dad's ability?"

"Unfortunately yes, and she thinks it makes her queen of her forty-year-old universe."

I smiled at the idea of a little sister pestering him.

I knew we'd found his room before he said a thing. Everything about it was him. Immediately upon entering, it was impossible to miss the entire wall of CDs accompanied by all the means to enjoy such a collection of music. A skyline of speakers, amplifiers, and pieces I didn't even recognize were stacked high to the ceiling. The afternoon light spilled onto the floor from the right, and next to the window was a finely crafted acoustic guitar. His bed was large enough for two and seemed to be the only seat in the room, so I made myself comfortable.

"You know," William said, mulling over music choices. "Whatever you decide is okay with me." He sighed and his eyes drifted to mine. "My dad's right. This isn't my choice, it's yours. I'll be there for you no matter what happens or what you choose."

"Let's just not talk about it." Even if it was only for one night, I was desperate to escape the choices that followed me. Just for now I wanted to pretend none of it was real.

"All right," he agreed. "I just need you to know that."

After he'd selected the perfect background music, I made room for him, slipping my sandals off and moving to lean my back against the wall. He moved close to me, taking a pillow and lying casually in my lap. With his glorious face so close, so easy for my eyes to find, I became overly aware of his affect on me. Even without the pulling power of his ability, I still felt drawn to him.

William left his head in my lap as we listened to his music, insisting each track was better than the last. Lost in a daze that drifted in and out of the lyrics of each song, I gently combed my fingers through his hair and tried not to think about my future. His eyes stayed peacefully closed as I examined the unique details that made him so irresistible. I traced the outline of his jaw, the shape of his eyebrows, the bowed curve of his lower lip with my finger, and eventually William dozed off into a sort of half sleep.

My hand moved on, grazing the skin around the collar of his shirt and down his freckled arm. Even the strangest parts seemed attractive to me. The delicate skin in the crook of his elbow, his strong thick knuckles, there wasn't a single inch of him that didn't appeal to me. As I glanced back to admire his face once more, his eyes were open ever so slightly.

"Feels good." He stretched, burying his head into my stomach as he woke up. "My turn."

He sat up and went casually for my neck, sliding his fingers up into my hair and making me melt into the bed. His lips, soft as the skin of a rose, danced lightly over the top edge of my collarbone. The sensation his touch could generate was somewhere between a pleasant tickle and a deeper more intense sense of pleasure that nearly drove me wild for him. It was hard to enjoy the light tickle without letting the latter overcome me, but this time it did. I reached for his face and drew it to mine with a burning need to feel his lips. The kiss was everything I wanted it to be and more, exhilarating and satisfying, but I hadn't thought about what was to follow, and I began to panic. In reaction to my overly zealous kissing, his hand had found the bare skin of my lower back and I froze internally at the feel of it. My mind told me to pull away, but my eager body, greedy for more contact, disobeyed.

"Wait," I breathed.

His reaction was quick. He pulled away, eyes wide and filled with regret.

"I'm sorry," he stammered.

"No." I shook my head. "Don't be." Clearly I was the eager one, moving things faster than I even knew how. "It's just, I've never done this . . . with anyone. I've never had a boyfriend. I mean, you were my first kiss, so I don't really know what I'm doing." I was rambling now. Clear things up Elyse, get to the point. "I'm just new at this—"

"Hey," he cut my rant short. "It's okay. We'll go slow."

I took a deep breath. "Okay."

I knew we were supposed to be soul mates, but everything had just moved so fast. William sank back against the wall, propping himself up with pillows, and I followed, laying my head against his chest.

"So, I was really your first kiss?" he asked, running his fingers through my hair.

"Yeah, pathetic huh."

"No. You're a good kisser, actually."

I looked up at him. "Really?"

"Yeah, my first kiss was with Sue Crape on a dare. Trust me, it wasn't pretty."

"Have you ever had a girlfriend or anything?" I asked, eager for more juicy details of his love life.

"Once," he admitted.

"Well?" I prompted, poking him in the side.

"Well . . ." he repeated. I could tell that he was smiling. "It was Juliet Harrison. She's living in a different community, but people here know her. I'm not too proud of it."

"What happened?"

"She's manipulative," he sighed. "Her bloodline is Athena, and being descendant of the goddess of wisdom, she sort of knows everything. Can you imagine how irritating it would be to have a girlfriend who claims she knows everything and actually does? She basically convinced me that we were supposed to be together, which in the end obviously was a lie."

I had questions, but I kept quiet.

"I should probably take you home," William said, when I didn't say anything. "I feel weird sleeping in the same bed when my parents are here."

I lifted my head and pushed myself up. "Why do you still live here, anyway?"

"Why do you think? All they think about is war and the prophecy. They're too paranoid to let me leave."

Lying next to William in my bed an hour later kept me distracted for a while, but when he fell asleep, my conversations with Iosif, the Nickels, and Anna began to play over and over again in my head. I watched William's peaceful face as he slept, not wanting to confront the fact that time was not on my side. I tried to remember to enjoy these moments, even if they were slipping away like water through sand.

19.

I WASN'T AWARE of how comfortable I'd gotten to William's warm body beside me in bed until I woke up to the feeling of his absence. All he'd left was a note on his pillow with the words, "I have a plan. I'll be back on Monday. Be careful."

Immediately, I thought of Anna. I hadn't seen her since I'd found out about the cancer. I explained to her it wasn't safe, but safety wasn't the only reason I'd been avoiding a visit. Once I saw her, I would be forced to face everything I'd been pushing into the back of my mind. William's protective presence was the perfect excuse not to go, but now that he was gone, I knew I had to.

I thought about what William would say as I drove my neglected Nissan over the bridge to Oakland. *What are you thinking?* I imagined his worried expression. I was a little nervous about the repercussions, but we were both flagged. If I didn't go now when I had the chance, I knew I'd regret it later.

It wasn't until I pulled off of the freeway that I realized I was being followed. I recognized the black Lincoln from the start of my trip as it exited after me and mimicked my right turn. The car stayed close behind as I made my way to Anna's without the slightest attempt at being inconspicuous.

I began to worry. Something wasn't right. Instinctively I took a wrong turn, diverting the pursuer off the road to my friend's house, and seconds behind, the vehicle followed. I drove steadily, slowly, not sure what to expect. My mind was frantic.

In my panicked state, I began to speed up from 35 to 40 and then to 50 zipping through the residential neighborhood. I turned down every other street, hoping to lose them, but the Lincoln stayed persistent and determined. The adrenaline seemed to take control of me, the fear acting on my behalf. I was too paralyzed with fright to cry or to react in any other way than to run, but when I glanced in my rearview mirror to judge the distance between us, the car was gone.

I kept my foot on the accelerator, still too nervous to slow down. I had to make sure I had lost them. I turned randomly down street after street before I made the decision to stop the car in an alleyway behind a row of houses.

The panic began to slowly fade with each second that the black car failed to appear. Was there someone really after me, or was it all just a prank? Maybe they had realized they had the wrong person, but considering my situation, that would be unlikely. I shuddered at the thought of not knowing at that very moment where they were, or worse, what they were plotting.

I turned around in my seat to look out the back window, not trusting the mirrors. My wide eyes searched, and I waited, but still there was no Lincoln. I sighed heavily, wrapping my hands tightly around the steering wheel and leaning my head back against the headrest.

I was still on edge when I left, but I couldn't hide forever behind those houses. Besides, it would take me another hour or so to wind my way out of the maze of streets I had burrowed myself in. A pursuer would have no idea where I was headed.

By the time I arrived at Anna's, after a lengthy journey including two stops for directions, I was so grateful to be there that I didn't think to approach the place cautiously. I parked the car, grabbed my things, and was already heading for the door when I caught a glimpse of the black car waiting for me a few spaces down across the lot.

I went rigid at the sight of it, almost not noticing the slender figure leaning against the wall nearby. I could tell it was a woman by her petite frame, which made me feel foolishly more at ease, but her face was cast in shadow from the ledge above. I wondered, as I stood unmoving, whether or not it was the same car that had followed me, whether or not the girl was just waiting for someone. Maybe that someone was me. I told myself nothing was wrong, to remain calm, but just as I made my first decisive effort to continue on, something blindsided me, knocking my senses—a voice.

Elyse.

My own name sounded in my head like it had been spoken deliberately into my ear, familiar, but unrecognized. I immediately whirled around expecting the girl to be standing right behind me, but she remained still and unchanged beneath the overhang. Fear began to seep through my pores, forming tiny beads of sweat that chilled my skin, and although she hadn't advanced, I could tell she was looking in my direction. My eyes combed the lot for some reasonable explanation, but there was nothing suspicious about the scene, nothing but her. As she emerged from the shaded wall into the sun, I made the connection. It was Kara.

I smiled with relief, and immediately perked up as she walked to meet me. At least it was her and not Ryder.

"Hey," I beamed, but she didn't reciprocate my excitement at all. Her face stayed flat and serious, almost, professional.

Her clothes were much more formal than I remembered. A sleek black skirt and suit jacket fit her body nicely only to be contrasted by the same rough looking army boots she liked to wear. Her eyes, done up with dark rebellious makeup, stayed locked on me with intensity.

"Hey," she returned with detachment. Her voice matched the one spoken in my head. "Do yourself a favor. Get back in the car and go home."

"Why?" I asked, thrown off by her unfriendly tone. "Why are you still following me?"

Don't be stupid.

Her lips didn't move. The words were spoken in my head like they had been uttered through a set of invisible headphones. Suddenly things clicked into place. The black Lincoln had been her all along.

I disregarded her last statement. "If you knew where I was going, why would you chase me down, Kara?" My words sounded accusatory and aggressive. I had thought of her as a friend after she saved me from Ryder, but apparently deception came easy to these people.

I was hoping to scare you off, to keep you from coming here in the first place.

"Get out of my head, and talk to me like a person," I spat. I felt angry and defensive, and apparently those emotions were enough to break through my nervousness. I didn't feel scared of her, though maybe I should have been.

"Don't get snappy with me, Elyse. I'm trying to make sure you don't get yourself killed."

"I thought I was flagged, and so is Anna. So what are you here to do? Arrest me?"

She laughed a short breathy huff as if that was a ridiculous idea. Her black curls bounced around her face as she shook her head.

"Well, what then?"

"I just don't understand why you'd do something you know would put you at risk with The Council. People are stubborn and stupid. I see what happens when you cross them. Trust me. Don't."

"How am I putting myself at risk? I'm going to see my sick friend. Frankly, I don't see what is so taboo about that. I've done nothing wrong."

Yet. The word pushed through my thoughts, obtrusive and unwelcome.

"What's that supposed to mean?"

Do you think I can't see what you're considering?

My promise to Anna rushed to the forefront of my mind,

and she nodded her head confirming that was what she had meant.

"What does it matter to you? It's none of your business."

It's my job. The Council makes it my business.

I wasn't sure what to do, or if her involvement would mean there would be consequences.

"What will they do to me if I see her today? They can't punish me for just visiting, can they?"

Ryder's on a job. He'll only know what I tell him. A defiant grin crept to her lips, and she seemed pleased with the fact that she had some of the power to herself. *Consider this a warning.*

She turned away from me without a goodbye and walked toward the Lincoln.

"Kara," I called after her. She stopped but didn't turn back. "Thanks."

***

"You know, normal people like to use bookshelves," I teased from the couch in Anna's living room. William hadn't called me all morning and I was starting to worry, but at least it gave me more time with Anna. The more time I spent with her, the more I realized I couldn't trust what she said about her condition. She would always brush things off light-heartedly like they were no big deal. I could tell she was twisting the truth.

I picked up an old copy of *Moby Dick* and thumbed through the worn pages. "I thought you didn't even like to read."

She laughed as she dug through a box at her feet. "Yeah, when I was twelve."

"True," I said with a smile.

Her hands shook as she shuffled through the dusty memorabilia—a music box, some photo albums, a round tin full of trinkets. Her breath was shallow and labored, and I could tell she felt tired, but I kept quiet. I knew what sort of response I would get if I were to offer help, suggest rest, or ask if she was all right—a stubborn smart alec remark that would play it off as nothing.

"I know they were in here," she mumbled to herself.

"Who cares, Anna? You don't need to find them right now."

Seeing her work so hard to do the smallest of things made my stomach cinch up with knots. She was getting worse.

"Here they are," she said, completely ignoring my concerned eyes. "I can't remember the last time I looked in these yearbooks." The smile that stretched across her face was worth the trouble to find them. "Wow."

"What?" I asked, moving to share her recliner.

"Look at us. We were so cute."

She was looking at an old grainy black and white photo. We were in line for recess, arm in arm, jump ropes in hand, and happy as two kids could be.

"Is that Collin in the back?" she pointed.

Collin. The name surfaced like a bubble of air in water. His hair kept long in the winter would whip back and forth as he ran the black top at lunch, hypnotizing me with fascination. I had forgotten about the boy. He was only there for a year before he moved.

"We sure spent our share of nights on him," Anna laughed.

"Days too," I added.

Days were simple back then. Well, maybe they were never

simple, but they were a little easier for a while.

Next, she pulled out the photo albums. "I've been looking through these a lot," she said with a reminiscent smile, "after Chloe goes to sleep."

I sat with her as she relived the bitter sweet moments of her life. She was so beautiful in her wedding dress, her face youthful with a healthy glow, and full of life. Her smile seemed to stretch across the room, she was so happy. She wore her hair up in curls that billowed around a veil trailing down her back. The dress revealed strong arms and a neckline that didn't expose her collarbone the way it stuck out now. "Too bad the jerk left two years later when Chloe came. Some men just can't handle the joys of life. It's been twelve years, and he still hasn't even called her."

"I told you, I had a bad feeling about him."

"Well, at least he gave me my daughter. Everything happens for a reason."

I nodded. "Yeah, that's true." Everything did happen for a reason, and as I watched her look back on her unfinished life, saying goodbye to her memories, I considered maybe my ability to heal happened for a reason. Maybe I was given this gift for one reason only, to save her.

"Okay, here's me pregnant," she laughed. "Not quite as flattering."

Her face was round and rosy to match her belly, which pushed the middle section of her overalls to the max. Her pant legs were rolled, and she was barefoot with a paintbrush in hand. She was painting the walls baby girl pink while her husband stood stone faced in the right corner of the photo.

"I don't think he was too happy we were having a girl," she admitted.

"I was," I said, remembering. "You were so sure it was a boy."

She laughed. "I know. I named her Wyatt and bought everything in blue."

"I knew the whole time. You wanted a boy too badly. It was bound to backfire."

"No, Kurt wanted a boy. I didn't care either way." She flipped through the pages. "She was so cute," Anna bragged, grabbing the next album. "And so good. Never cried."

It was nice flipping through her memories. In every picture there was a smile, and it was good to see her happy. She was too young for this torture. This cancer was a thief robbing her of everything. There was no escape. None, except for me. I had to save her. I would never forgive myself if I didn't.

"I found out how to cure you, Anna," I admitted gravely, "but it's . . . complicated."

The silence caught me by the heart, and I could feel her want to hope, but not sure she should.

"It's okay," she said with grim understanding. "I've accepted—"

"No," I interrupted. Seeing her had decided it for me. "I'm going to do it, but there are consequences." It was the best way I could put it without telling her what I'd have to do.

"Oh." She sounded unsure of how to react without the specifics. "What are they?"

"They're . . . worth it," I answered honestly. "But can you give me some time? Hold out a little while?"

It was cruel of me to ask, and I had no excuse other than one simple fact. I was scared, scared and in love.

"Yeah," she answered, "but just promise me you'll be smart about it. Don't do it if it means putting yourself in danger."

"I'm a big girl," I teased, trying to lighten the mood. "Almost ninety, remember? I think I can handle it."

Her hopeful smile was all the reassurance I needed.

20.

"MISS ME?" William asked when he surprised me Sunday night at my apartment.

I smiled. "Maybe."

He scooped me up and threw me onto my bed.

"So what's your big plan? I've been waiting all weekend to hear about it. Thanks for calling by the way."

He crashed down next to me. "Yeah, well the guy I went to see is more than just a little paranoid. No phones allowed."

"So, who is he?"

He looked at me apologetically. "I can't say."

"Oh come on," I said sitting up. "I'm not taking part in any plan I don't know the details of."

"It's just an emergency scenario. We might not even have to go through with it."

"And if we do?" I asked, hoping to get a little more out of him.

"I'll tell you when we get there."

I gave him a playfully displeased look. A grimace that said, *I'm only half joking, the other half doesn't like this at all.*

"Hey, I'm trying to keep you safe. It's not like I'm trying to make you my love slave or something."

I lifted my eyebrows mockingly, daring him to try. His smile grew wider as he moved closer, but I lurched away with a reactive scream, and he pounced after me. His low rumbling laugh taunted me from behind as he chased me throughout the apartment, ready to tackle and wrestle me to the floor. I maneuvered my way in and out of my room, around the table and eventually into the living room before realizing I wanted to be caught. I whipped around only to be launched onto the couch and tickled until I couldn't breathe.

"Wait. Stop," I gasped, laughing uncontrollably. "This isn't fair." In truth, I didn't want to be able to escape. I wanted to be trapped by him, for there to be no way out of his web of affection. He looked me in the eyes as he ran his fingers through my hair, and moved in for the kiss. The feel of his lips still got my heart racing, and the sensation rushed through me to the tips of every extremity.

His lips stretched tight into a smile, breaking the seal our mouths had formed.

"That was too easy. I didn't even have to use my ability."

I looked into his emerald eyes and tried to figure out what made them so different from mine, how they managed to yield so much power. "What is it like when you use your ability? I mean how do you even do it?"

He sat up and took on a thoughtful expression. I was glad I had an excuse to watch him. Whether it was his ability or not, something had a hold of me, as if looking away from him would be to deny my eyes of the very origin of beauty, to be blind to the glory of the finely sculpted terrain of the earth or the gentle light of the dawn.

"Nobody has ever asked me that before. I'm not sure exactly how I do it. It's like any other command your brain tells your body." He opened and closed his fist, watching his fingers curl and uncurl. "You're not sure how, but when you want to move a part of your body it moves. I just look at whoever I want to affect and do it."

"Is it hard?" I asked, more than happy to continue ogling.

"It can be hard if I'm tired or distracted."

"You have to use your eyes though, right?" I asked immensely curious.

He looked at me with a sinister smile, as if to threaten me playfully with his dangerous gaze.

"Yes, my eyes essentially direct the flow of whatever causes the infatuation," he answered. "I have been working on using my peripherals though."

He turned and looked away, leaving me a bit confused, but when the familiar feeling of his spell began to permeate my body, and I couldn't bring my eyes to look away from him, I realized what he'd meant. I tried to fight it, not because it bothered me, but because I wondered how strong a hold he had on me. It was useless. Slowly but surely I sank into the euphoria.

I let my eyes follow the finely structured contours of his cheekbones down to the hard corner of his jaw and traced the edge with my eyes to the tip of his squared off chin. The skin on his face, a light almond color, was smooth and flawless as if it were brand new and freshly exposed. I considered touching his cheek, just a slight brush of my hand to push back the loose strands of hair that had fallen into his eyes. I would have given anything for it.

"Did it work?" he asked, releasing me from his influence. "I didn't want to look."

"Yeah, it worked," I laughed. My head was still not entirely clear. "But you know that isn't necessary."

He shot me a perplexed look.

"Oh, come on. You've got to know by now that you have me wrapped around your little finger."

"Good to know," he teased. "Now I have you right where I want you."

As soon as William was back in town, it wasn't long before the whole gang came knocking at my door looking for him.

"We have a new spot," Rachel chimed.

"Want to come?" Sam asked from my door step. It was still a shock to see him, the new older-looking version of the boy I'd been introduced to.

"Sure," I accepted for the both of us.

It felt refreshing to be out at night. The yellow glow of the streetlights changed the color of things, and I watched the world in sepia as the group of us headed for the N train. The trees that lined the streets formed a canopy of leaves that made the moonlight scatter on the sidewalk. Nics and Rachel laughed and danced boisterously ahead of the rest of us, while Paul and Sam seemed deep in conversation.

This was what it was like to feel young and alive, to have

friends and be happy. I stole a quick glance at William, knowing that it was truly him that made me feel this way. His beauty was sharp in the dull light of the night, like the full moon against the pitch-black sky.

"I wonder where we're going," I said as the train took us deeper into downtown.

William shrugged. "No idea."

"It's a rooftop in the city," Paul answered from the seat next to me.

When we got there, the lobby of the building was empty, with only a few security cameras to keep watch. Nics made sure all of us got up to the top floor unseen by any surveillance, and we took the stairs to access the roof. I realized once we stepped out onto the top of the building why this new place was worth the trek. The view was spectacular. The city lights stretched out like the sea.

I hugged my elbows close to my body in the chilly night air. "Wow, this place is amazing."

"Told ya," Rachel said with excitement.

"All right, you guys are good to go," Nics said to Rachel and Paul, and the two of them took off into the air.

Sam leaned an old rusty stepladder under the knob of the roof access door. "At least it will give Nics a warning if someone tries to get up here." He grabbed four folding chairs from behind a vent and set them out for us.

"So," Nics said, looking at William. "Have you heard the rumor yet, or should we tell you?"

"What rumor?" I asked.

"I guess that means you haven't."

William shrugged and shook his head. "What is it?"

Nics looked at Sam before she spoke. "People are saying Dr. Nickel's son is dating the last healer." Her eyes fell on me, searching for answers. "Is it true?"

William looked at me, letting me be the one to decide what to say. "Yes," I admitted. "It's true."

"The dating part or the prophecy part?" William asked with a smirk.

I blushed and had to look away. "Both."

"What?" Rachel demanded, slamming down next to us.

"Seriously, how could you not tell us?" Nics complained.

"He told me," Sam added.

William glared at him. "Thanks. That helps a lot."

"You told Sam but not us?" Rachel scoffed.

"I'm his best friend," he defended William.

Nics gave Sam a shove. "I thought I was your best friend."

"You're my best girl friend."

"Okay, first, I am not your girlfriend—"

Sam rolled his eyes. "Are you kidding me?"

"Who cares who is best friends with who?" Rachel jumped in. "We're all friends. He should have told all of us."

"If I would have known I was going to get a verbal beatdown by the two of you," William said, holding back a smile, "I might have actually considered it."

Paul laughed. "You didn't see this coming, huh?"

"So, what does this mean?" Rachel asked. "Is there going to be a war?"

"I don't know," I answered honestly. "I don't really know what everyone expects me to do."

"I think you should get out of here," Nics said seriously. "You saw what they did to Sam."

"Thanks, Nics," Sam scoffed. "She acts like I look like a grandpa."

"Sam," she whined. "That's not what I meant."

Rachel had to take over. "She's just saying if The Council finds out—"

"They might already know," William interrupted. "I told her we should leave, but she doesn't want to."

"Why?" Rachel asked.

All five of them were staring at me. "You guys don't understand." I couldn't expect them to. If I were in their shoes I'd probably say the same thing, but Anna needed me, and I wasn't going anywhere, no matter what any of them said. "Besides, I'm flagged. If they wanted me dead, I'd be dead."

"She's got a point," Paul said as he hovered a foot above the ground. "She hasn't done anything to prove that she is who everyone thinks she is. Maybe they're waiting for her to make a move."

Sam nodded. "Maybe you're right. Why start a war over someone you aren't sure is your enemy?"

"You think if she just stays quiet they'll leave her alone?" Nics asked.

"Well, think about it," Sam continued. "If she doesn't do anything to cross them, why instigate it? If they came after her, it would be like setting fire under our feet. People would go crazy, pick sides, start fighting over nothing."

"They don't want to be the ones to throw the first punch," Paul added.

"I'd say they already did," Rachel said. "We heard about your Evasion test."

"That was Ryder," William clarified. "I don't think Christoph had anything to do with it."

"So what do you think, Elyse?" Nics asked. "Will you swing first?"

"I guess we'll see won't we," I answered, thinking of Anna. Surely The Council would consider that an offense, even if it was my one and only move against them.

21.

WILLIAM'S FRIENDS AGREED to keep things quiet and to discount any prophecy rumors that may have been traveling the halls. On my first day back at The Institute since the Human Evasion test, I noticed a difference immediately. People stared, and those who intentionally looked away walked on the opposite side of the hallway.

"Just say the word and we're out of here," William said, holding my hand protectively.

"It's fine," I answered, brushing it off. Part of me still hoped that in one of my classes I would learn of a way to save Anna without having to die in her place. If it meant tolerating a few looks, so be it.

When I walked into Abilities Defense, Helen greeted me with a smile. "You survived."

"Barely," I said, remembering the traumatic event. Had everyone heard about my Evasion test?

"Well, you've inspired my lesson for today. It should be

fun."

"I think she confuses the word fun with insane," William whispered to me as we headed for a giant blue beanbag. "Last time we did something 'fun' Nics cracked her head open."

It turned out William was right. Ms. Stanzic was crazy.

"Today we are going to play Get Out or Go Down," she announced to the class.

William nudged me with his elbow. "Fun or insane?"

"Each person will have a chance to get out the door of the classroom. I will choose a group of three to try and stop you. Those who make it get ten points."

"Insane," I mouthed to William, who smiled to himself.

"I'm hoping this lesson can teach you how to get out of situations when it seems like all odds are against you." She looked at me with a pleased smile. "Volunteers?"

Nobody jumped up willingly, but this was not an optional assignment, and in the end it was James, the boy who could throw electricity, Paul, and Stan, who's ability to cause sleep nearly killed Nics the last time—all three of them against Rachel.

"Three boys against a girl," Paul complained to Ms. Stanzic. "It's not a fair match."

She just laughed. "That's the point of the exercise."

"I can take them," Rachel challenged with sass.

The entire battle took less than thirty seconds. As soon as Ms. Stanzic said go, Rachel immediately snapped into a tiny multicolored ball of light. She flitted around the room like a fairy, taunting the boys as James shot off streams of crackling electricity, and Paul chased madly after her. Light bulbs burst, and Stan's head whipped back and forth as he tried to focus his sight on the illuminated form that zipped around faster than his eyes could move.

After she'd had her fun, the light bulleted for the door and was out before Paul had even changed directions.

"Told ya," Rachel bragged as she re-entered the classroom in full form.

"Excellent job, Rachel," Ms. Stanzic said.

The next match-up was a freckly brunette named Penny, who had the power of invisibility, Sam, and Nics, against Stephan, a muscular jock type that was descendant of Eris, goddess of discord.

"At least they aren't fighting each other," I whispered to William as we sank deeper into the blue beanbag chair.

"Yeah, we'll see," he said, smiling.

When Ms. Stanzic said go, I expected Stephan to make a run for it, but he stood his ground facing the three with a mischievous grin.

Sam glared at Nics. "Do something," he demanded.

"I am," she shouted back. "He's blind. What else to you want from me?"

"Work together," Ms. Stanzic advised.

Penny had disappeared. I expected her to come up behind her over-confident opponent and block his way, turn him around in the pitch-black space Nics had built around him, but instead Sam went flying backwards into the wall.

"What the hell?" he screamed at Nics.

Her face became enraged. "It wasn't me," she spat.

Suddenly Sam was fumbling around in his own world of

darkness that Nics must have thrust upon him in retaliation. Then it was Nics who began to stumble and slur, and when they came into contact in their altered states, the two of them wrestled each other to the ground, cursing and screaming. It wasn't until the invisible Penny began to antagonize the both of them, pulling hair, jabbing ribs, that I realized Stephan was using his ability to cause this conflict.

"This is amazing, Stephan," Ms. Stanzic praised him as he stood in the exact spot where he started. "William, can you counteract this?"

William sat up, causing me to slouch into the giant hole he'd created in the beanbag. He lasered in on his wrestling friends, but despite his attempts to stop them, the fighting continued.

"I hate you," Nics screeched.

"Get off of me," Sam bellowed as they rolled across the floor. "You're crazy."

Penny's invisible hand pulled Sam's hair hard enough for his head to extend backwards.

William shook his head in frustration.

"Keep trying," Ms. Stanzic urged. "Stephan, no need to leave the room. Don't let up."

It was the screaming that stopped first, then the wrestling, although Sam still had Nics trapped between himself and the floor.

"Wooo," Paul whooped from a green foam couch across from us. "Kiss her, Sammy!"

They stared at each other—whether it was out of hate or love was the question. Sam's face lowered slowly toward her.

Their eyes closed.

Ms. Stanzic gave a nod in our direction. "All right, William. Thank you."

Nics's eyes snapped open as William relaxed back into the cushiony chair, setting them free of his influence.

"Get off," Nics said with a scowl.

"Oh relax," Sam said, letting her up. "It wasn't like I had a choice." He made sure to raise his eyebrows at William disapprovingly.

"What?" William said with a shrug.

I couldn't keep from smiling.

The class went by quickly, maybe because today everyone made it through without any injuries. As the students began to shuffle out of the classroom into the noisy hallway, I decided this was my chance to ask about Anna, possibly my last hope.

"I need to talk to Ms. Stanzic about something," I told William as we headed for the door. "Meet you at the car?"

"Sure," he said, before continuing his banter with Sam and Nics. I was glad he was too distracted to ask why.

I waited for the last person to leave the room.

"Hi," I said, approaching her desk.

"Hello, Elyse," she greeted me. "So, how was the lesson? Did you like it?"

"Yeah, it was great," I answered honestly. "I have more of a personal question, though."

She waved her wrist, stopping the persistent tick of the wall clock.

"Go ahead."

"You were my mom's best friend, right? I am assuming I

can trust you."

She smiled sweetly. "Of course you can."

I really didn't feel comfortable explaining my plans to anyone, but I didn't see any other option. I sat down in front of her desk, mustering the courage to speak.

"If I want to heal someone with advanced cancer," I began, but as I broached the subject her mouth closed tightly, and she looked away. I chose not to continue.

"You want to heal a human." Her words were quiet but sure.

"I didn't say that."

"Descendants don't get disease, Elyse," she said apologetically. I could see she was sorry for deciphering my secret.

My eyes dropped to the floor. "Is there any way to survive?"

I forced myself to look at her again, and she stared back at me.

"You shouldn't be asking me this."

"*You* shouldn't expect me to start a war without breaking rules," I countered.

Her eyes widened, accepting my point.

"Your mom did it," she said suddenly, "only once. You need a backup, someone to heal you when you've lost too much."

I was hoping she wouldn't say that. I needed a better option, something I could do on my own.

"There isn't another way?"

"No." She shook her head. "Blood out, blood in. That's the only way. Trouble is, these days you aren't going to find a Descendant willing to risk their life for a human they don't know. I'm sorry I can't help you. I have children and a family."

I sighed, disheartened. The only person willing would be Chloe, and she was in the dark about my ability to heal. I couldn't put her in danger with The Council. "I can't ask somebody to do that for me, not when The Council would kill anyone that's involved."

"If The Council finds out, they won't just kill your back up. They'll kill you. They'll kill your friend." Her eyes were sad, communicating her worry. "It's not worth the risk."

I shook my head, still thinking. "No, we're flagged." The Council was aware of what Anna knew. I'd gone to visit her. I told her everything. Nothing had happened.

"How?" she asked in surprise. "That doesn't make sense. Why would they protect their enemy, and a human?"

"I don't know why she's flagged, but she is. My whole life we've been friends and no one's touched her," I answered. "I'm flagged because I'm the new mother."

Her lips parted in shock. "I suppose that would be a good reason, wouldn't it?"

"If I have no other choice," I decided, "I'll just go through with it on my own."

"You can't." She nearly yelled the words. "Don't you realize the moment you die, she won't be protected? She's flagged because you're flagged. Christoph won't need her anymore."

"What does he need her for now?"

"I don't know. Maybe he's trying to win you over by sparing her, but the minute you're gone, she will be too."

Her words knocked the wind out of me. How could I not see that coming? I'd spent so much time worrying about how and when I would do it, what would happen to me, and William, that I had completely looked past what would happen to Anna after she was healed. Still, I wasn't going to let that defeat me.

"So I'll tell her to run. I'll have a plan. Maybe I can do it without The Council ever knowing."

"Don't be a martyr, Elyse," she scolded me. "I know you obviously have grown to love whoever it is you want to heal, but think of how many people are counting on you. Think about what your mother and father gave up to keep you alive. Don't forget that."

How could I argue with her logic? My parents had given up their lives as Descendants to ensure I stayed safe. Killing myself in place of Anna would mean their sacrifice was made in vain. Even so, Anna was my family now, and I had to do what I could to save her.

"I can't just watch her die," I insisted, "not when I have the cure."

"This is part of the process. As a Descendant and a healer, you have to learn that you can't save everybody, Elyse. Your mother struggled with the same thing, and I'm sure the rest of your ancestors did as well, but you can't take the weight of the world on your shoulders."

"But it is on my shoulders. Everyone expects me to save them from The Council, and I have no idea how to do it."

"Trust your instincts, and the prophecy will fulfill itself."

"My instincts are telling me I need to cure her."

She nodded, accepting my decision. "Then find someone who loves you enough to be your backup, no matter what the consequences."

22.

THE CLOCK BEGAN ticking, and I stepped into the empty hallway without paying attention to my surroundings. I watched the floor as I made my way to the elevator and caught sight of a familiar pair of shiny black cowboy boots that didn't belong in this place.

"You're too easy to find." Before I had time to look up, Ryder threw me across the hallway like a ragdoll. I smacked hard against the surface of the wall. Pain shot through my back, but I could still move. I scrambled to my feet and tried to make a run for it.

"I don't think so," he said, stopping me in my tracks. It was false hope to think I could escape so easily.

He walked casually up to my immovable form and tipped me over like a sleeping cow, letting me fall flat against the linoleum floor. It knocked the wind out of me. I couldn't breathe.

"Is it true?"

Where was everyone? How was this entire place empty? I pleaded desperately for someone to appear as Ryder straddled his legs over me, sitting on my stomach. What little breathing power I'd managed to regain from the fall was diminished by the weight of his body. *Please someone*, I thought silently, *come into the hallway.*

As if he had read my mind, the Human Evasion professor opened the door to his classroom. He poked his tiny blond head out, and looked directly at me. I could see the shock in his face, and tried with all my might to speak with my eyes—*save me*, but after one look at Ryder, he shut the door, and the lock snapped behind him.

Keeping me restrained beneath his body, Ryder released me from his hold. As soon as I could move, I struggled, but that was all I could do. I opened my mouth and tried to scream, but somehow he still had control of my ability to speak, and nothing came out. I threw myself around violently, trying to wriggle my way from under him. I should have expected the thick fist to knock my head sideways, but the blow was quick and hard. I didn't see it coming, and the side of my face smacked against the floor.

"Now stop that," he said, as though talking to a child. "I asked you a question. Is it true? Do we have a little prophecy princess on our hands?"

I stared straight at him, trying to mask my fear with hate. He didn't really expect me to answer that did he? I opened my mouth to see if I could scream, "Hel—"

His heavy hand came down over my jaw before I could finish the word, and yet again, I found myself frozen still.

"You know, I did a little research," he said, as if talking to himself. His full weight continued to crush me as he leaned over and looked into my eyes. "I couldn't find another healer. Turns out *you* are the only one. I never actually believed the prophecy, but . . ." he shrugged his heavy shoulders up and down casually, "maybe I was wrong. Problem is I've never actually seen you heal anyone. I wanted to see for myself." His smile was frightening, and I knew if I was physically able, I would be shaking.

I flinched internally at the sound of his switchblade. He let it glisten in front of me before he touched the metal to my right cheek, and slid the sharp edge of his knife across my face. My body remained still, but I was thrashing inside, screaming, pleading.

I felt both tears and blood drip down the surface of my skin and could only watch as he wrapped his own hand around the blade, gripping it tight enough to cut his palm. Then with unnecessary force, he slapped his bloody open fist to my cheek, taking pleasure in half suffocating me with his fingers.

When the cuts healed, Ryder laughed to himself wearing an evil grin. "And here I thought the Nickels were trying to pull one over on us, but you're the real deal, sweetheart."

I felt the air fill my lungs to capacity as he stood and began to walk in circles around me.

"I'm really resisting the urge to kill you right now," he said with a sneer, "but I know Christoph has plans for you and your little human friends. You may think you're safe, but it's only a matter of time before you get what's coming. He has his reasons for keeping you alive until he gets what he wants.

And when he's done with you . . ." He turned my head with his foot and stared down at me with bloodlust in his eyes. "You're mine."

The tip of his boot smacked against my ribcage, rolling me onto my belly and leaving my face smashed against the floor.

"In the meantime, don't cross me. I can find ways to get to you. Accidents do happen."

He left me there, belly down on the scuffed and dirty tile as he walked away, his boots clicking, whistling a cheery tune. Even after I could move, I lay there quietly sobbing to myself over more than just the physical pain. The fear, the looming uncertainty of the future, the consequences of my actions, my existence, all of it poured out of me in the form of uncontrollable tears.

When I finally pulled myself together and gained full control of my body, I made my way to the bathroom. I couldn't let William see me like this. Both Ryder's blood and my own were smeared all over the right side of my face, and in the dim florescent light, it looked like the scene of a horror movie. I turned on the cold water and rinsed my skin clean, avoiding looking myself in the eye. I knew it would only make me cry. *Be stronger*, I told myself. *Don't let him win. Don't let him tear you down.*

Once the blood was off of my hands and face, I rinsed it out of my hair. I used the hand dryer to dry the wet strands and combed the front part over my cheeks, trying to hide the fresh pink skin that was flushed and new.

"I know," I heard William exclaim with excitement as I made my way through the parking garage. Sam and Nics were leaning up against William's Honda as he talked exuberantly with his hands. "I've never made two people fall in love with each other before."

"Who says you did?" Nics said with a guilty grin.

"I do," William answered. "Come on, Sam. Are you going to let her deny it?"

"No way." He shook his head. "I'm staying out of this."

William threw his hands in the air. "You do realize there were about thirty witnesses, don't you?"

"I'm telling you, it didn't work," Nics insisted.

"All right. Let's try it again then."

"No," Sam and Nics responded in unison.

"He did manage to keep you from fighting," I said, trying to put on a happy face. William slid his arm around my waist, and I jerked as his hand grazed my bruised ribs. "That's got to count for something."

The four of us agreed to meet at Cearno's where the plan was to have Rachel and Paul weigh in.

"You okay?" William asked once we were in the car.

I flipped down the sun visor and looked in the mirror for blood on my face. "Yeah, why?"

He looked at me suspiciously. "Just wondering. What did Ms. Stanzic have to say? What did you need to ask her anyway?"

"Oh," I stammered, not ready for the question. I thought about making something up, but maybe this was the perfect time to broach the subject. "Since the Evasion test, I've been thinking about healing a lot, and I just wanted to talk to her about what would happen if I were ever forced to heal a human."

William's eyes went immediately serious. "You can't." His voice spiked. "You know they'd kill you."

"Well, technically I'm flagged," I began to argue.

"Even so, and they'd just kill the human afterwards."

"What if The Council didn't know?" My voice was quiet, hopeful.

"I can't even believe you're thinking about this. Are you nuts? You are. You're nuts—"

"You don't know what it was like," I interrupted. "I could have healed that little girl."

"They would have killed her anyway."

"Yeah, well what if Anna or Chloe needed help? What then? Would you just expect me to sit back and do nothing?"

He stayed focused on the road, unable to answer my question. Neither of us spoke, and it felt like an eternity of silence.

"Do they?" William asked without looking at me. "Need help?"

"I said *what if*," I answered, hoping to protect him from my burden. "I'm just having a hard time with this, okay?" I couldn't ask him to help me. Not only would it put him at risk with The Council, but it could backfire. What if he tried to stop me or got in my way, thinking he had to protect me? I felt so hopeless.

"All right," he accepted as he reached for my hand.

I let my head lean back against the seat and watched the city pass through the window of the car, wanting the conversation to be over.

"So, what do you think?" William asked, changing the subject. "Did I make Sam and Nics fall in love or what?"

I smiled through my worry, thanking him for letting it go. "Definitely."

"It's a pretty hard skill to develop," he said proudly.

"You might have had some help, though. I think they are secretly in love already."

He nodded in agreement. "I was afraid of that."

Talking to him pushed everything out of my mind, even thoughts of Ryder. The pain in my ribs didn't seem as bad when we were laughing, and he looked so happy it rubbed off on me. *We* were so happy. The thought of it ending made my throat sting.

"Elyse." He looked at me genuinely once he'd parked the car in front of Cearno's. "I love you," he said. "You know, I've been waiting for you my whole life." His eyes softened as he looked at me. "I don't know, sometimes I feel like every moment before you was wasted. Now that you're here, even though things seem bad, and we have the prophecy hanging over our heads, at least we have each other." He pressed our warm palms tighter together.

The tears that I had been hoping to save for when I was alone started before I'd given them the go ahead. Part of me was happy to hear him speak of me as I often thought of him, but another part knew it was exactly what I shouldn't hear.

"Why are you crying?" he asked, his face visibly feeling my pain.

Any other time I would have felt so elated by his words, but instead they tore at my heart. Why now? Why when I faced such sacrifice did he have to unload his feelings on me in such a way that made me need him? Everything seemed so uncertain, so unfair, all but one thing. We were destined, fated, meant to be.

"I feel the same way," I said quietly.

He mistook my tears for happiness and kissed my cheeks with a smile as they rolled down my face. Having him close felt good, like comfort and home, but each gentle kiss reminded me of what I'd be losing if I healed Anna. His lips moved to my mouth, still wet with tears. I gave into it, though I knew it would mean more pain later. I couldn't face the cold truth in this moment. It was too hard to bear.

With the remnants of William's kiss fresh in my mind, I was desperate for a solution, one that didn't put anyone at risk or require I give up my life. There had to be another answer—chemotherapy, alternative medicine, another opinion, something. I needed a miracle.

23.

"JUST SPEND THANKSGIVING with us, Elyse. You are being ridiculous," William groaned. "It isn't safe."

I sighed and threw myself onto the couch. "William, I want to see her. She invited me. What, should I just say no I don't want to?"

"Yes," he answered easily.

"She's my best friend. I *do* want to see her."

"It's not about that. It's dangerous. You saw what happened to Sam, and Ryder wasn't exactly easy on you either."

I hadn't told William about the hallway incident, or the fact that The Council officially knew I was the one who was supposed to fulfill the prophecy, and I was glad I didn't. I couldn't imagine what sort of a fight he would put up if he knew.

"Well, if not now, when?" I pleaded my case as he paced around my living room. "We're both flagged."

"Elyse, that doesn't make you invincible. What about the

Evasion test? You almost died. Clearly the man has ways of getting to you."

"I already talked to Kara. Ryder is at a bar every Thanksgiving. He'll be passed out."

He gripped the back of his neck, trying to control his anger. "You don't know that for sure."

"It's worth the risk to me." I looked up at him from my spot on the couch, willing him to understand.

"Well, it's not to me. At least let me come with you."

I shook my head, giving myself time to come up with an excuse. What was I supposed to say? He couldn't see her sick. "No. I don't want to get you involved. Besides, you should be with your own family."

He combed his fingers through his hair. "You're being unreasonable."

"Don't worry. It'll be fine."

"Don't tell me not to worry," he said exasperated. "I'm the one who had to watch you nearly beaten to death, who thought I might not make it in time when you were bleeding out on that street corner. How can I not worry?"

"Well, you can't tell me I can never see her again. I won't accept that."

He sat down next to me, taking my hands in his. "I'm not saying that," he said in a soft voice. "I'm just saying you should wait a while, and go when . . ."

"When, William?"

His brow wrinkled with worry. "I don't know."

"I'm not going to just push her out of my life. She's my only family."

He stood, walking toward the window, purposely avoiding eye contact.

"What if it's for the best?" He turned back to look at me.

I couldn't believe he said that. "I'm going," I said with force.

"Fine," he said through tight lips, and he walked out my front door, slamming it behind him.

***

I proceeded hesitantly, unsure of my decision to come, but as soon as I saw Chloe's face light up, I knew I'd made the right choice. The smell of a baking turkey spilled out of the house as she opened the door.

"Chlo bug," I beamed, as she threw her arms around me.

"Finally," she joked. "I've been waiting all day."

"Well, are you going to invite her in?" Anna laughed from the living room. I hadn't noticed until she spoke that she was lying in a bed made up on the couch.

My attention moved immediately to her as I walked through the door. "How are you? Are you okay?"

"Yeah, I'm fine," she lied. "Chloe here won't let me do anything. I'm on strict orders from her not to leave this spot."

They looked at each other with endearing smiles, Chloe happy to be helping make her mother's life a little easier, and Anna appreciative.

"You better start peeling those potatoes," Anna said, giving directions from the couch. "When you're done with that, come back and I'll tell you what's next."

"Okay," she said with excitement before darting off to the kitchen.

As soon as Chloe was out of earshot, I looked at Anna. "So

how are you really?" I asked, sitting at her feet.

Her eyes fell, revealing the truth. Her cheery disposition was all an act. I let her be silent for a while, to take a break from having to be or say anything that wasn't genuine.

"You know, the illness, the pain, it's hard. I'm not going to lie, but the worst part . . ." She sighed, leaning closer to me. "It's her."

She glanced at the swinging door to the kitchen, eyes welling with tears that she was determined to hold back. Guilt pummeled me from every angle, like I was losing a boxing match. I rested my hand on her shin, but I was sure the feeling gave me more comfort than it did her.

"She's only fourteen," Anna continued with heartache. "It's just such a burden on her. I mean she's making Thanksgiving dinner, and she's just a kid."

"It's okay," I tried consoling her. "The burden would be much heavier without her mother—"

"It's not okay," she cut me off bitterly. "I just wish it would happen already so she could move in with my sister and be a kid again."

"What?" I whispered with an edge to my voice. "Anna, don't talk like that."

"I'm sorry, it's . . ."

"No," I said forcefully. "I told you. I'm going to heal you. It will be soon it's just . . . I mean, I need more time." Seeing her erased all doubts in my mind about my decision to heal her. If I had to give up my life, I would, but if I had a little more time, maybe I could still find another way. I hesitated too long, and she saw right through me.

"What will happen if you heal me, Elyse?"

I looked down at her thin frame beneath the blanket. "How much time do I have?" I asked, avoiding her question.

She ignored me. "If you won't tell me, I don't want you to do it."

"Well, I can't tell you."

She closed her eyes, losing hope. "Why?"

"Because you'll try and talk me out of it."

"You're probably right, and if that's the case, then don't do it."

She was so stubborn. I didn't bother fighting back.

She sighed, lying back down. "I'm so tired."

"So rest," I said getting up, stretching her legs out for her. It was my decision to make anyway, not hers. "I'll go help Chloe."

She didn't argue, and as she closed her eyes, I was glad I was there to give her a little reprieve. After all, she was suffering while I took my time coming to terms with the situation. It was hard to see her in so much pain, and I would have done it right then and there if it weren't for William. I owed it to him to say goodbye, and more than anything, I was scared.

"Hi," I said walking into the kitchen. Seeing Chloe was always a little jarring for me. She looked so much like the younger Anna I remembered. "Can I help?"

She smiled. "Sure."

I grabbed a knife and began to peel potatoes, watching her from the corner of my eye. There was so much of her mother in every move she made. I had always felt love for her, but now something deeper compelled me to protect her as if she were my own.

"So, what are you this year, a freshman?" I asked.

"Sophomore," she answered. "You know that."

"Yeah," I admitted. "I still don't believe it though."

"Three more years," she said with a mischievous smile. She had to remind me every time I saw her, confronting me with how close we seemed in age. It was strange. She seemed so young, so impressionable.

"Four more years," I corrected, "and don't think that means you don't have to listen to me. I'm twice as old as your mom. Remember that."

"Yeah, yeah," she teased.

I shoved her with my shoulder as she picked up a knife and started peeling beside me.

"So, give me the latest gossip. How's school going?"

Her eyes stayed down. "I don't want to talk about it."

"Why?" I asked, picking up on her discomfort.

She shook her head. "There are these girls."

"What girls? What are they doing?"

"You know, locking me in the bathroom, sticking gum in my hair, pretty much making school my own personal hell."

I put down the knife, angry at the thought of such cruelty. Didn't they know her mother was dying? "How long?"

She still hadn't looked at me, and I could tell she was embarrassed. "Since last year," she mumbled.

"Does your mom know?"

"No. I haven't told her." Her eyes snapped up, intent and serious. "And I don't want you to tell her either."

I sighed, struggling with the decision to keep this from

Anna, but Chloe's expression was desperate. "All right," I agreed.

"Is she feeling okay?" she asked nervously. "I know she acts better than she feels with me."

I turned to put the freshly peeled potatoes in the boiling water, trying to avoid eye contact. The question had sort of blindsided me, and I wasn't sure how to answer.

"Yeah, she's fine," I tried to say as casually as possible.

"Do you think I should go check on her?"

"No, let her rest," I said with my back still turned. "Don't wake her."

"All right." I could hear the stress in her voice as she opened the oven to baste the turkey.

I tried to compose myself, but hearing her worry and fret over her mother's condition tore me apart. I knew what it was like to lose a mother. It wasn't fair, not this young, and I wouldn't let it happen to her. I had to give her some peace of mind, tell her that it would all be all right.

"Chloe," I said softly.

"Yeah," she turned to look at me, her eyes heavy with sorrow.

"Your mom is going to be fine. She'll make it through this."

The words were a promise solidifying my decision, but to her they were nothing but a false consolation. Tears fell silently down her cheeks, although she spoke with a smile.

"No, she won't."

"Trust me," I said, trying to speak more with my eyes than with my words. "I won't let it happen."

I could tell by her expression that she knew I was trying to say more than I was, but she didn't understand. How could she? Over the years, Chloe had learned about my age, but Anna and I had kept the day we healed between us. Without discussing it anymore, we continued to prepare the food, grateful of each other's company.

24.

WILLIAM NEVER SAID anything about my Thanksgiving with Anna. If he was still angry, he kept it to himself. I did catch him checking over his shoulder every so often, but Kara must have kept the visit a secret, because I hadn't seen any sign of Ryder.

"We should do something this weekend," I thought out loud as I popped some frozen waffles in the toaster. In the past week, the two of us had taken to confining ourselves to each other's company, unaffected by the world outside.

William was sprawled out on the couch, head buried in the weekly Headquarters newsletter.

"No can do," he said without as much as a glance away from the article. He didn't offer any more explanation than that. Did he taunt me with his ambiguity on purpose, or was it just in his nature to maintain a certain level of mystery?

"Why not?" I finally asked.

"We already have plans."

"What plans?" I asked predictably. Without a beat, he answered, as if he'd been waiting to tell me for days, but didn't want me to know it.

"We're going somewhere."

"Well . . . where are we going?"

"It's a little out of the way, so we'll be staying for the weekend," he added without acknowledging my question.

I grabbed the waffles as they popped up and made room for myself on the couch, shoving William's feet aside with my hips.

"So, you're not going to tell me?"

"Nope," he answered simply.

"Will you tell me if I guess?"

"Sure," he said with a smirk as he set down his newsletter. "You'll never guess."

"Well, how will I know what to pack?"

"You're already packed." His sinister expression only added to his already stunning good looks, making it hard to be annoyed.

"How?"

"I packed for you last night when you fell asleep. The bag is in your closet."

I nibbled one of the berries off of my waffle. "What if you forgot something?"

"I didn't." Confidence was never something he had to dig very deep to find.

"Swimsuit?" I questioned, hoping for a hint.

He shrugged. "Might need it."

"What shoes did you pack, flip flops or tennies?"

"Both," he grinned widely.

"What about underwear?" I blurted out.

"Yep."

"You seriously dug around in my underwear drawer?" I asked completely mortified. What did he see? I wasn't exactly the lingerie wearing type of girl. Horrifying images of pink Tuesday cotton briefs and old Hanes that had been washed too many times made me groan with embarrassment.

He laughed. "Don't worry. I just grabbed and stuffed. I didn't see anything."

"Good," I shot out, not really believing him.

As the day crept on, lingering in suspense of what was to come and when, none of my guesses got me any closer to our mystery destination. Between loads of laundry, I found out that we weren't going out of state, but he wouldn't tell me where in California. I had eliminated Los Angeles, San Diego, and Orange County, but I wasn't exactly certain he *would* tell me if I had stumbled across the right answer.

Overly antsy, I'd finished all the dishes, vacuumed, mopped, dusted, and William even helped me scrub the bathroom from top to bottom, making the place officially immaculate. Finally, after showers and dinner, he opened my closet and grabbed my bag.

"So, are you ready to go?" he asked.

"Well, how am I supposed to know if I'm ready if I don't know where we're going?"

"Nice try," he said, beaming with excitement. "We've just got to stop downstairs before we leave. Nics and Sam are meeting us at Cearno's."

Without letting me look in my duffle, William took off to get the car with it in hand.

Nics and Sam were waiting on the sidewalk as I locked up my door, and I wondered why they weren't inside enjoying a mocha blast or a strawberry sun tea. It wasn't until I walked over to meet them that I saw the red and white CLOSED sign hanging from inside.

"Hey." Sam spoke through the car window as William drove up. "Cearno said we could park in his spot. You wanna drive around back so we don't have to lug our gear out here?"

"Gear?" I asked, picking up on the terminology.

"Yeah, it's heavy," Nics said as she slid into the back. Sam followed right behind leaving the front seat for me.

"So why is Cearno's closed?" I asked a little worried for the future of the place. "It's not closed for good, right?"

"What? No," Sam laughed. "He always closes down for Lenaia."

"Sam, come on," William groaned.

"Lenaia?" I asked completely lost. "What is that?"

"What?" Sam hiked his shoulders up defensively. "You haven't told her? How was I supposed to know?"

"Whatever. Just help me load the stuff into the trunk."

I could hear the two of them bickering quietly from the back about what had just happened, but all I really had was a name. I realized that I hadn't even seen what William had packed in the trunk. I had no idea what was being shifted and shoved around back there as they tried to fit everything in.

"So, you've never even heard of Lenaia?" Nics asked from behind me.

"No," I admitted, turning to face her. "Should I have? It's not some initiation thing is it?"

"No, it's just a holiday festival. It's really fun actually."

"Oh come on, Nics, you too?" William complained as he re-entered the car. "Are you both completely incapable of keeping things to yourselves?"

"I just told her it was a festival, jeez. She was all worried you were dragging her off to some initiation ceremony or something."

"Really?" he laughed. "Well, in a way it is. You'll never forget your first Lenaia."

As we continued down the seemingly infinite straightaway into the nothingness of the I-5 freeway, the evidence of the ever-present city began to taper off. I couldn't imagine where we were going, but I realized this might be a very long drive. The blackness deepened as we left the city's lights behind, and the mountains silently tucked themselves away effortlessly into the night, so well that I couldn't tell where they ended and the sky began.

After several hours of driving through small town after small town, William exited unexpectedly. It was an exit that most would overlook. There was no street name or promise of distant civilization, just an anonymous cutaway that wound into the abyss of open space. Despite the apparent lack of any sort of gas station or pit stop, William showed no signs of stopping or re-entering the freeway. He simply kept on while the lights of our car were swallowed up in the natural folds of the terrain. Only after a few sharply bending curves did I catch sight of several other sets of taillights blinking in the distance like an airline runway outlining our path.

I looked around in all directions at the black emptiness surrounding us. "Where are we going?" I asked.

"You'll see," William answered quickly, before the others could give anything away.

I raised my eyebrows, unsatisfied with his answer.

"Don't worry," he added. "Those are other Descendants ahead of us. We're not the only ones headed this way."

"Hardly," Sam said.

"So I take it this is no back road to LA then?"

"Not so much," Nics answered with a grin.

"Seriously, guys," I urged. "What, is there some secret city out here in the middle of nowhere? I mean this isn't even a paved road."

Sam laughed at my paranoia. "I don't know, William. I don't think she likes surprises."

"No, I do, I just . . . How do you know other *people* won't follow us out here?" I asked, moving the conversation away from the topic of me.

Nobody answered.

"I guess we don't," Sam said from the back seat. "Nobody's ever followed us before."

"Like you'd notice," Nics teased him.

"I'd notice," he said defensively.

"Yeah." She sounded unconvinced. "Like you *noticed* when Gino Piloske tracked you for three whole days for a class project."

"Okay," Sam countered. "First of all, Gino's bloodline is Artemis. His ability is tracking."

He paused for a while, satisfied with his response.

"And second?" Nics asked, egging him on.

"Do I even need a second?"

I smiled to myself, resisting the urge to turn around and watch them banter.

"Well, you said 'first,' which implies you have a second."

"Fine. *Second*. I *did* know he was tracking me. I just didn't want him to fail his project."

"Yeah right," she exclaimed.

"Shut up, Nics."

"Oh, I'm just kidding around, jeez."

I let the sound of their bickering fade to background noise as I mulled over my unanswered question. It was nice to know that I wasn't the only one who didn't know every little detail about how they lived.

"I'm sure they have security," William said, glancing away from the road with a reassuring smile. He'd still been hanging onto my last words. "They have a major committee set this thing up every year. They would never let it go unprotected."

"How long have you had Lenaia? I mean how long have you been celebrating it?"

"As long as anyone can remember."

"Hey," Nics interrupted belligerently from the back.

"Wow," William reacted.

"Well, he's reing bediculous."

"What?" I asked aloud.

"Being ridiculous," William interpreted.

"Sstopet, Sam," Nics slurred. "I know what you're tryindo."

"Sam," I said mildly scolding. This time I did turn around.

"Is she *drunk*?"

"She was annoying me," he returned with a shrug.

"You think just because I'm a little *tipsy*, I can't fight you?"

Suddenly my vision blacked out, like the deep night sky had swallowed up the world around me. Everything was gone, but somehow still there. I clung to my seat, registering the fact that I could still feel.

"Hey," I shouted. "What's happening?" But my words were drowned out by the sound of everyone reacting at once. I wasn't the only one who was blindly hurling through the black space that surrounded us.

"Nics, stop. We can't see," I heard William yell, but by then it was too late. She lifted her shield just in time for us to watch the car plow nose first into a ditch.

"Shoot," Nics muttered as we looked around at each other.

"Is everyone okay?" I asked. Nobody seemed hurt.

"Yeah," Sam answered, rubbing his head which had bumped against the window.

"Dammit, you guys," William snapped after seeing no one was injured.

Nobody spoke. The silence seemed to deepen as he put the car in reverse, only to find that accelerating dug us further into the soft billowing dirt.

"Now what?" I dared to ask with harmless interest.

"I don't know," he answered. "I haven't seen a car in the rearview this whole time."

"I told you we should have left earlier," Sam said.

"That has nothing to do with it. If you wouldn't have gotten so aggressive," Nics spat.

"So this is my fault now?"

"Well, it's not all my fault."

"Hey," William interrupted. "Didn't Rachel and Paul leave after us?"

"Yeah," Nics answered.

"So call them," Sam barked.

"Why don't *you* call them," she shot back.

"I'll call," William said, letting me in on a subtle eye roll. "Or maybe I won't. Does anyone get a signal out here?"

After three noes, it was decided that we would just wait for the next car. After all, it was sure to be someone going in the same direction.

William shut off the lights to save the battery, and we all got out to wait in the dark, Nics and Sam making a point to put as much room between each other as possible. With her sulking on the hood of the car and Sam propped up against the slightly raised rear bumper, William and I settled down on the ground mid-distance between the two, trying not to take sides. Without the hope of headlights in the distance and not much conversation to partake in, it was easy to listen intently to the sound of the night. I didn't dare break the tension between the three of them. Crickets chirped their hypnotic songs and the wind carried a steady hum in and out of the dry grass and rustling sagebrush. In the distance, something set off the balance, a foreign resonance that cut through the rest. I focused in on it, trying to pick it out. Its uneven pattern seemed too controlled for nature, unnaturally deliberate. The broken pieces of murmured sound could only be one thing—voices.

"What?" William spoke through the stillness, noticing I was suddenly alert.

"Shhh," I hushed him. "Do you hear that?"

I had caught Sam and Nics's attention, who played only mildly interested. The voices were getting clearer, coming closer, but I was still reluctant to give us up. What kind of people wandered around out here at night? People who didn't want to be seen.

"I think I can hear something," William whispered.

"What?" Nics asked, moving in to make sense of the commotion.

This time William shushed her, and Sam was soon to join in. We all listed intently as the voices became distinct. There were two of them, a man and a woman. It was obvious he was older and tougher, with a thick rough voice like a television mobster. Hers was just as angry, but younger and with the hint of a dramatic tone that had yet to be stripped away by age.

"Oh don't give me that, Sal. How many jobs have we done together?" The words were clear, but distant. I could just barely make them out. "I can see right through you, and you don't like it any better than I do. You may look tough, but no one likes killing people, not unless they've gone nutzo."

"I know," he responded, a little exasperated, "but what can we do?"

"Nothing," she answered matter-of-factly, "and that's what really burns me."

The conversation hit a lull, making it hard to tell how much closer they were getting. Luckily, the car had hit the ditch just in front of an overgrown patch of sagebrush, giving us enough cover to not be seen. If they had been approaching from the opposite direction, they would have spotted us immediately.

"You know, I shouldn't have to drag some poor sap and his wife a mile into the brush. That's your job."

"Hey," his gruff voice rattled defensively. "I thought you were saying it shouldn't be nobody's job."

"Yeah, but especially not mine. I access the mind. I give you the information you need to know, and that should be it. Dead bodies are your jurisdiction."

"Well, I hadta get ridda the car. It ain't no piece a cake tuggin a car through this brush neither."

"Last year there was nothing like this. I was actually excited when they gave me the assignment this time. I thought, finally, something easy and clean. Give my conscience a break, right? Little did I know, I'd be luring innocent people off the road just so the community can have a little party."

"Eh, quit your whining. You're just mad 'cause we hafta take the first shift. Here comes another one."

A pair of headlights gleamed in the distance, making the pit of my stomach clench up with tension. Was I about to witness a murder here? I watched anxiously as the car crept closer, and aside from William's comforting hand in mine, I was completely unaware of the three around me. Before the car was close enough for us to make out any sign of its make or model, the woman spoke words that put me at ease.

"They're Descendants," she said.

"Well, what else? At least keep me entertained," he requested.

"Um, it's a boy and a girl," she answered, playing a game that they had obviously been using to pass the time. "He's of Hermes. She's of Iris. Ages eighty-four and eighty-eight. They're dating, pretty in love actually. They're both flyers so the car ride has been rough."

As the car came nearer, none of us dared move at the risk of being seen by the two lookouts. We chose to watch it roll by only to see it skid to a stop a few feet down the road.

"Why are they stoppin'?" the man asked.

"It's Paul and Rachel," Sam whispered.

The three of us waited in terror for the woman's response, knowing full well she could read their minds, which would ultimately give away our position.

"Uh . . . there's some . . ." the woman's voice sounded surprised.

"Well?" he urged.

"They are picking up their friends who are crouching in front of their car by the road."

"Really? I didn't see nothin'. How'd you miss 'em?"

"Well, excuse me. I was burying Mr. Smith. Where were you?"

"Gettin ridda the car," he growled. "Can they hear us?"

It was apparent she considered her answer before delivering it.

"No, they can't hear us. Let them go."

"Hey," Rachel yelled from the open door. "What are you guys doing out here?"

"Nics here drove us into a ditch," William yelled back, keeping the scene free of suspicion.

"Me?" Nics whined.

"Can you pull us out?" William shouted.

Nics and I stayed behind, in the cover of the brush, while the boys went to work. Both of us still listened carefully for any continuation of the previous conversation, but the two stayed silent and so did we.

"Come on," Sam beckoned when they were finished. "Let's go."

I had never been so eager to leave somewhere before in my life. As soon as Sam said the word, I jumped to my feet and dove into the front seat. Even as my heart skipped wildly in my chest, making me sweat through the chilled air, part of me wanted to look back, to stare the murderers in the face and tell them, *I know what you've done.* When I turned my head, I immediately wished I hadn't. The man stayed hidden in the shadows, but a familiar face was illuminated in the red glow of the brake lights. Our eyes met, and I went rigid. The woman was Kara.

The four of us drove in silence at first, following the taillights in front of us closely.

"So I guess that answered your question, Elyse," Sam said breaking the silence. "Some security."

"I'm sorry I asked," I said with genuine regret.

Their conversation moved on to something casual and non-threatening, but I wasn't paying attention. Instead, I drifted off, contemplating their reaction to what was nothing less than a murder confession. The thought made my mouth sour with disgust. How could they act so nonchalant? It seemed so easy for them to accept it as unfortunate, as though nothing had happened, but it wasn't easy for me. Kara's face was burned into my vision. Even my open eyes couldn't escape it. I pressed my forehead to the cold glass window and tried to force her out of my mind. This was the second time she'd murdered a human, that I knew of. The truth buckled in on me, folding me up like thin paper until I felt small and vulnerable. No matter what sort of relationship we had, her first priority was to The Council, whether she wanted that or not. She could never be a friend, not when what she stood for would always be an enemy to me. William was right, things were complicated with her. She wasn't on our side, and I shuddered when I thought of what she was truly capable of.

"You okay?" William asked gently, noticing my change in mood.

"Yeah, just a little shaken, I guess."

Clearly he hadn't realized it was Kara who was out there. Her voice was different, lower and tough. I had only recognized it when I saw her face. I opened my mouth to tell him, but my breath caught in my throat. It would ruin his night. I took a deep breath, holding in my secret.

"Well, we're almost there. Believe me, the festival will take your mind off of it."

"Yeah," I said without agreement. I wasn't sure if it would take my mind off of it, or if I even wanted it to. Maybe it was my duty to think about it, to remember it. Nobody else would.

"Finally," Nics sighed from the back, and at that moment, I saw exactly what it was she recognized. The overgrown road curved one last time, bringing into view the mouth of a cave settled at the base of a rocky mountainside. Its opening was visible only by a soft glow of light that spilled out from somewhere deep inside.

"We're going in there?" I asked in disbelief. I hadn't expected a cave, but where else could we be headed?

"Yep," Sam answered. He leaned forward to look at me. "Not what you expected, huh?"

"Where is the light coming from?" I asked before realizing it was probably the other cars. I was wrong.

"Mr. Williamson," said Sam. "He's descendant of Helios. He helps with light every year. It's sort of an honor to be on the committee. People get all excited about it."

"Unless, of course, you're given the task of murdering those who get in the way," I said with cold bitterness in my voice.

The car went silent for at least half a minute, and I could feel the raised eyebrows glaring at me uncomfortably.

"Sorry," I mumbled before anyone had the chance to speak, my cheeks burning out of embarrassment. "I should have kept that to myself."

"It's okay. I guess we're just . . . used to it," Nics said.

Used to it? As if that was an excuse. I couldn't hold back my reaction.

"That's crazy," I let out, swinging around to face all of them. "How could you ever be okay with something like that?"

"It doesn't mean we're okay with it," Sam added quickly. The worried look on his face was hard to combat. I didn't want him to think I thought badly of him.

"But you live with it?" I clarified. "I mean humans are just dispensable, and everyone just looks the other way? How did things get like this?"

"Not a day goes by that I don't ask myself the same question," William said with a grim tone. His lips tightened into a line as he looked at me. "Welcome to life on the other side."

With that, we entered the cave, into a world that I now had to call my own, a world where there was no turning back.

25.

THE ROAD WAS not paved, but the dirt was smooth, and it cut through the mountain with ease. Once we were in the tunnel, our headlights washed away the subtle glow that had led us here, and we followed the single path as it led us deeper underground. I'm not sure what I expected the mystery light to be, maybe a miniature sun or an illuminated Mr. Williamson, but I never would have imagined what we saw when we turned the last corner. It was too simple, too ordinary. Extravagant, yes, but nothing like what I'd been thinking.

The road was lined with trees and elegantly designed streetlights from the '40s, as if, despite the general cave-like atmosphere, we had driven into the past. Wooden signs protruded from the mountain walls and hung like storefront advertisements: "Welcome to Lenaia." An attendant dressed head to foot in 1940s attire was waiting for us at the end of the entryway. He had fallen asleep in his chair, with his newsboy cap tipped down over his eyes and his long lean body stretched out in front of him.

"Hey," William shouted out the window. The boy jumped to his feet, defensive and alert, only to meet William's greeting with a smile. "How'd you get stuck with this gig, Charlie?" Obviously they knew each other.

"Volunteered," he answered, walking toward the car. "Hey guys." He tipped his head up acknowledging the rest of us.

"Why? You're going to miss the birth of our existence, you know?" Nics said, peering through the two front seats.

"The what?" I whispered into William's ear, but all he had to offer was the same loose-ended response—"You'll see"—his careful grin testing the limitations of my curiosity.

"How's avoiding an ex-girlfriend for an excuse?" Charlie answered.

"Yeah, that's good enough for me," Sam laughed.

"You've never had a girlfriend," Nics joked with careless insensitivity. "How would you know?" I saw Sam's face flinch at the intentional jab.

"Still," William recovered for him, "it can't be easy being on Jillian's bad side. Isn't she of Dolos?"

"Yeah," Charlie answered with a regretful look. "I'm trying to just stay out of her way." He tapped the hood of the car, wrapping up the conversation. "Well, you guys are on your own from here on out. Grab your packs out of the trunk, and follow the road to the right. You know the drill."

"You got it, boss," William said, tossing him the keys through the window.

William insisted on carrying everything he'd packed for the

both of us, so being the only one with a free hand, I turned and waved goodbye to Charlie.

The trees grew thicker the deeper we went, pressing their burly branches against the walls of the tunnel, as if they were bearing the load of the heavy mountain. The gentle roar, that could only be the sound of a thousand jumbled voices, grew louder with every step, until at last the source came into view like a painted picture come to life.

I stopped dead in my tracks. "Oh my God."

William, Nics, and Sam all had their eyes locked on me, and satisfied grins gave away their enjoyment in watching my reaction.

The trees that lined the tunnel were pale in comparison to what stood before me. The space had opened up into an enormous cavern that was filled with nothing less than a fully matured deciduous forest. The overgrown trees were gigantic with trunks the size of tractor tires and roots that protruded from the ground that were as high as I stood. The branches tangled themselves into each other, creating a canopy of leaves that showered down like slow falling snow covering the ground. The floor of the forest was carpeted with an array of green plants, and dirt paths provided a way around the trees.

Despite the magnificence of the phenomenon, people were everywhere, acting as if such a scene was nothing to make a fuss about and could easily exist inside the hollow space of a mountain. To the left I could just make out a clearing where groups had started to gather and sit. To the right, scattered throughout the trees, were countless tents, and Descendants casually made their way in and out of them as they came and went.

"Come on," William said with a grin that made me blush. The others had moved on ahead while I stood gawking in awe. "We've got to get to our spot."

My gaping mouth curled into a smile, and I ran ahead to catch his hand.

"This is amazing," I beamed.

"Yeah, they did a great job this year."

"How are we going to find a spot though? Tents are everywhere."

"I use the same spot every year. Nobody goes there. It's a little secluded."

"Perfect," I said with a suggestive smirk. He laughed it off, and kept moving.

As we walked through the crowds, I noticed the groups of eyes that turned my way, and realized the rumors must have spread.

"Ignore them," William whispered, as he glared at those who stared.

I chose to focus on the scenery. Large trees and flowered plants sprung up from the dusty floor thick into the distance. I wasn't sure how far it went, but eventually the greenery tapered off, and the surface of the rock walls began to show smooth and misshapen like large sheets of petrified wood. Vines crawled along the uneven planes of the earthy stone, and the trees dissipated.

"Do you like it?" he asked, clasping his hand tighter around mine.

I swung our arms back and forth. "Of course," I answered.

"I just thought you'd like the privacy seeing as you're apparently the talk of the town, and it's nice to have a place to run off to when it gets too crazy. We can move closer to everyone if you want."

I smiled. "No, it's great."

"Good." He moved toward me. I caught a hint of his crisp cool scent as he held me close. "So," he said with a slight blush, "I uh . . . made something for you. Lenaia is sort of our version of Christmas."

"Why didn't you tell me that?" I complained. I had no gifts for him.

"I didn't want to spoil the surprise," he answered, handing me the wrapped square.

"It's a CD," he said, excited as I opened it. "All our stuff, you know. I added a few new ones, too."

"Thanks," I said, unable to show how truly happy it made me.

"And, I know you like poetry," he added, "so I printed out my favorite. It reminds me of you."

He waited quietly, judging my expression as I unfolded the paper and read his message to me.

Sonnet CVII

Not mine own fears, nor the prophetic soul
Of the wide world dreaming on things to come,
Can yet the lease of my true love control,
Supposed as forfeit to a confined doom.
The mortal moon hath her eclipse endured,
And the sad augurs mock their own presage;

Incertainties now crown themselves assured,
And peace proclaims olives of endless age.
Now with the drops of this most balmy time,
My love looks fresh, and Death to me subscribes,
Since, spite of him, I'll live in this poor rhyme,
While he insults o'er dull and speechless tribes:
And thou in this shalt find thy monument,
When tyrants' crests and tombs of brass are spent.

- William Shakespeare

"Happy Lenaia," he said, apparently pleased with the fact that I was bright red. "If you can, forget about the prophecy and everything else." He sighed and reached out to touch my cheek, and my eyes lifted. No one had ever looked at me the way he did. "Try to enjoy it, okay? This might be the only time you get to."

I smiled and nodded, knowing he was right. By the next one, I might be dead.

"You're too perfect," I said, hugging him long and hard, trying to push away those thoughts. We kissed only briefly, a soft brush of the lips. "So, Lenaia gets crazy, huh?"

Just at that moment, the roar of a crowd sounded from within the depths of the forest.

He shrugged and laughed. "Yep."

"I don't know if I'm ready for this," I teased.

"Too bad. We've got to go meet Nics and Sam. They're probably waiting for the show to start like everyone else."

"Show?" I asked.

"The birth of our existence. They re-enact it every year. It's sort of a tradition. You'll see."

Without warning, the sound of trumpets burst through the trees, breaking the delicate silence between us and prompting the distant masses to cheer.

He grinned with excitement. "It's starting," he said, and before I knew it, he had me by the hand racing in and out of the trees.

"What about my stuff?" I yelled from an arm's length behind.

"Forget it." I heard the words from somewhere ahead of me.

As we rushed toward the sound of people, kicking up the dirt path behind us, the smell of wood and earth filling the air, I realized for the first time how truly fulfilling Descendant life could be. Finally, all the sadness of my past had been washed away by the present, and although an ominous blackness lurked somewhere in my future, I could not feel the weight of it now. All I felt was excitement.

I could hear an announcer's voice getting closer as we approached. Sporadic bursts of laughter and grouped applause answered the man's witticisms, and I could tell they were just through the brush ahead. The crowd came into view as we reached the precipice of the sunken arena, a sea of people filling an enormous ancient Greek amphitheater that dipped into the floor of the cave like an empty swimming pool. I followed their eyes, all seemingly glued to a single place far below, center stage, and I found the announcer. He was not in a tux as I had imagined, but in classic Greek garb, draped in white cloth that partially covered his bare chest and hung to his feet. I felt the urge to stop and watch as the anticipation emanated from the air like an erratic wind, but William tugged at my hand, which was still locked in his, and we took our seats next to Sam and Nics.

"Tonight is no ordinary night," the man's voice echoed with enthusiasm throughout the theatre. "After all, tonight does not even exist. How could it exist before the very birth of your existence? But fear not, for that all begins now."

At that, the place went pitch black. I thought Nics was the culprit, but a strange humming sound seemed to be growing slowly louder all around me. When I heard William humming next to me, I realized it was the people who were creating the noise. It grew louder and louder until eventually the crowd sounded nearly out of control with hoots and hollers. Then it clicked. They were creating Chaos, the first presence in Greek mythology.

Just as I thought the crowd was about to explode, they yelled in unison, FIAT LUX, and the lights snapped back on like someone had flicked a switch.

"What was that?" I asked William.

"'Let there be light' in Latin," he laughed. "Get used to it. There is a lot more audience participation from here on out."

"From the primordial void we all emerge, but we have no earth to stand upon," the announcer added as he began to float into the air, "without Gaia."

The show was magnificent, unlike anything I had ever seen, taking us through the stories of the gods, some very different than what I had learned of in books. William whispered all the audience parts into my ear before they came so I could yell the cues out with the crowd. It was like watching live theater infused with spectacular special effects that had me questioning all I thought I knew about science and history. It was amazing.

"So?" William asked, his eyes alight with the anticipation of my response.

"I loved it," I answered truthfully.

"I knew you would."

Nics and Sam stayed put, even as the sea of people around them began to flow like a current in all directions.

"So now what?" I asked. "Where is everyone going?"

"Now it's whatever you want," Nics answered.

"Most people head for the food," Sam added with enthusiasm. "That's where I'm going."

Food sounded good. In fact, the mention of it had my stomach rumbling.

"Okay. Let's eat," I agreed.

"You heard her," Sam said, jumping up and taking off at a full run into the woods behind us.

"Sam," Nics yelled back, and before I knew it, she was chasing after him.

"Race ya," William shouted using my leg to propel himself out of his seat.

"William, wait," I laughed. "I don't even know where I'm going."

"So you better keep up," he teased, yelling over his shoulder. His strong legs were quick as he maneuvered in and out of the trees, but I never lost sight of him. My body moved faster than I knew it could, as if some desperate instinct had kicked in at the thought of him slipping through my fingers. When he stopped up ahead of me, I felt my heart settle as he looked back with a wild smile.

"I won," he said, rubbing it in as I approached.

I rolled my eyes playfully.

"I thought I was going to lose you."

"You'll never lose me, Ellie," he said with an unexpected brush of his lips on mine. "I'll always find you."

I let myself enjoy the moment despite the truth, despite the fact that what we had was impermanent. Maybe he would, though. Maybe he would find me in the next life, on the other side.

"Promise?" I asked with downcast eyes.

His finger lifted my chin so that I could look nowhere but at him. "Promise."

"What are you guys waiting for?" Sam yelled from the clearing that stretched out in front of us.

Just then, the smell of a thousand different flavors overcame me, and I noticed the feast awaiting us. I had never seen so much food in my life. Tables upon tables were filled with everything from burgers to filet mignon. A separate section was even set up for traditional Greek delicacies that I had never seen before.

"You've got to try this," Sam said more times than I could remember. He seemed to think of himself as a connoisseur of sorts when it came to the array of Greek dishes, taking it upon himself to give me a tour of the food.

Once we had our plates, we settled down below a giant

birch at the edge of the clearing.

"So where's Nics?" I asked as I ate my ambrosia and nectar.

"She took her food over to the bonfire with Rach and Paul," Sam answered.

"Why didn't we go?"

William shrugged. "They're probably already gone. They like to get to The Cavern before everyone starts packing in."

"Yeah, but if you get stuck in the center like they do, you're not getting out until it's over."

"What's The Cavern?" I felt like I'd asked a million questions already, but the two of them didn't mind answering.

"It's the place where they have the . . . what would you call it, William, a dance?"

"More like a tribal celebration," he laughed.

"Basically everyone has their fair share of traditionally brewed moonshine, and they all go nuts on the dance floor," Sam clarified.

"The music is pretty unique," William added. "Probably unlike anything you've ever heard."

"Really? Like what?" I asked, imagining a variety of musical instruments straight out of Dr. Seuss.

Suddenly, a thud reverberated through the entire cave so strong it shook the dirt we sat on.

Sam laughed. "Speak of the devil." Two more thuds sounded in succession.

"It's starting," William said, unfazed by the powerful booms. "You wanna go?"

"What's starting?" I asked, a little startled as the ground shuddered once again. "Is that the music?"

The Cavern was just beyond The Kitchen, as they called it, past the array of feasting tables and through a narrow corridor that sloped deep into the floor of the mountain. The intricate drum beats got louder as we got closer, and when the small closed-off path opened up, the full impact of it was spectacular. The entrance put us high above the dancing masses, so we could see the whole display of activity happening before us.

There was no attempt to mask the natural appearance of the stone mountain walls. It was amazing in its own right. Stalactites that must have taken centuries to form hung decoratively from the ceiling attaching themselves to equally impressive stalagmites that rose from the ground like pillars encircling the dance floor. The musicians played from a platform that protruded out from the cave wall. William was right. The music was unlike anything I had ever heard. They beat massive wooden drums with large hammer-like sticks, and smaller ones like bongos for the quicker rhythms. There were several flutes and miniature harp-shaped string instruments that hung from straps around several women's necks. The singer used no microphone, but somehow his deep humming carried throughout the space loud and clear. He sung no actual words, but instead, used his voice like an instrument that tied all of the music together.

It wasn't until William asked if I was ready that I realized people were moving past us down the winding cut-away that trailed down to the dance floor.

"Sure," I answered, eager to join the moving masses for the first time. As we headed down the path, I could feel the energy emanating from them like heat, and as we got closer, I realized that a large portion of the music was coming from the people themselves. Some sung their own tune as they danced, but most hummed along as one to a single repetitive melody.

"I'm not sure what I'm supposed to do," I said, speaking over the music. I stood stiff and awkward as people swayed in rhythm around me.

"Just dance," he smiled, pulling me into the crowd of bodies.

I had never been dancing. I didn't know how.

"But is there a certain way?" I asked, unsure.

Without another word, he drew me in by the waist, tight against his body and began to move like everyone around us in a slow dipping motion that reminded me of the movie *Dirty Dancing*. He bent my body back over his arm and swung me low, sweeping my hair across the dusty floor.

"I feel ridiculous," I laughed.

"Who cares? Just have fun," he said, our hips still rocking to the beat.

I looked around at everyone feeling the music, moving in any way they pleased, and it seemed almost more ridiculous not to dance. I opened my mind to the alluring rhythm and let it move through me.

"You're right," I said, more confident. "Who cares?"

At first I stuck to a subtle sway, but before I knew it, we were both dancing as though we were a part of the sound—the physical representation of the music.

We danced until we ached and couldn't possibly keep on.

"Come on," William whispered in my ear. "Let's go back to the camp site. I have a surprise for you."

"Sure," I agreed, wiping the sweat from my brow.

We looked around for the others, but they were nowhere to be seen, so the two of us left unannounced.

"That was incredible," I raved as we trekked through the trees. "This whole place, the show, the food, the music—I can't get over it."

He laughed at my overly exuberant ranting. "I told you. You'll never forget your first Lenaia."

Stepping past the large roots, I expected to see the empty space we'd left behind and gasped as William's surprise came into view.

"What's this?" I asked in amazement.

The bare ground of our campsite had been transformed into an oasis of wild flowers and willows that canopied over a deep pond. Cherry blossoms showered down off the exotic trees onto the surface of the water, where they floated like lily pads blanketing the pool with shades of pink.

"It's for you."

My eyebrows raised in shock. "You're kidding, right?" I stepped forward and dipped my hand into the cool water, scooping up a petal. "You did this?"

"Well, not myself," he admitted. "I had my mom's friend Lily do the trees and flowers, and Sam's mom did the water while we were at the show."

The beauty of their work weighed on my conscience. They had gone to so much trouble for me, and for what? So that I could abandon them and their prophecy, their next generation oracle, and break William's heart?

"I don't deserve this, William," I said, dropping the petal

to the ground.

He looked at me with power in his eyes and threaded his fingers through mine. "Yes, you do."

I could see that arguing my point wouldn't exactly show my appreciation, and I wanted him to know that I loved it, that I loved him.

"Thank you," I said, ignoring the gentle yet persistent ache in my chest. "Really, for everything."

"Hey, I'm just glad you're having fun." He smiled and kissed my cheek. Then suddenly his eyes brightened as an idea surfaced. "I packed our swimsuits."

He let go of my hand, leaving it cold and empty, to grab the suits out of the tent.

"I figured, since we'd get all sweaty from dancing, it would be nice to wash off."

He was right. My skin was still sticky from the heat of The Cavern, my hair still wet and stringy, and my heart, which was constantly egged on by William's close proximity, still pumped hot blood through my warm body.

After changing behind a tree, I emerged timidly with my arms wrapped around my stomach. The last time I wore a bathing suit was fifteen years ago, when Betsy still had the strength to get into a pool. William, already swimming gracefully in the still water, glanced instinctively in my direction when he saw me coming, but turned away politely while I slipped into the pool.

"Is it too cold?" he asked as we swam toward each other.

"No. It feels good. Refreshing."

Once we reached the center of the pond, the depth seemed

to diminish and we were both able to stand.

"It's beautiful," I said, watching the cherry blossoms float like feathers onto the water around us.

He tucked a nearby blossom behind my ear. "So are you."

I sighed deeply, trying to release the pent up emotion that tended to build in me whenever William was around, but his lingering hand made that difficult.

It wasn't necessary anymore to pull me closer. We seemed to draw to each other naturally. Water dripped down his face from his wet hair. Our moist lips met, and he kissed me gently.

"What if we had never met?" I asked, reflecting on all the past events that had led me here. I held him tight against me and buried my face into the warm skin of his shoulder.

"We did," he said simply, resting his cheek against the top of my head.

"No, seriously." I looked up. "What if I hadn't moved in upstairs, never came in to buy coffee?"

"You were moved in to that place for a reason, Elyse, not by chance. I would have made sure to talk to you, even if you hadn't come in for coffee."

"What if I would have stayed locked up there all day?"

He shrugged. "And what if red was blue and blue was green? What does it matter?"

"I don't know. I've just been wondering if you can recover from heartbreak. I mean, do you really think it is better to have loved and lost, than to never have loved?"

"Yes, but who's going to break your heart, Elyse? It definitely won't be me."

My fingers made ripples as I combed them over the surface

of the water. "Not even if you had to do something you couldn't turn your back on?"

"Never," he said, sure of the fact. I stared into his eyes, hoping to see something waver, but they were honest. "I know I'm young, and you probably think I don't know anything about love or what it means, but I've known since the first day I saw you that I was in love with you. I've never been so certain of anything in my life."

The way he looked at me, like his life depended on our love. It was that look that made it hard for me to accept my choice. I couldn't imagine how I would ever be able to walk away from it willfully. Even so, my throat felt tight with devastation, as though I'd already lost him.

***

On the last day, the fireworks exploded with deafening thuds that hit me in the chest like a bass drum as we all watched the final show. The bright flares of light illuminated the high walls of the cave with their color, and I watched in awe. William had made himself comfortable in the seat just below, leaning back between my legs like I was his own personal lounge chair. It still caught me by surprise the way he acted toward me—so casual and intimate, like we'd known each other our whole lives. I hadn't figured out how to handle what his touch did to me. The feel of his body's weight on my legs sent my heart racing three times its normal speed. I didn't dare make a move. The slightest sign of discomfort might cause him to sit up, and I wanted more than anything to stay like this as long as I could. I ran my fingers through his hair and kissed his forehead from time to time, just to prove to myself that I could, briefly thinking, *I might never get over this feeling.*

"Did you see that?" my new friends screamed at me with enthusiasm between the oohs and aahs. The display was quite spectacular. Fireworks were fireworks, but fireworks infused with abilities were a whole different category. Raindrops became tiny little pops of sparks as they fell, bursting just before they reached us like shattered glass. A tiny star no bigger than a baseball shined brightly over the crowd only to explode outward from the center like the big bang stretching through the universe. Palm trees grew in seconds from the ground below only to be lit like a bomb at the base of the trunk shooting upward into amazing blossoms of greens and yellows.

Suddenly, in the dim light of it all, something drew my eyes away from the entertainment. Just as a firework erupted, casting off its ember-red glow onto the faces of the crowd, I saw her. She stood just above the seated masses of people, halfway concealed in the woods. Her gaze was deliberate, and it hit me dead on. As the red light fizzled out, she disappeared with it into the blackness leaving me with a cold and unsettling feeling I couldn't shake. With William desirably close, and in such a wonderful moment, I didn't want to think of her. I turned back to the show, but she reappeared in seconds as she had before.

What do you want? I spoke the thought in my head, hoping she would hear it.

Follow me, she responded. *Come alone.*

I hesitated, wondering if I should listen. Alone. It could be dangerous. There was no telling who would be with her—

maybe the man who had accompanied her earlier, maybe Ryder. Besides, I didn't want to talk to her, not after knowing what she'd done.

Why? I attempted, but there was no response.

Kara had already vanished into the trees, so I didn't have much time to make up my mind. But why should I follow her?

Then, without warning, she spoke the one word that decided it for me—*Anna*. It was the last word she offered, despite my eager plea for her to explain. In the end, I had no choice.

How was I going to get out of this? There was no question that I would follow her, but I had to think. William wasn't going to just let me leave.

"Hey," I yelled over the booming. "It's a little loud. I'll be back okay?"

"I'll come with you," he said, getting up.

"No," I insisted. "I'll be fine. Stay. You're having fun."

"Are you sure?" he asked, unconvinced.

"Yeah, don't worry," I reassured him. "I'll just be standing in the back." And before he had time to protest, I was headed in Kara's direction.

I had lost sight of her, but if I ran, I might be able to catch up. With one last glance back at William, who was completely absorbed in a sparkling waterfall that was erupting at the base with fireworks, I cut into the forest at the last spot I'd seen her. I immediately began whipping past the trees and overgrown greenery, unsettled by the fact that I had to associate with her at all. As I ran, searching for her face in the forest, I felt the overpowering urge to confront her with the question that had been eating away at me—*why?* Why had she killed two more innocent people? When I was so desperately trying to save a life, murder seemed like such an unforgivable offense, no matter what her reasoning. Couldn't she have just told them to turn around?

I stopped to listen for her footsteps, but she was gone. I looked in every direction, and just as the last ounce of hope began to fade, she spoke.

Keep going straight. Turn right at the cave wall. There's a crevice. Squeeze through the opening. I'll be there.

Why can't you just tell me what you want like this? I thought, speaking intentionally to her. My mind was quiet as I waited for her to respond, but she said nothing.

Frustrated by her lack of explanation, I kept on, my only options being to turn back or follow her directions, and I couldn't turn back. I ran fast, feeling a sense of urgency with each step. There was no breeze to cool my warming body, and the stale air stuck to my skin. When I finally came to the cracked space in the rock wall, I pushed my hair, damp with sweat, from my face and stepped through.

"Why did you lead me out here?" I asked, defensive and agitated as I caught sight of her. Instinctively, my eyes scanned the space of the tiny crevice we occupied for any sign of company, any threat. "Why couldn't you have just talked to me in my head? You seem to enjoy it." I could hear the anger in my voice when I spoke to her. The image of her face lit up in the taillights of our car interfered with my thoughts. In my mind she was a killer, no matter what the reasoning.

"There are too many abilities here. I needed to get you away from the crowd, just in case, to protect myself." Her eyes were weak and full of shame, but her voice was strong and defiant. "Do you want to hear what I have to say or not?"

I'd almost forgotten why I'd followed her in the first place—Anna. My palms began to sweat, and my throat ached with fear. I didn't want to think of what she could possibly want to tell me about her. Knowing who and what Kara really was meant that it couldn't be good.

"What is it?" I asked.

Suddenly her familiar voice was in my head, taking me off guard.

She's dying.

The pit of my stomach burned with resentment for her.

"I know," I sneered, trying to shake her voice out of my mind. "Did you bring me all the way out here just to rub it in? I mean, do you enjoy seeing innocent people die?"

Understanding crossed her face, and a look of disgust followed shortly after. It was clear to her that I wasn't going to forget what I had heard. There wasn't a trace of friendship left between us, nothing to hope for or grasp at—just anger.

"You don't know anything about me," she spat.

"Well, I do know one thing. You're a murderer."

She came at me before I had time to move. The air in my lungs was forced out by the impact my soft body had against the hard ground. She was on top of me, and tears welled up in her terrified and angry eyes as she held a knife against my neck.

"You're right," she said softly, her expression cold and

vacant. "I am a murderer."

Her body never faltered from the dominant position she had taken in her attack. She was strong, skilled, and precise. Ready to strike if necessary.

"I could kill you right now if I wanted," she added, still hovering above me.

It felt like an eternity pinned beneath her knife, panic coursing through me, my heart about to burst. I was afraid, not for myself, but for Anna. Without me, she had no hope—she would die. Maybe William wouldn't even know what happened to me. Death would mean a wasted life. No purpose, nothing to give, just a quick ending to a pointless story. The thought awakened me from the fear, and tears came without warning.

"Look, I don't want to kill you," she said, irritated with how this had turned out. "I just wanted to warn you."

"I know she's dying," I said as she let me up. "I know." I rubbed the place on my neck where her knife had been.

"Not about that." She shook her head. "Warn you not to heal her."

My eyes narrowed as I tried to figure her out. I couldn't imagine she would care if I died.

"Why not? Because of the prophecy?"

"No," she said with force, "because they'll kill her, right after you do it. Don't be stupid."

"I'm going to warn her, tell her to run," I protested.

"You think that will work? They'll find her."

I tried to stand strong. "Well, they only know what you tell them at this point, right?"

She looked away. "I might be able to buy you some time, but . . ." Her face became harder. "I won't promise anything. If others get involved, I'm not risking my life for you or some human."

I swallowed the sick feeling back into my stomach. "Just buy me time. It'll work."

"You need to go soon if you'll have any chance," she said as she walked away. "Tonight."

As soon as Kara left the cave, my legs lost their strength, and I sank to the ground with my face in my hands. The heaviness in my chest made it hard to breathe.

Tonight.

26.

THE DRIVE BACK from Lenaia was solemn, but I wasn't the only one feeling down. Everyone was sad to leave, and I was glad I could hide behind that excuse, that I didn't have to explain why I was so disheartened.

The car was silent most of the way, with only William's music to fill the empty air. It gave me time to prepare myself. I refused to accept Anna's fate. No matter what Kara said, at least healing her would give her a chance. I'd already written the letter telling her to run, change her name, take Chloe and start a new life. I'd been carrying it around in my purse, ready for this moment. I wasn't going to let them win.

If it had to be tonight, so be it. The waiting was over. I looked over at William's face, his striking features highlighted by the light of the moon, and he smiled at me. It was a smile that could challenge the heavens, radiant and heart-stopping. I looked into his dangerous eyes, always tempting me to put it off a little longer, and tried to memorize the way they held me.

It was 10:30 when we finally got in. We went straight to bed, both eager to be close. His body felt warm and soft under the sheets as he moved to be next to me. His strong hands found my face and pulled it in to meet his lips. The gentle brush of his mouth as it passed over mine was enough to take me down. Any resistance I may have had was defeated. He could have me.

I knew it would be wrong to let things go as far as I wanted them to, simply selfish. Being closer than we already were would hurt him more in the end, but his touch robbed me of the breath I needed to protest. I was selfish, so be it.

I peeled the T-shirt off of his body, and he did the same for me. His broad shoulders held me delicately despite their strength. His eyes were serious and dark with intensity as he lay me down on the bed, sliding his sharply defined physique over me. He stared into me, like I was as vast as the sky.

"Kiss me," I spoke the words softly, and he obeyed.

His body pressed against me, as his lips, smooth and delicate, fell into rhythm with mine. I wanted nothing more than to let myself go, but I couldn't. I didn't deserve the love he had to give. I should have pulled away long ago. It wasn't right to lead him down a path that ended in such sorrow. It was wrong, and to take it any farther was just cruel.

"What's the matter?" he asked, catching sight of the hesitation in my eyes.

I took a breath, not sure how to explain. "It's just . . . I want to. I *really* want to, but I can't, William."

He lowered his forehead to mine, our noses touching, and

let out a slow chuckling sigh.

"It's your fault, you know. Do you see what you do to me?" he teased. "If you weren't so irresistible I might be able to control myself." He rolled over onto his back, staring at the ceiling.

He thought it was him, that he had moved too quickly.

"No, you were fine. You know me. I'm just shy."

He turned on his side to face me with an accepting smile.

"I guess we should go to sleep anyway. It's late."

"Yeah," I agreed reluctantly. I didn't want the night to end, but I knew it had to eventually.

"Goodnight, Ellie." His body slid in behind me, his arms curled under and over me, and his legs tangled themselves into mine, as if he was rooting himself to me like a tree clinging to the earth. I held on tight to the moment as I lay wrapped up in his body, feeling the roots of his soul growing deeper within me. What would happen in the morning when he realized I was gone? The pang of unrelenting guilt brought on a subtle nausea. I swallowed hard, pushing the feeling out of my throat.

If only there was another way. My mind never stopped, always plotting, thinking, hoping for another option, but there was none. I had to accept my fate. All I had was this moment, this last precious moment with him that hurt like the end of all things, with the weight of a thousand heartbreaks wrapped up in its brief insignificance. Still, I had to be grateful for it, grateful that I had met him. He had shown me what it was to be in love, and what else was there really, besides love? In the end it is all there is, and despite the heartache that accompanied my ending, it was worth it.

When his breathing slowed, I opened my eyes. There would be no sleep for me tonight, not until it was my last sleep, eternal sleep, and I would close my eyes forever. I held tight to the feeling of his heavy arm on my chest, his sweet, hot breath on my neck, before working up the courage to escape from his tangled limbs. I took a deep breath and moved slowly and silently inching away from his body under the cocoon of sheets. Once I was free, I turned to look at him through the darkness. The gentle moonlight that managed its way into my room helped me make out his features, calm and content as he slept. I quietly hoped death would be just as peaceful.

The air in the room was cold as I slid off the bed and onto my feet. My eyes fell back on him as I stood, looking for any sign of movement, any notice of my absence, but he slept soundly. I lingered and watched his breathing long after I knew he'd been undisturbed, but the clock pestered me with its nagging tick, reminding me of each second that had passed. As I walked to the dresser, I lifted my toes so they wouldn't crack with each step. I was soundless and opened the drawers without waking him, pulling out the last shirt I'd ever wear. It didn't matter which one, and once I'd put on my jeans, there wasn't much left to do but say goodbye.

I wrote the note as slowly and clearly as I could in the dark, hoping he would see that this was a deliberate choice, not a spur of the moment decision.

William,
I love you . . . I keep waiting for the tears to come, for my

anxiety to stop me, but all I feel is gratitude—for every breath, every memory, every short-lived smile, every day.

I'm sorry. I had no choice.

I folded the paper in two and placed it on my bedside table, taking my time, giving myself a reason not to leave. I had to pull myself away from that very last moment, but eventually I turned and walked out the door with slow quiet steps, leaving before my longing to stay overpowered my need to go.

I thought it would finally hit me during the drive. But this was my purpose, to heal. Eighty-nine years of life was more than I could ask for, and to end it with such sweet memories of love and bliss seemed like the perfect time to go.

I had my regrets, my doubts, my worries. Would he forgive me? Would he recover? Would he understand? But none of it mattered. After years of watching my loved ones die before me, standing helplessly by as my condition continued to plague me with loss, I finally had the chance to set things right. The old should die before the young, and though my appearance created the illusion of youth, I was old—far older than Anna, by nearly half a century.

That was the logical way of thinking about it, an argument for those who would oppose my choice, but in truth, this decision was one of the irrational heart. Even if my age was not a factor, I couldn't stand by watching Chloe relive the pain I'd known, not when I could prevent it.

As I drove, the silhouetted skyline climbed up the dawning blue sky, waiting for the first sign of the sun. The moon still glowed full and silver in the gray early morning light like a shimmering coin at the bottom of a pool. I must have stayed longer than I thought, but the timing seemed perfect. The open road, left abandoned by the sleeping citizens, seemed to reassure me that the path I'd chosen was the right one.

I used the spare key Anna had given me at Thanksgiving, opening the door as soundlessly as I could. If I woke Chloe, things would get complicated.

Even with the few lights that were left on, the apartment was dark and gloomy, as if the atmosphere had absorbed her sickness. Silence set the mood as I prepared myself to climb the stairs to her room. I needed to see her first, to say a proper goodbye before I ended it.

Chloe's bed was empty, and she wasn't in the living room. If she *was* here, she would be sleeping with her mother, and I hoped with all my might that she was at her aunt's.

I released a silent sigh when I saw the single body lying motionless in the bed—Chloe wasn't home. Careful not to startle her as I approached, I walked slowly and took a seat on the edge of the mattress. I found her hand and gently placed it in mine, but the only response she gave as she struggled to lift her lids, was the hint of a smile. She was weak, almost gone, and I had come just in time.

"You know, Anna," I spoke with a shaky voice. "All my life I've had to carry around the burden of being the one who lives, watching everyone I love age and die. You don't know what that's been like, to feel powerless as the world steals everything right out from under you. Well, maybe you do. But I won't let that happen to you, to Chloe."

Her frail body lay still and unresponsive as I spoke, but it felt good to talk to her, to say what I needed to say. Part of me was glad she wasn't able to communicate. I knew she would only resist, and that would be a waste of her precious energy. I kissed her forehead with love. Soon she would feel better, and all of her suffering would come to an end.

I made my way downstairs heading straight for the kitchen. I had already run through how it would go. A knife would be my tool of choice. The bracelet wouldn't produce enough blood. As I opened the drawer to the right of the stove, hoping to find the sharpest one I could, a chilling voice invaded my head.

Elyse. Her tone was calm but stern, and it was nothing less than a warning.

With my hand wrapped tightly around the handle of a knife, I turned to face her.

"Kara, please," I whispered.

27.

THE STILLNESS IN the room was as sharp as the blade in my hand and bound by fragile tension that could shatter at the first sign of attack. I stood, weapon in hand, ready to face my enemy, to defend my cause at any cost. I didn't dare let my eyes veer from direct contact, and hers stayed locked on mine, but nothing in them was looking for a fight. Nevertheless, I felt the muscles in my body tense.

She stayed calm as I calculated how I could kill her, or at least stop her from getting in my way. Her posture, far too relaxed, told me she had either accepted her fate or that she felt confident she would win the struggle between us. Neither made me feel any more at ease.

"You know," she said breaking the silence, "I never wanted this life."

I didn't care enough to respond. Her feelings were the last thing on my mind. I tried to stay focused on the attack that was sure to come.

"I told you," she continued, "if they try and hide on their own, it won't work. They'll find her."

Hatred seeped out of every one of my pores as I suppressed the urge to lunge forward and take her to the ground. If I wasn't so worried about losing my precious blood, maybe I would have already done it. Instead, I only gritted my teeth and held my tongue.

"I could help you though . . ."

My heart stuttered. Had I heard her wrong? I looked for the insincerity in her face, the joke behind her words, but her expression remained strong and defiant. *Help* could mean so many things. Could she help me survive the process? I couldn't keep the hopeful tone out of my voice.

"How?"

She nodded and smiled to herself before answering decidedly. "Be your backup."

My chest nearly caved in at the thought, and I took a deep breath full of relief.

"Kara, I . . . are you sure?" Deep down I didn't want to hope for something too good to be true.

"I think I am."

"What about your family?"

"I've already warned them, told them to leave. They'll be at risk, but the prophecy is the only way to really save them. They've had to live in fear for too many years."

Everything seemed to fold into place just a little too well. How did I know this wasn't some Council scheme to get me to kill myself and leave Anna and Chloe for them to murder?

"Why are you helping me?" I asked, keeping my eyes on

her. "Why put you and your family in danger? I don't mean anything to you."

I tried to be subtle as I evaluated her sincerity, and watched her brow sink into a hateful scowl.

"I've been working for The Council since I was fifty-six. I never had a choice." She looked away from me as she spoke, as if she were afraid her disloyal words might travel too far. "It's about time someone took a stand against them."

"Exactly," I agreed. It was gratifying to know that we would not only be saving a life, but that it would stand for something. Still, the unsettling thought wouldn't leave my mind. How did I know for sure this girl was on my side? All she had given me was her word, and the word of an enemy was as trustworthy as a foundation of sand. "But how do I know you're telling me the truth?"

I could see her processing my perspective, swimming through the uncertainties that had inspired my doubt. With open access to the workings of my thoughts, there was no telling what she was looking for, but she seemed to understand my need for proof.

She exhaled decisively. "I'll show you. Give me your hand," she said, stepping forward with caution.

Still a little wary of her closeness, I set the knife down and reached forward, allowing her to pull my fingers back and expose the bare flesh of my palm.

"If I let you in, you'll see more than you may be ready for, but I suppose it's for the best. You need to see why I'd choose to defy them." She looked at me and pressed my hand to her forehead.

I assumed I was about to experience her ability in reverse, but the transition was difficult to comprehend. Being inside her mind was like being in a dream. My thoughts were still present somewhere in the distance, but hers occupied the forefront of my consciousness. Images spilled past me in chaotic, jumbled spurts like a music video or a life-encompassing slide show set on fast-forward. Unfamiliar faces and places I'd never seen whirled about, unrecognized, and I felt for a moment as if I had amnesia.

Try and remember, she advised.

Remember what?

Use my mind to remember what you want to know.

As I tried to decipher my own intentions amidst the collection of her thoughts, an outside image of myself popped into view, pushing everything else aside. At first, I was watching from the driver's seat of the black Lincoln that had followed me from the city. I saw things from her eyes as she closely observed me without my knowing. In the coffee shop, at home, on many occasions when I thought I'd been alone, she had been there.

Each memory encompassed a whole range of feelings, thoughts, and emotions, none of which embodied the malice I had expected from her. Instead, she watched me with curiosity and bitter resentment for the task she had been given—to report everything she knew about me to The Council.

There was jealousy for the freedom I had, for William, and confusion as she wondered why I would die for a human, let alone one who had lived so many years. Then there was hate, not for me, but for The Council. I found myself interested in what could conjure up such hate and chose to seek out the origin of her anger.

Once I'd reached the core of the emotion, I was peering out from her twelve-year-old eyes at two loving parents and a little sister clinging to each other in overwhelming sadness as she was being ripped from their lives.

The hatred continued to blacken with each mission assigned to her. The memories became brutal and violent as they progressed. Murders, experiments, torture. She had seen unimaginable things. The flickering photos of her mind stopped to focus in on one singularly disturbing instance.

She was in someone's apartment, and it was just turning dark out. A man stood tall and brutish, blocking my view of the woman on the couch. I knew from her recollection that this man was what they called a Hunter. She had been allocated as his lookout as she was often assigned to do, given her unique ability to access the mind. If the Hunter needed help extracting information, of course she would be required to assist, but Hunters were usually sent for one reason—to kill.

I noticed that she kept clear of the woman's mind, opting to stay out of it, and I searched for the reason. Then it hit me, a sense of dread that nearly made my knees buckle—she didn't want to know the fear that was to stand before a Hunter.

"Kara, go check the rooms," the Hunter grunted.

"All right," she said, glad to escape the horrific scene that was sure to take place.

I wanted to know what would come of the faceless woman, but her eyes only provided me a view that led away from them. She turned the corner to the sound of the woman's muffled scream, and didn't look back.

Checking rooms was an easy task that usually provided refuge from the horrors at play. Hunters knew their victims well and picked times when they were sure to be alone. Not once in ten years as a lookout had she ever met an unexpected human, but I could feel the anticipation of what was to come, and I knew this was what she wanted me to see.

The apartment seemed completely deserted as she assumed it would be. All the lights were off, and aside from the continued agonizing moans of the poor woman, there was nothing but dead silence. Even after years of bearing witness to these sorts of atrocities, her stomach still felt like it was full of rocks. Sweat beaded across her forehead as she became sick in the toilet of the guest bathroom, the last unchecked room. I watched her retch, feeling the climax of the memory growing nearer. Then I saw it, a small bare foot, visible just outside the coverage of the shower curtain. My heart nearly stopped with hers as she digested the image. Hunters left no survivors.

Hello, she whispered, although the words were unspoken. *I won't hurt you, but you have to be very quiet or he'll hear you.*

As she peered around the curtain, she was taken aback. The child was so young, a little girl of only four or five. The girl recoiled slightly out of fear. Her wide eyes were a soft brown that oddly resembled the little sister of her memory, and although they were wet with tears, she stayed quiet.

The woman's faded cries had ceased, which meant he'd be wrapping up. She didn't have a lot of time. He'd come looking for her.

Listen, the child's teary eyes made her ache with sympathy. *I'll be back for you, okay? Don't worry.*

And with that she pulled herself together to face the Hunter.

"What took you so long?" he barked as she re-entered the living room.

She put on a gruff face and stepped back into her "bad guy" role. One thing she had learned from the beginning was that in this business, there was no room for weakness, no time for tears, and no reason to be civil. The only way to survive was to be somebody you weren't, to slip into an alternate identity that was strong enough to handle it all.

"What? You gotta get home to paint your nails or something? I was looking for money, what do you think?" Her voice came out harsh and cold.

"Find any?" But before she could answer, the man's eyes averted. "Lookie here," he grunted, and I felt the hairs on Kara's neck stand up. She turned around just in time to see the bullet hit the little girl right between the eyes.

***

Anna didn't move when I entered the room. She lay still and peaceful, for the moment, escaping the pain. A part of me began to worry as I watched her, and my stomach flinched with fear. I prayed she was still holding on. I sighed with relief as I saw the subtle staggering breath that fought with her slowly rising chest. I wasn't too late.

I sat down beside her, taking her hand while Kara waited just outside the door. Anna's eyes parted briefly, and her breath deepened as she began to feel my comfort. Everything would be all right.

"People don't understand," I confessed in a low voice. "What you mean to me will never be understood by anyone other than us, but I don't need it to be. We know."

I lifted myself off of her bed, and took the knife from the bedside table. There was nothing left to say really, only one last sweet intake of breath before I cut deep into my flesh. The cherry-red blood glistened with vivid pigment against my skin, painting bright crimson patterns on the surface of my hand. It dripped from my fingertips onto the dull colored carpet, each drop a hidden ruby in the sand. The pain was clouded, washed up in the pure shock of it all. It was only a side effect, an afterthought in all that mattered to me in that moment.

Come on, Elyse, Kara coaxed gently as she stepped inside the room, and I moved my wrist to Anna's mouth.

I felt compelled to fulfill my purpose and unafraid to follow through. Maybe I was put on earth for this one deed, this one moment, and everything else was just a collection of stepping-stones that led me here. Whatever the case, there was no going back, not now. All that was left was the mystery of what was to come of me, and the prophecy. I felt almost certain it was working as the blood left my body and flowed into her mouth. At first she tried to resist, confused by what was happening, but when she realized it was saving her, she became desperate for it, grabbing hold of my arm with wide eyes.

"Okay, that's enough," Kara said out loud so Anna could hear. "Give me the knife, Elyse."

"No," I said forcefully through the fog. "Just a little more."

"Well, at least give me the knife."

I heard Kara wince as she made a smaller incision on her own wrist. "Are you done, I—"

As her words cut out, I felt my body freeze. The sensation was all too familiar, and I knew we were in trouble. I stared into Anna's terrified eyes and noticed she was frozen as well, lips still locked around my wrist.

"I told you I'd find a way to get to you," Ryder sneered. "They can't pin it on me if you voluntarily bleed to death."

I couldn't turn my head to see him, but I heard the crack of his fist against Kara's jaw. "What a deceitful little brat you turned out to be. Was it worth it? For a human?"

Anna and I were only able to listen to her guttural moans, as another blow forced all the air out of her lungs. I hated him. My mind was screaming, desperate to make my body move, but it wouldn't. Would he kill her? Kill Anna? I was helpless, and as more blood left my body, I was running out of time.

"There are always consequences," Ryder bellowed. Kara's bloody face came into view and smashed against the floor.

Then it all began to fade, and my existence came tumbling in around me like the heavy night sky, crushing me between itself and the floor of the earth. My senses grew weak and blurred together in a fog. The sound of Kara's beating dissipated, and I was lost in a place of shock that left me unaware of what was happening around me. Time was a foreign thing. I had no concept of how long it had been. Had it taken minutes, hours, or even days for me to die? There was no way to tell.

Life. A labyrinth of crossroads and blind turns that you're never really intended to find your way through. Full of defining moments and significant landmarks that could at any time take you by surprise, turning your whole world upside-down. Whether I'd lost my sight or control of my consciousness was unclear, but it didn't matter, soon it would be over, and so I let go of my last ounce of strength and waited for the end. Then, nothing. The blackness carried me away, and I lost touch with where I was, who I was, what I was waiting for.

Nothing.

28.

TIME TRICKLED ON like spilled water, slowly and in all directions, so when I felt myself moving, weightless in the world around me, I couldn't guess how long it had been since I was last conscious. But was I conscious? The dizzy, numbing weakness that had me whirling told me yes. Whether in life or in death, or maybe somewhere in between was uncertain, but I was aware of my body and its distress. I had not left it. My mind was still imprisoned by its solid form, registering the agony of its complete inability to function. I was unresponsive, only able to process pain, confusion, and the sound of quick, uneven steps that belonged to somebody else. Then, through the haze of my broken and disjointed thoughts, I realized I was being carried.

Each breath that dragged in and out of my lungs was a struggle as I instinctively began to panic. Where was I? Where was Anna? I couldn't remember what had happened. Did it work? The footsteps quickened to a run, reacting to my panicked breath, sending blinding pain through me with each jolt forward. I wanted to open my eyes, to beg them to stop, but instead, it became too much. Darkness, soothing and peaceful, took me in once again.

***

Waking from the blackness was sharp and abrasive. The light seeped in like fire, shattering its coddling tranquility. All I could see was white. I didn't understand why I fought against it. Light was good. Light was the other side. It was hope, and though my eyes ached from it, I forced them to open and stare into the source.

Fear pinned me down and stole my breath as my surroundings came into focus. Goosebumps crawled up my arms and legs as my skin recognized the cold sting of the metal table I was stretched out on, or maybe it was just the fear that sank in when I realized where I was. Three lights hung like still pendulums above my head. To the right was a blacktop counter covered in beakers and chemical solutions that had been left to process. I was in a lab.

As my senses returned, I noticed that the only real discomfort I felt was the IV plugged into the crook of my arm. Remembering the deep incision I had made into my right wrist, I checked for the wound, but there was nothing but my bracelet. Not even a scar. My first instinct was to tear out the IV and make a run for it. There were no windows, but maybe I could sneak out the door, assuming there weren't any guards. I still felt the need to escape, despite the fact that I was healed and apparently alive. I had no way of knowing the intentions of whoever had me here, but before I had the chance, I was interrupted.

The sound of a squeaky door opening stopped the blood in my veins, and I slammed my eyes shut. The click of hard heels came closer. Nothing was spoken, but I could tell it was a man. He hummed aloud as he busied himself with the beakers, pouring one liquid into another. Then, without warning, he turned his focus on me. His fingers found the pulse in my neck and ran the length of the invisible scar that should have been an open wound on my arm. A cottonball was pressed against the inside of my elbow as the IV was removed. He was surprisingly gentle, but I still cringed internally at his touch. What did he plan to do with me? Before I had time to consider my next move, the door creaked again.

"She's awake," said the man standing over me. My ears perked at his familiar voice—Iosif.

"Finally," I heard William say. Had I imagined him? My eyes acted before I had time to contemplate it. I had to know. They snapped open and found his face, laden with worry. To think that I was never going to see him again, never going to feel his touch or hear his voice, seemed unimaginable. He was as essential to my being as air and water.

He was beside me before I had a chance to speak, lacing his fingers through mine and reaching for my face.

"William, I'm so sorry," I said sitting up, feeling the need to explain.

"Whoa whoa whoa," he said lying me immediately back down. "Take it easy. You've been through a lot, Ellie."

His sad eyes showed so much hurt, and I felt it ten times over for causing it, but I couldn't say I regretted my choice. It was a painful one, but Anna would live a long and healthy life now, and that meant the world to me. I wondered how she was, where they were, and finally realized I had no idea how any of this had played out. How did I get here? Why was I with William? How was I alive?

"Anna and Kara?" I asked, preparing myself for any answer. "Are they alive?"

He nodded with a comforting smile. "Yes. They're together, but I had to bring you here," he answered with tender eyes.

"How did you find me?" I asked, hoping to pick up on where he had come into the picture.

"When I woke up, you were gone. Your note helped me put the pieces together. I knew it had to do with Anna. The day you mentioned having to heal her, I knew there was more to it. I remembered her address was on your refrigerator."

"I couldn't have told you, you . . ."

He nodded in agreement. "I *would* have tried to stop you," he admitted.

I sighed, thankful he understood.

"When I got there," he continued, "the door was wide open, and I heard noises upstairs. I almost went right up, but I heard Kara in my head. She told me Ryder was there, and that he was going to kill all of you. So, I tried to be as quiet as I could, grabbed a knife from the kitchen, and surprised him from behind. I stabbed him in the back, straight in the heart before he could freeze me." It seemed hard for him to explain, and I could tell that reliving it was difficult.

I couldn't believe all of it had happened while I was unconscious.

"So, he's dead?" I asked. It was hard to picture William killing someone, even if it was Ryder.

"Yes," he answered, "very dead."

The thought was such a relief. "Thank you." The words seemed so inconsequential. He couldn't imagine how my heart overflowed with gratitude for saving us.

"When I saw you, I thought you were dead," he said, remembering.

The walls of my heart fell in at the thought of him finding me that way. How he must have felt, what he must have thought of me.

"I'm sorry," I choked, falling into his arms. "I had to."

"I know," he whispered, holding me as long as I wanted him to. When I pulled away, he knew it was because I wanted him to continue.

"You lost so much blood. I don't know how you survived, Elyse," he trailed off in disbelief.

"Her body has an amazing ability. It can withstand a loss far beyond the normal capacity." Iosif spoke for the first time since I'd opened my eyes. I wondered why he had stayed to watch William and I reunite, but something told me he played a large part in my survival, so I was nothing but thankful for him. "Even so," he continued, "I would say it was amazing you survived, but we all knew you would. There was never any question of that. Your sacrifice set things in motion. Now it's only a matter of time."

His prophetic talk always threw me off a bit. I never knew what I should take to heart and what I should disregard as babble, but Iosif had been right all along. He'd told me whatever path I chose would lead me where I needed to be. With Anna cured, Kara protecting her and Chloe, and Ryder dead, it seemed to be *exactly* where I needed to be.

"You survived because you were meant to," he concluded with finality. "To fulfill the prophecy."

"And because I'm your cure," William added, holding up his arm. A cotton ball was taped over the inside of his elbow. "I want a little of the credit."

"You healed me?" I asked, touched by the thought of it.

"Well, once we got you here, Iosif and my dad donated too. You lost a lot."

I moved to sit up, this time slow and easy so they'd let me stay that way.

"Kara said she was planning on healing you, but she was beat up pretty badly, so I cut my hand and gave you a little of mine. You regained consciousness for a second. You said 'funny how trees are people too, huh.'" He laughed a little as he recollected, now that I was okay. "Adorable, even when you're dying."

I took a moment to smile. His laughter meant he had forgiven me. Something I had toiled over up until the moment I thought was my last.

"Your power was magnified by my touch." He took my hand, reminding me of the warmth that was supposed to protect us. "I think that's what really saved you, because even after that, you needed more, apparently lots more, and neither Kara or Anna were capable of it. I drove as fast as I could, and Iosif did the blood transfusions when we arrived."

The thought was terrifying. I only hoped it was all worth it.

"So, even though I survived, do you think it worked? I mean, do you think I healed her?"

The question was mostly for me. Of course he wouldn't know, nobody would know. The plan was that no one would need to. In a perfect world, I would be sitting next to my best friend, basking in her transformation from near death to renewed with life. Instead, here I was, recovering from my own near-death experience, guessing how she was.

"Where are they?" I asked.

"The thing is, Elyse. I killed an agent, you healed a human. It's too risky to stay here," William confessed. "When they figure out Ryder's out of the picture, there will be an investigation."

I looked up at him. "So, what should we do?"

"Kara is going to play it off as though she came across the three of us already dead—you, me, and Ryder—and that she killed Anna and Chloe when she realized Anna had been healed."

"So they think we're *all* dead?" I asked, confused. "How is that going to work?"

"Well, we can't stay in San Francisco," William answered truthfully.

"What about Anna and Chloe, though? Are they coming with us?"

"Kara is hiding them for now, and they'll meet up with us after we leave."

"Dr. Nickel will be taking care of loose ends at Headquarters and The Institute, and I will be speaking to your landlord," Iosif chimed in. "A funeral will be arranged for the both of you, closed casket of course . . ."

"William, I . . ." there were no words to explain how sorry I was for everything. "It wasn't supposed to be like this."

"Oh, yes it was. Everything that happened needed to happen. This is the first of many foreseen events to take place before the war," Iosif said mysteriously. But there was no time for more of an explanation.

When the door creaked for the third time, I expected it to be Dr. Nickel or Kara, but instead a woman entered. I recognized her, maybe from a dream. Her face was aged nearly as much as Iosif's, but her eyes were gentle. I noticed right away because they were locked on me intently, as if she knew me. Her wispy white hair hung freely around her delicately framed shoulders.

"Hello." She turned her attention to Iosif when she spoke. "It's time. They're coming." Although her words were a warning, she spoke them with a smile.

Her warning wasn't directed at me, so I didn't think to consider who was coming or what it was time for. Instead, I looked at Iosif to respond.

"Your father's arranged a car. It's waiting out back," he urged, suddenly on alert. He grabbed two vials off of the counter containing the clear green liquid he had been brewing and placed them delicately in William's hand, wrapping his fingers around them as if the liquid was of high importance. "Do you know how this works?" he asked him with uncertain eyes.

"Yes," William answered anxiously. The tension had spiked. I could tell he was eager to leave at the woman's warning, and I got the feeling there was something I didn't know. "Come on. I'll explain in the car."

William slid his strong forearms under my knees and behind my back.

"Where are we going?" I asked as he carried me out the door and down the stairwell.

His voice was rushed and worried. "We have to get out of here."

"Why? What's going on?"

When we got outside to the alleyway behind the building, he set me on my feet, and I saw the car waiting there as Iosif had said—a black hearse sitting idly just outside the door.

"That's the car?" I asked in disbelief. This couldn't be happening now, right? I wasn't ready to accept it. The sight of it made me shiver.

In place of an answer, William opened the back. "Come on, get in."

"Whoa, wait. Now?" I reacted with shock. They had told me a funeral would be arranged. That registered somewhere, but now? Here, so suddenly?

"Yes, now," William urged.

The panic seemed to be emanating from him, and it made my mind swim with frantic questions. What would this mean? We hadn't discussed what we would have to give up, where we would go, how things would be.

"What's the plan after this? I mean, is this it? Where are we going?"

"Elyse," William said with urgency. "You don't understand. They're coming."

"Yeah, you're right," I said finally frustrated. "I *don't*

understand, because nobody has told me anything."

"Look, we don't have time. The Council is checking up on things. I don't know the details. I don't know where we are going, so I can't tell you what's going to happen." His words were hurried and frantic, and the distressed look in his eyes made me fold. I tucked my questions away for later and ducked into the back of the cab.

The moment William closed the hatch behind us, I felt claustrophobic. The white tufted fabric that lined the walls of the hearse was foreboding and uncomfortable. Death seemed to follow me like a dark cloud always hovering overhead. Two coffins crowded the space, and William and I crouched between them on the floor of the car. The more feminine one was black and sleek with shiny enamel and brushed nickel trim, aesthetic and elegant. Despite its beauty, the idea of playing out my death as if it had actually happened left a sick feeling in my stomach. If William had arrived a few minutes later, this would have been my coffin.

"Lie down," William instructed as he pulled a white curtain across the back window.

"In the coffin?" I asked, my voice spiking a little in surprise.

"On the floor," he said, laying down close beside me. "So they can't see us."

"What's going to happen?"

My heart raced as I imagined how far they were behind us. I kept imagining what I would do if the back door swung open, and I were to be dragged out by the feet, ripped away from William before we had a chance to get away. I had the urge and the will to fight back, but I had no defense. Still, I knew I could be ruthless if they threatened us, and maybe I would have to be.

"Nothing's going to happen," he assured me. "Everything will be fine."

I turned my head to face his, our noses inches apart. "Do you think they'll come out here?"

"I don't know."

All was quiet as we lay flat on our backs, hidden from view, our heavy breath in place of a conversation. William was the first to break the silence.

"We have to get in the coffins."

"I know," I answered.

". . . and I need you to drink this."

In his hand was one of the vials Iosif had given him.

"Trust me," he said. "You remember the elixir Juliet drank to make it seem like she was dead?"

"Yes," I said skeptically.

He held up the vial of green liquid. "This works the same way."

I raised my eyebrows, wondering how such a thing could really exist, if it would work. "Have you ever taken it before?"

"No." His voice was honest and understanding. We were both unsure, but there wasn't really any other choice.

I tried not to think as I lay my body down on the pillowy satin fabric of my coffin. I repeated William's words in my head. Everything was going to be fine. Wasn't it? I held the vial to my lips, staring up into William's eyes and fully trusting him despite my fear.

"Farewell," I said, quoting Juliet's last words before her

death-mimicking sleep, "God knows when we shall meet again."

"Don't say that," he said with pained eyes.

I smiled. "Come on, it's fitting."

"No, it's not," he said solemnly.

"I love you." If I had to choose any last words, those felt right.

"I love you too," he said, and kissed my lips, speaking more than we could ever say.

I drank the liquid and William closed the lid, sealing me in blackness. It was then I realized that things hadn't turned out so well for Juliet. A shiver shook my shoulders and I began to float. Not being able to see my surroundings made the floating sensation overwhelmingly intense and uncomfortable. I thought about calling out to William, who was no doubt feeling the same unsettling side effects in his coffin beside me, but I couldn't chance it. They might be outside by now. Instead, I hoped and wished for sleep to come. I felt my pulse slow and my breath shorten, and then I heard the rear hatch of the car open.

"I've been waiting for this day," said a husky sinister voice. "If she hadn't been flagged untouchable, I would have killed her myself."

"And I would have helped you," said another man with hatred in his voice.

"Too bad she offed herself. Would have been my pleasure to do the job."

I could hear the smile on the husky voiced man as he spoke and played out the murder in his head.

"Although, I'll always wonder if she would have joined us," said his counterpart. "Now we'll never know."

"We do know. There's nothing about her joining us in the prophecy. Trust me, she needed to die. The Council was banking on empty hope. She would have brought us down."

There was a pause as the two men considered what was just said, but it lasted too long. My hearing had started to fade along with my consciousness into a gentle sleep. Pieces of conversation faded in and out like someone was turning their volume up and down.

"Open them up," said one of the men.

". . . not really necessary . . ." Iosif's voice was followed by his agonizing scream, and although I wanted to help, I was sinking deeper. Unable to move, unable to hear, unable to react, all that was left for me was sleep.

29.

THE WIND WOKE me up. The soft breeze picked up my hair and traced it across my face tickling my cheeks and nose. Above me, an umbrella of branches provided shade, letting in small patches of sunlight that danced in patterns on the ground below where I lay. For a second, I thought I might be back at Lenaia, but between the shimmering gold and red leaves, I could see the blue of the sky. I sat up, dry foliage and dirt sticking to my hair and back, and tried to figure out where I was. William was there beside me, sleeping soundly and unaware of our new surroundings. No need to bother him. The rush of slow air through the trees was the only sound, like rushing water.

My last memory was of the inside of the coffin, black and alone, but I knew we had been headed somewhere for a purpose. I scanned the area with my eyes, looking for anything that might help us figure out what we were supposed to do next, where we were supposed to go. There was nothing in the distance but more trees.

Suddenly, a heap of dead leaves smashed against the top of my head and began raining down on me from above.

"What the . . ." I looked up trying to find the source, but William's belly laugh gave it away.

"You should have seen your face," he managed, still rolling with laughter on the ground next to me.

His cheerful mood was contagious, and I laughed at my own reaction.

"So," he said, once we had both gained control of ourselves. "Wonder where we are."

I looked around again. "No idea."

"Do you want to walk around, check the place out? We're not going to get any more lost than we are now." He didn't seem the least bit concerned about our situation. In fact, he seemed quite the opposite. He was happy we were lost.

"You're not worried at all?" I asked, feeling a little uneasy myself. "We have absolutely no idea where we are?"

"Not *absolutely* no idea. I know where we are in theory. This was *my* emergency plan after all."

"What is that supposed to mean? In theory we are on planet earth. What good does that do?"

"Okay. We're in a safe haven."

"Yeah, that's much clearer," I said rolling my eyes.

"My uncle's bloodline is of Soteria, goddess of safety. He can do amazing things. He created this for us."

"The forest?" I asked, confused.

"No, the haven," he corrected. "Think of it as a set of boundaries set up around this place. Only we are allowed in, and whoever we agree is trustworthy. To everyone else, everything that is contained within the borders is invisible."

"So, is it real or not?"

"It's real, but it isn't infinite. It has limits, and beyond those limits is . . . well, wherever he put us. We just can't see it."

With nothing else to lead the way, we followed the distant sound of trickling water coming from a nearby stream. I let my mind wander, speaking up only when something piqued my interest or when concern overshadowed my want to push my worries aside.

"Do you think they're all right?" I asked through the sound of cracking twigs beneath our feet.

I wondered if I should tell William about Iosif's scream. Maybe he had heard it too. The haunting sound seemed to resurface no matter how much I wanted to avoid it.

"Who?" William answered, knowing very well I may be referring to a number of people.

"Everyone, I guess."

"I don't know," he said. "I hope so." With a single glance, I knew I had pulled the unwelcoming thought to the front of his mind. For a moment he stopped his boyish gallivanting, throwing rocks and hanging from tree limbs, and looked back at me to consider. "At least you're safe."

Suddenly his focused changed, and his solemn expression settled into one of concentration.

"What is it?" I began, but he cut me off.

"Shh." His careful eyes met mine for a brief second and focused again on something in front of us.

I wasn't sure how I didn't see it myself. The beautiful doe

moved slowly and gracefully across our path, her thick brown coat blending into the maple brown backdrop of tree trunks and fallen leaves. William and I stood frozen in our places, not wanting to scare her away.

Out of nowhere something coming vaguely from the right flew past us and plunged itself deep into the neck of the animal—a dart. I gasped and jumped back startled. Where had it come from? I looked around and saw no one. The graceful doe let out an unnatural moan as it tried to leap its way to safety, but the dart had disabled her, and she fell to the ground with a staggered jerking effort.

It happened so fast. As I struggled to understand, I felt William's hand around mine, pulling us into hiding behind a tree.

"Let her go, William," said a rough and disorienting voice coming from a direction we weren't expecting.

"Uncle Mac?" William sounded surprised, but relieved as he loosened his grip around my waist.

"I said let her go, William." The man emerged from behind a wide trunked tree, his voice a warning. He was thick bodied and solid like a mule, the stubble on his face so thick it could be dirt, but his appearance wasn't what I found most threatening. The double-barreled shotgun in his hands was pointed my way.

"Wait," William stammered nervously. I felt his grip tighten again. "Uncle Mac, it's us. What are you doing?"

The doe squirmed stiffly, obviously in pain. My eyes flew between the gun and the animal, confused and scared numb.

"I need proof," he said angling the gun toward William

himself.

"Wow, Uncle Mac. Wait, what proof?" He was starting to panic. My eyes turned to the doe. She was dying.

"Heal her," he demanded, the hollow barrels looking me straight in the face. "She could be a Council spy. I need to know it's her."

I don't think I could have moved if William shoved me forward. I was still frozen in shock. The doe was motionless, little life left in her eyes.

"What?" William couldn't hide the hint of doubt in his voice, and I thought maybe he actually believed I was with The Council.

"Come on, before it's too late," the man yelled.

"Can you do it?" William asked, desperate and unsure.

"I don't know," I blurted out. Could I heal an animal? What if I tried and it didn't work? Was this man really going to shoot me? I glanced at him briefly to judge his sincerity, and there was no hesitation in the way he held that gun. I had no choice but to try.

She reacted to my approaching steps, a futile effort to escape what she surely thought would be her death. Her muscles flinched, tensing under my palm as I stroked her side before pulling out the dart in one fluid motion.

"It's poison," I mumbled to myself, assessing the situation. The poison was in her veins, so the doe would have to ingest my blood like Anna. I touched the bracelet on my right wrist, thankful I had a way to extract it. Who knows what other option Uncle Mac would have come up with? Shoot me in the arm, I guessed.

I pressed the two gold buttons and felt the blades shoot into my flesh, then twisted it a little to the left and pressed again, hoping it was enough to do the job. I lowered it to her mouth, letting the steady quick drops run over her tongue, and to my relief, she began licking instinctively. It took several minutes, but after a while, she began to breathe steadily, and once she had the strength, she rocked onto her feet and darted off into the brush.

"See now, that wasn't so hard," the big man grinned, genuinely pleased.

"What the *hell*, Mac?" William yelled throwing his arms into the air.

"What yourself? I thought you'd expect I'd want proof. What'd I tell you about fifty times last time I saw you?"

"Trust no one blindly," William answered, still in shock over the whole ordeal. "Why didn't you need proof from me then?"

"I believe you just gave it to me." He propped the gun over his shoulder, in the most casual way and turned to leave without another word.

William and I stood unmoving, my heart finally beginning to slow back to its normal pace. He turned to me, his shoulders hiked shaking his head. He had no words to express his outrage.

"Well, are you going to keep up?" Mac yelled from a distance.

"I'm sorry," William managed. He looked in Mac's direction and sighed. "Come on."

"Wait," I said, catching him by the wrist. He seemed too

comfortable following the armed man into the forest. "How do you know we're safe?"

"We're safe," he said taking my hand. "We're as safe as we can be . . . for now."

ZOVA BOOKS
LOS ANGELES

zovabooks.com
zovabooks.blogspot.com
facebook.com/ZOVAbooks
twitter.com/ZOVAbooks